**Other works by Walter G. Esselman:**

- **Superhorror Max** (Dark Myth Publications, 2021)

  Winner of the Open Contract Challenge. A darkly humorous collection exploring fear, survival, and absurdity in equal measure.

- **Liberty's Run: Book One** (Dark Myth Publications, 2021)

  The first entry in Esselman's post-apocalyptic adventure series about hope, loyalty, and the human spirit.

- **Liberty's Run: Book Two** (Dark Myth Publications, 2022)

  The saga continues as humanity faces new threats and deeper moral choices in a fractured world.

- **Liberty's Run: Book Three** (Dark Myth Publications, 2024)

  The climactic conclusion to the Liberty's Run trilogy.

- **Cowboys vs. Nazis** (Dark Myth Publications, 2023)

  A pulp-style Western horror mash-up filled with grit, gallows humor, and impossible odds.

- **A Dragonson Anthology** (Dark Myth Publications, 2023)

  A sweeping collection of dragon-themed stories that mix fantasy, action, and mythic resonance.

- **Catmandu** (M-Kids Press, 2023)

  A children's adventure featuring courage, imagination, and the magical bond between animals and humans.

## Anthologies

- **The World of Myth Anthology: Volume III** (Dark Myth Publications, 2018)

  Contributor of short fiction to the celebrated anthology series.

- **Monsterthology Volume II** (Zombie Works Publications, 2019)

  Contributor to the second volume of the horror anthology line.

- **The World of Myth Anthology: Volume IV** (Dark Myth Publications, 2021)

  Contributed multiple short stories showcasing his sharp wit and macabre imagination.

# SUPERHORROR MAX

A Novel

## WALTER G. ESSELMAN

DARK MYTH
www.darkmythpublications.com

Dark Myth Publications, a division of
The JayZoMon Dark Myth Company, LLC.
145 S Glenoaks Blvd. Unit #3149, Burbank, CA 91502

ISBN: 979-8-9925038-6-9

Second Printing October 2025

Dark Myth Publications is a registered trademark of The JayZoMon Dark Myth Company, LLC.

11 10 9 8 7 6 5 4 3 2

# Dedications

Dedicated to my Papa, Walter Henry Esselman.

And also to my wife Amy, my Parents and friends, Jai, Jason and Alana, for all their support over the years. Thank you!

## Special thanks to 'Team SuperhorrorMax' for making this all happen

Kristofor Harris and Zoie Montoya in the Art Department, Ian Fuller in the Marketing Department, and our Publisher Dave Montoya for making this all possible. Also, Rebecca Ilich for editing the book, and Sandy Fuller for getting me help in marketing.

And, to all those who helped Dave get my book out, Thank You too. I might not know who you are, but I really appreciate all your efforts.

# Foreword

I never read the 'Forward'. I always like to jump straight into the words of the author.

So, I'll put any interesting-type, info-ee stuff at the end, and let you dig in. Hope to see you at the finish line!

If you'd like to read more, please go to waltergesselman.com for horror, light fantasy and more, because I have Worlds upon Worlds upon Worlds for you to travel in.

Email: waltergesselman@gmail.com

Website: waltergesselman.com

Facebook: https://www.facebook.com/Dragonsontales

Instagram: https://www.instagram.com/uncle_walter_1/

Tumblr: https://52worldsofwaltergesselman.tumblr.com/

DeviantArt:
https://www.deviantart.com/reverendwhiskeygecho

# SUPERHORROR MAX

A Novel

# 1

The Secretary of State walked down the halls of a deliberately nondescript government building. Her Stuart Weitzman shoes—picked out by her daughter that morning—clacked along the tile floor. She and her temporary deputy secretary followed a young marine who looked apprehensive with his first big assignment.

Pushing aside her concerns, the Secretary of State took on a motherly tone and spoke to the young man. "What's your name?"

The marine looked a little surprised at the question.

"Um. Private Jim Parks, Madam Secretary," he replied.

"Have you been in Virginia long?" asked the Secretary of State.

"About two months, Ma'am." replied the marine, as some of the tension left his shoulders.

"D.C.'s great." smiled Madam Secretary. "You'll enjoy it here."

"Can't complain so far." said the marine with a hint of a smile.

"Doesn't do you any good anyhow," retorted the Secretary of State jokingly.

"True," replied the marine with cheer, but then he

hastened to add. "Ma'am."

"Can you tell me how many people are here?" asked Madam Secretary.

"Dunno Ma'am," said the marine uncertainly. "Not a small group."

"Any military. Lots of medals?'

"Why yes, Ma'am."

The Secretary of State made a thoughtful noise. "That's not good."

"Why do you say that?" wondered the temporary deputy secretary, Vicki. She was covering the post while the regular deputy secretary got acquainted with her newborn son.

"Well, you know, the more medals in the room, the bigger the trouble," replied Madam Secretary.

The Secretary of State took out a scrunchie—which she had snuck out of her office—and pulled back her blond hair. She did not even look at her temporary deputy secretary but said in a sigh.

"That's enough out of you."

Vicki blinked nervously. "What? I didn't say anything."

"You were thinking it pretty hard," replied Madam Secretary.

Wincing, Vicki looked embarrassed.

The Secretary of State was the only one on her staff who approved of her scrunchie usage.

"If I have to be in that meeting for God knows how

long," said Madam Secretary. "I want my hair pulled back."

Vicki had so much energy, she skipped a pace and then glanced at her boss.

"What're we doing here?" she asked.

"I don't know."

"I've never seen this building before," said Vicki, and then her voice lowered. "It looks *confidential*."

Vicki had always reminded the Secretary of State of a miniature sun, thermonuclear and all. But while Vicki was a little young for Deputy Secretary, this short-lived assignment showed tremendous potential in the girl.

The Secretary of State looked askance at Vicki. "Do you remember how we talked about embracing silence?"

Vicki winced.

"This is one of those times, isn't it?" murmured the young woman.

"Bingo."

Vicki crept for precisely 42.6 seconds.

"But wait! If this is about the revenants, isn't that a domestic issue. And the Secretary of State principally deals with foreign affairs."

Madam Secretary held back a smile. She had asked the President that very same question just this morning.

"Whatever is causing these outbreaks — And we do know it's not man-made — doesn't care about borders," said the Secretary of State. "We've had outbreaks in Germany, Japan, Tasmania, and now Michigan."

Vicki's breath hitched.

"And it's only May," she finished.

"Exactly! We need to start dealing with this on a global scale."

The marine stopped by a plain door and stood aside.

"In here, Ma'am," he said.

"Thank you," said Madam Secretary sincerely.

The Secretary of State went into the beige room, followed by Vicki.

The dimmed lights presented the rows of partially filled metal chairs.

As they sat, the Secretary of State's eyes fell on the only person still standing.

Voluminous hair—lit by the monitor behind him—gave the impression that Dr. Emile Corva had a halo. The Secretary of State might be the only one in this room who had been to the doctor's office at the CDC's dark science facility, Kipperling Falls.

Corva brightened up. "Madam Secretary, thank you for coming on such short notice."

"My plane doesn't leave for South Korea for another four hours," said the Secretary of State. Because she respected and liked Corva, she did keep her voice neutral.

"Believe me, I wish this were not the case, but this *is* vital," said Corva earnestly. He motioned to the other people in the room. "And I'm sure you know the other people here."

Vicki took that moment to scan the room. She was trying

to put names to the faces quickly.

However, Madam Secretary had done that the moment they walked in. There was a very select list of political and military leaders in this room, which chilled her to the bone.

"This had better be good," growled the general.

"If we're all here, it's not," said the Secretary of State solemnly.

"Indeed," replied Corva. He went to the back of the room and rapped twice on the door. "Everyone's here."

After a moment, a man in a grey suit walked through. He had big shoulders, a wide, flat nose, but Madam Secretary noted the kind smile on his face.

However, his blue eyes were haunting.

"Well, let's get this show on the road," said the man in the gray suit. "The following meeting is Confidential..." He stopped with a wry smile. "Except, when it comes to us." And he tapped his gray suit. "I don't have to say the perfunctory, 'Don't talk about us, or we'll destroy you,' do I?"

That got a gravelly chuckle from the general, but Vicki leaned towards the Secretary of State.

"He's kidding?" asked Vicki. "Right?"

Madam Secretary just shushed her.

The man in the grey suit continued. "This is dealing with Soundsville, Michigan. And more specifically, Fallen Oaks penitentiary. Ah! I see by your faces that some of you have already heard the whispers around the campfire. Very soon, the Department of Homeland Security will release footage taken during the incident. Then it'll be plastered all over the airwaves. My job here today is to give you all the facts of the incident, disturbing though they may be."

# 2

M*om?" called out Max.*

*The boy stepped onto the carpet, which he and his mother had rescued from a garbage bin when they had first arrived in Toledo, Ohio. He cautiously crossed their tiny apartment.*

*Thud.*

*There was that sound again from his mother's bedroom.*

*It was dull as if someone had collided into the wall by the door. Max stopped as soon as he reached the door. There was a sudden silence from inside her room.*

*Mom had come home last night after a terrible day. One of her co-workers had bitten her. By the time she had gotten home, she had just wanted to hug him and go to bed. He had put up a fuss at the hug. He was almost thirteen!*

*"Mom?" called out the boy again. Worry coiled in his belly. He knocked at the door.*

*Almost in response, there was another heavy thump against the wall, which made Max jump. Immediately, he was mad at himself for jumping. It was just his Mom.*

*"Are you decent?" he asked. When no reply was heard, he*

*tried the handle. The door swung open into a dark room.*
*"Mom?"*

*Hands snatched at him.*

# 3

L et me go!" demanded Max.

But the fifteen-year-old was slammed back into a tall wooden cabinet.

The memory twisted the boy's guts. However, he held back nausea at the memory and dug in his toes. The Chinese-American boy tried—once again—to break the blockade of taller boys surrounding him.

The lead bully, Craig, casually pushed him back. Hitting the cabinet again, Max felt a poster of Gandhi tear behind him, but the boy was so furious that he barely noticed. Craig, on the other hand, looked down on Max with a serene expression.

"We just want to know," asked Craig with a too-reasonable voice. "Is that so difficult?"

Max bared his teeth. "It's none of your Goddamned business!"

"Now, that's not nice," said Craig, and his syrupy tone got even more smarmy. He was a big kid—just over six feet tall—with close-cut brown hair. "We only want to know if your Mom did become a revenant?"

One of the boys, Simp, furrowed his bushy eyebrows. "Wait? What's a revenant again?"

"It's another name for zombie," said Craig offhandedly. "Now shut up."

The bully looked back at Max. Craig's was desperate to grow a mustache, but it looked like a distressed caterpillar right now.

"Now, just tell us what happened," ordered Craig. "Was she bitten? Did you have to put a bullet through her head?"

"Leave him alone!" snapped Tammi from behind the bully boys. The petite blond girl barely reached to their shoulders.

Max stiffened when he heard her voice. Because the boy had not hit his growth spurt yet—and he was wondering if he ever would—he had to duck under Craig's arm to look at her.

"Tammi, I got this," hissed Max with teenage embarrassment.

Craig looked over one wide shoulder at Tammi.

"Yeah, Tammi," sneered Craig. "He's got this."

"Don't talk to her that way," spat Max.

"What way?" asked Craig innocently as he looked back at Max.

"In that slimy, I'm just trying to help, even though I'm an asshole voice," said Max.

Craig's face stormed over with outrage and anger.

"What did you call me?" asked the bully.

"He said, 'sit down so the class can begin.'"

Max and Craig blinked at each other, and then they looked for the source of the new voice.

Leaning inside the door was a big man in a crisp, gray three-piece suit and a royal blue tie. Over one shoulder hung a tan satchel.

"And you are?" asked Craig with narrowed eyes.

"The substitute teacher," said the man, who then put steel into his voice. "Now...Sit...Down."

The hostility on Craig's broad face scuttled away, and feigned helpfulness immediately replaced it.

"Of course, sir," said the bully with an oily voice.

Craig nodded to his bully-boys, and they all started to move, except for Simp.

"Move it, Simpton," growled Craig.

"But he didn't tell his story yet," whined Simp.

Craig just gave Simp a shove. The bully led the guys to the back of the room, where their desks were clustered.

After Craig was gone, Max and Tammi moved over to two empty desks, which were near the front of the class. Pulling the silver Tigers jacket off his narrow shoulders, Max hung it onto the back of his chair.

Tammi sat and curled her legs under her.

Once everyone settled down, the Substitute Teacher went to the chalkboard and wrote his name: Mr. Lovecraft.

Simp chuckled at this but was immediately silenced by Craig.

Dropping his suitcase onto the teacher's chair, the substitute—Lovecraft—moved around to the front of the desk with a folder. He set his reading glasses on a wide, flat nose.

"Hi everyone. My name is Mr. Lovecraft, as you can see," said the Substitute Teacher. "Mr. Forrester is out sick today, so I will be filling in."

Half-sitting on the edge of the desk, Lovecraft took a red, sealed envelope from the folder and dropped it onto the desk. As he took a moment to scan the teacher's notes, Tammi pointed at the large, red envelope.

"What's that?" asked the girl.

"Fire drill type stuff," said Lovecraft offhandedly as he continued to scan the notes. Finally, he looked up at the class. "Okay, you guys were talking about..."

"We're not all guys," insisted Missy, with a prim and proper voice.

"Pardon?" asked Lovecraft.

"There are women here too," sniffed Missy, who looked like a porcelain doll. She sat before her boyfriend, Craig, the bully. "So, we're not all guys."

"Of course, I meant 'guys' in a gender-neutral way, but regardless," conceded Lovecraft. "Ladies and Gentlemen—as I was saying—Mr. Forrester had been talking about Local History, correct?"

"Yes, sir," said Patrick dutifully, who was seated next to Max.

Patrick leaned forward eagerly. His big hands, which he had not grown into yet, fidgeted with his pen.

"Right," said Lovecraft. He spotted Craig whispering to Missy but decided to ignore it for now. "You had just gotten to the building of the jail on the edge of town."

"We want to talk about the revenant outbreaks," interrupted Missy in a demanding, nasally voice.

"Yeah!" agreed Craig as he eyeballed Max's back. "Especially any first-hand accounts."

Max's ears—under his shaggy blond hair—went red.

"Ah, Current Events," mused Lovecraft for a moment. "Nope, we have work to do."

"Why can't we?" whined Missy. She had a soft face framed by tight brown curls and real ruby earrings. Missy turned her head in a cute—but calculated—way. Lovecraft was sure that the maneuver had ended a lot of opposition from many people in the past.

However, the Substitute Teacher ignored the teenage girl.

Missy's eyes went wide in outrage. She swiveled around to glare at Craig—as if it was his fault—while Lovecraft kept speaking.

"Right, so the jail was built in 1863 by Charles Pierce and originally housed prisoners of war during the Civil War," he said.

"That place is scary," said Tammi.

"Well...it is a prison," suggested Lovecraft gently.

"No. She doesn't mean scary like 'jail,' but rather scary like 'haunted,'" helped Patrick.

"Haunted?" asked Lovecraft in a tiny voice.

11

Patrick continued eagerly. "Yeah. There had been rumors of spirits there even before the jail had closed. The last group of ghost hunters to go in there ran screaming from the place. In the middle of the day!"

Simp said in a thoughtful tone. "But Pop said there was no such thing as ghosts."

"Yeah?" said Craig. "Your Pop was never a guard at that jail. My Grandfather worked there, and he won't talk about that place. He just gets this weird look in his eyes when it's mentioned. Of course, that means we have to mention it all the time."

"Well, I'm not here to talk about urban legends," interrupted Lovecraft. "The jail is considered one of the first supermax facilities in the country. And it conducted capital punishment by hanging. Wait that can't be right."

"Oh, it is. The jail would not change to lethal injection or the chair," explained Patrick. "It caused a big stink with the Department of Justice when they hung the last inmate there, but that was also the day of the last riot. So, the riot was a reason to close the prison."

"How many people died there?" asked Simp.

"It doesn't say," said Lovecraft as he glanced over the teacher's notes.

"the state executed five people after the reinstatement of capital punishment in 1976, but there were a lot more deaths than that," said Patrick. "The name of the jail was because lightning struck two oak trees and knocked them over. Something about the strike spooked the local indigenous people. So Charles Pierce—who built the jail— bought the land for a song."

12

"Lightning doesn't strike twice," sniffed Missy.

"That's an old wives tale," said Patrick. "Lightning hits multiple times with every strike. I mean, it's hit Roy Sullivan 7 times."

"Who's Roy Sullivan?" asked Missy.

"Someone who must've gotten hit by lightning," interrupted Lovecraft dryly. He waved his notes to get the conversation back on track. "According to this, the jail employed half the town either directly or indirectly."

"Who would want to work there?" asked Tammi with a tremble of fear.

"It's honest work," suggested Lovecraft. "Unlike the people who had to live there."

"Still...creepy," said Tammi.

"What if they sent us there during a revenant outbreak?" asked Missy.

"I wouldn't worry about that," said Lovecraft.

"It could happen," insisted Missy, with a bit of orchestrated panic.

"I heard that City Hall is supposed to be the meeting place," said Lovecraft. "*And*, that's only in case in case of emergency." He patted the red, sealed envelope that read 'Do Not Open.' "That's what this is. They handed these out this morning. And remember, it's only in case of emergency, and the odds of that...."

"How will we know?" asked Tammi.

"Tornado siren, I think," said Lovecraft.

"Can we open it now?" asked Missy.

"Hopefully, we never have to open it," said Lovecraft. "I only got one because I was playing teacher today."

"If the revenants come, Max will get to see his Mom again!" sneered Craig.

Max sprang up, spilling his desk. The boy swung to jump at Craig, who looked surprised. But just as Max was about to spring, Lovecraft grabbed him by the back of his shirt.

Hauling the boy backward, Lovecraft dragged Max towards the hallway.

"I want everyone to read Chapter 11 until I return quietly, or you'll all be writing essays tonight," said Lovecraft.

"But we're only on Chapter 5," said Patrick.

But Lovecraft just glared at the student.

"Reading chapter 11," squeaked Patrick, and he stuck his nose in his book.

Lovecraft pulled Max out into the hallway. The Substitute Teacher closed the door behind him with his foot.

"Let me go," snarled Max, and the Substitute Teacher did so.

The boy stepped away from the Substitute Teacher and pulled at his shirt until it lay right again. Then he turned to glare at Lovecraft.

"Why'd you stop me?" demanded the boy.

Lovecraft leaned against the peach-colored lockers and looked thoughtfully at the boy. Max was skinny with a head of unruly hair. But there was a fire burning in the

14

boy's eyes that had nothing to do with the bully back in the classroom.

"Because he's an idiot," said Lovecraft patiently. "And you don't need to drop to his level."

"Why not?" asked Max. "Just this once."

"I know it's tempting," sympathized Lovecraft. "But no."

"He mentioned my Mom," said Max, voice grinding with rage.

Lovecraft winced. "That was jerky of him. And I'm sorry to hear about your Mom."

"I...I just...," started Max, and his eyes began to tear up.

"I understand," said Lovecraft.

Max snapped. "How could you?"

"I know more about the revenants than you think," said Lovecraft. "And how hard it is for survivors afterward."

"Dragged back here again," grumbled Max as he looked down at the blue-gray tiles of the hallway. "Because my grandmother still lives here,"

"Are you originally from here?" asked Lovecraft.

"When I was young," said Max, almost to himself. "Mom and I went to the city. Something new after my father went to Fallen Oaks Jail." The boy suddenly looked up in surprise. He had not meant to say that out loud. "Please don't tell the others!"

"I won't," said Lovecraft sincerely. "Promise."

"My grandmother's nice," said Max hastily, but then he

15

stopped, and he gave a shrug. "But..."

"But it's not the Big City," suggested Lovecraft.

"It's not the Big City with my Mom," amended Max.

"I understand," said Lovecraft, but he let his face harden. "But that doesn't give you the right to start a donnybrook in my classroom."

"Donnybrook?" asked Max.

"Fight," supplied Lovecraft.

"But he...," started Max.

Lovecraft interrupted. "...is being a jerk. That's no excuse for beating on him. Now take five out here. When you're ready to come back, I'll be trying to herd the cats in that classroom to talk about that jail."

Despite himself, Max smiled as Lovecraft walked back into the class. Everyone was silently reading or at least pretending to. Lovecraft picked up the fallen desk, and he put Max's shiny nylon jacket on top. The substitute retook his spot, leaning against the desk.

"Now, where were we?" asked Lovecraft rhetorically. "The town jail was built—at first—by prisoners of war, which can't have been easy. There were accidents and even some deaths."

"Did you know that the Native Americans never settled on this land," interrupted Patrick.

"Do we know why?" asked Lovecraft.

"They...," started Patrick.

"Who's 'they'?" asked Lovecraft.

16

"The Native Americans," supplied Patrick. "They said it was because the soil wasn't good..."

"They're right about that," added Simp with an authoritative voice. "The soil's too rocky to make for good farming. It was hard enough to carve out my garden."

"But the real reason was that the land was cursed," said Patrick, trying to steer the conversation back to the pertinent point.

"Did they say that?" asked Lovecraft of the young man.

"Well, not in so many words," admitted Patrick.

"For this class," said Lovecraft gently. "We're going to have to rely on historical facts."

Patrick ducked his head down, chagrined.

"Now, the jail would go on to earn a reputation for being one of the most violent in the country. Had multiple riots— one of which resulted in the prison getting closed—and...," began Lovecraft when he heard the low moan of a tornado siren. Everyone stiffened.

"Is that...?" squeaked Missy.

"Relax," said Lovecraft steadily. "Don't panic. We have a plan."

"But what if...," started Missy.

"I'm going to take care of you! But you need to follow me, and do as I say!" said Lovecraft as he looked at her and then at the rest of the class. He spoke in a calm, relaxed tone. He picked up the red envelope from the desk and slit it open the top with his finger. "Don't worry. We're just going to take a quick bus ride to City Hall, as it says on..."

But Lovecraft stopped as he glanced at the paper.

"What's this?" asked Lovecraft, furrowing his brow.

"What's wrong?" asked Missy, and her voice nearly broke. She reached behind her to grab Craig's hand in a death grip.

"It's okay," said Lovecraft, and he calmly straightened up. "I'll be right back. I just need to check on something."

As Lovecraft headed for the door, Max came back in.

"Was that the alarm?" asked Max in concern, and he saw the letter in Lovecraft's hand. The boy nodded his chin at the letter. "Where're we headed?"

Lovecraft handed the boy the letter as he stepped out the door. Max's eyes followed the Substitute Teacher, who went out into the hall. There was a thrum of barely concealed panic in classrooms around him.

A door on the opposite side of the hall burst open. A flustered teacher, Chris Rayton, practically bolted out of his room. Spotting Lovecraft, the teacher dashed across the hall, waving his letter.

"Is this right?" asked Rayton. His voice was panicky, and his tight runner's frame vibrated with fear. Lovecraft took Rayton's waving wrist and stilled it so that he could read the paper. The designated school bus was different, but the address was the same on both letters.

"Damn," said Lovecraft softly, and he released the teacher's hand. "Mine says the same thing."

"Can we even go there?" asked Rayton.

"That must be where they set up the emergency shelter,"

said Lovecraft. "So, we have to go there."

"But...," said Rayton uncertainty.

Lovecraft looked Rayton square in the eye, and the Substitute Teacher spoke in a soft but firm voice.

"We don't have time to second guess," said Lovecraft. "Lives are on the line. Now, go get your class, tell them everything is going to be alright, and get them onto your designated school bus."

Lovecraft started to turn away.

"But...will it be alright?" whispered Rayton, and Lovecraft looked back.

"Yes," said the Substitute Teacher with unwavering steel in his voice.

Lovecraft turned back to his class. He did not let himself wonder whether he had just lied to Rayton. Regardless, the teacher had needed to hear that.

By the time Lovecraft got through his door, Rayton was already running back into his class. In Lovecraft's class, Craig was standing at his desk, and the bully had taken a step towards Max.

"What does it say, you idi...?" demanded Craig, but he stopped when he saw Lovecraft.

"The emergency shelter is in Fallen Oaks jail," announced Lovecraft.

A roar erupted as everyone in the class tried to speak at once. People began to jump out of their seats in panic.

"Follow me!" cried Lovecraft, and everyone stopped. He knew he only had a moment. "I will keep you safe, but only if we're calm, and you do what I say!"

Everyone paused for a moment, but then they saw that Lovecraft was serious. The students settled back into their seats, except for Max and Craig, who observed Lovecraft.

"But Fallen Oaks...?" whimpered Missy plaintively.

"...Has big walls and bars," said Lovecraft. "No revenant I've ever heard of is getting through there. Now, we're going to form an orderly, single line." He turned to Max. "What's your name?"

"Max," said the boy.

"Right," replied Lovecraft. The Substitute Teacher picked up the kid's Tiger jacket from the desk and tossed it to him. Max caught it and slipped it on. "Max is going to take the lead. We are going to walk single file down to the bus. Max at the lead, and me bringing up the rear."

No one moved at first.

"As a great philosopher once said, 'Don't Panic,'" said Lovecraft. "I will move Heaven and Earth to keep you safe."

The class slowly stood up and began to move towards the door.

"Single file people," said Lovecraft. "Max! Which bus are we going to?"

Max looked down at the paper in his hand. "Um...bus #7."

"7 is a lucky number," said Lovecraft. "Okay, Max. Take us to lucky bus #7."

"Okay," replied Max nervously, but he moved towards

the door. The boy took a deep breath and headed out into the hallway, but not before checking that it was clear of trouble.

Lovecraft took his suitcase and put it on so that the strap lay across his chest.

"Okay, everyone! Follow Max! Go on!" said the Substitute Teacher.

Forming a single file line, most of the students followed Max. However, there was a small knot of people still at the back, including Craig, Simp, and Missy.

"Why do we have to follow that idiot?" grumbled Craig.

"Oh Craig," said Lovecraft, as if the thought had just struck him. "Don't forget your textbook."

"What?" asked Craig with confusion on his broad brow. "Why?"

"You have a 500-word essay on chapter 11 due tomorrow," said Lovecraft.

"You're kidding?" asked Craig as his jaw dropped.

"750-word essay," corrected Lovecraft with a stern glare.

"We don't have to bring our books, do we?" asked Patrick dutifully.

"You don't," said Lovecraft, still looking at Craig. "Only people who mouth off."

Wisely, Craig grabbed his book and kept his mouth shut. He led the bully boys, and Missy, to the back of the line.

Patrick still grabbed his backpack with all his books. He moved behind the bullies but gave them plenty of elbow room literally since he did not want an elbow jabbed into

21

his chest again.

"Okay, people," said Lovecraft as he brought up the rear. "Keep moving."

After a glance to check that there was no one left in the class, he followed Patrick down the hall. He left the lights on and the door open so that the principal could quickly check that the room was empty.

Up ahead, Max was almost to the glass doors leading out.

Behind the boy, Tammi sputtered to him. Her voice a hurried whisper. "You...you survived this before?"

Max turned and gave her a confident smile.

"We'll be okay," he said. He pushed the door open and saw the line of buses towards the back of the school—per Federal law—in case of an emergency evacuation. He looked at the paper again to confirm that it said "Bus #7". Confidently, he went down the grassy hill to get there quickly and to a safe haven.

Deep in the city, there was a small explosion. Everyone jumped, and the line began to lose cohesion, but Max gave a shout.

"It's right over there!" cried Max as he pointed to the bus. "Just a little ways more."

Max moved a little quicker, and Tammi skipped to keep up with him. Everyone else followed, and Lovecraft smiled.

Good job, kid, thought Lovecraft. Don't give'em time to worry.

Max reached the edge of the bus, but he suddenly stopped. Tammi almost collided with him. She put a hand on his shoulder.

"What?" asked Tammi as Max knelt to look under the bus.

"Never go near a vehicle without looking under it first," recited Max mechanically, as if he had had it drilled into him.

"What?" asked Tammi.

"Ankle-biters," said the boy.

Confused, the rest of the class crowded behind him. The boy was to determine that there was indeed nothing under the bus.

Lovecraft froze. Checking under cars is one of the rules for surviving a Revenant Outbreak. He realized that the kids' tales of revenants were not made up to impress people. The Substitute suddenly felt a flood of sympathy for the boy. Max, unaware of all this, stood up and looked back at Lovecraft.

"Clear," said Max, almost professionally. Lovecraft nodded and walked up beside him. The boy looked up. "You want me to check the bus? I run fast."

"You all stay back, and I'll check inside the vehicle," said Lovecraft. The door was already open. He hopped up to the first step and peered down the bus, but there was no one in there at first glance.

Moving carefully, Lovecraft moved down the length of the bus, and he was elated to find it empty. He moved to the front of the bus and sat in the driver's seat.

"It's clear," said Lovecraft. "Everyone, hurry on in!"

To Lovecraft's surprise, Max stepped aside and motioned for people to go in. All the while, Max kept an eye out for danger.

The Substitute found himself liking the kid more and more. As the last student came on board, Max hopped up and dropped into the empty seat behind the driver's seat.

Rayton led his students in a tight bunch towards their bus through the students wandering out of the school.

In his seat, Max leaned forward.

"Where's our driver?" he wondered quietly.

# 4

The bushes near Bus #7 rustled, and—underneath the greenery—the driver's foot spasmed. Slowly, Ed Varney rose up. His body moved jerkingly until he was upright. Stabilizing, the bus driver looked around and saw Bus #7.

Sporting a bloody hand with a bite mark, Ed shambled towards the bus.

# 5

There he is," said Lovecraft happily. But then the smile

ran off his face.

"Um...," started Max.

"Something's wrong," said Patrick, who had sat in the first seat on the right-hand side. He stood and leaned over the stairwell leading down to the front door.

As the driver neared the door, Lovecraft stilled.

Ed reached the edge of the door and saw Patrick leaning over. The bus driver hissed and started to lunge forward when Lovecraft saw the driver's eyes. They were white with red halos around the iris, the eyes of a revenant.

Lovecraft shot past Patrick and kicked Ed in the face. The driver flipped backward. The class cried out at the sudden violence.

As Ed cracked his head hard against the pavement, Lovecraft leaped through the door. The Substitute Teacher dropped onto the revenant's neck, breaking it swiftly. Lovecraft leaned down, looking at the driver, who stared vacantly at the sky.

"Sorry," whispered Lovecraft to Ed.

Quickly, Lovecraft stood. Striding back into the bus, he looked briefly at the class. "Sorry about that. Poor guy was...well, we're leaving now."

Lovecraft sat down in the driver's seat and pulled the bus door shut. He shifted in his seat to get comfortable while he stared at the dashboard. Luckily, the keys were still in the ignition.

Max leaned forward in his seat behind the driver.

"You have driven a bus before, haven't you?" asked Max.

"I have a wide repertoire of talents," said Lovecraft loudly in a confident voice.

"Good," nodded Max.

The boy sat back as Lovecraft started the bus. Max blinked and leaned forward again.

"Wait," asked Max in a whisper. "Is one of those talents driving a school bus?"

"Nope," replied Lovecraft with quiet delight, and he ground the gears trying to shift. A few people cried out in surprise. He called back to the class. "Sorry! Been a while."

After a few false starts, Lovecraft got the bus moving forward. He pulled out of the parking lot as more students and teachers poured out of the school, some in a blind panic.

Reluctantly, Lovecraft had to trust that the other teachers would get their students onto their buses. If he tried to save everybody, he would save nobody.

"Max?" said Lovecraft. "You're my navigator! Where is this place?"

"Left," said Max as they came up to an intersection.

"Left it is."

# 6

Miraculously, Lovecraft only stalled the bus once at a

light. They drove through the edge of town towards the jail. The neighborhoods had tree-lined streets before pleasant, cookie-cutter houses. It was almost quiet and peaceful, and then the jail loomed up.

Against the suburban backdrop were two-story walls that looked like the remains of a gothic castle. Behind those walls was a four-story building towards the left.

On the right-hand side of the jail was a large iron gate. Lovecraft pulled up to it.

Before Lovecraft had even stopped, Max was out of his seat and looking out through the windshield. There was a larger gate in the middle, but set into one side was a person-sized gate.

"How do we get in there?" asked Max.

"There's a caretaker for the jail," supplied Patrick.

"I don't see them," said Max. "How do we get their attention?"

Lovecraft hit the bus horn. "That often works."

A round fellow, Stu, wrapped in an old brown coat, shot out of the jail, arms pumping. He sported a Still Life Carver hat over thinning brown hair.

"I'm coming," moaned Stu with a put-upon voice. "I'm coming."

Stu reached the gate and froze, a big keyring dangling from his hand.

Inside the bus, Patrick watched with disbelief. "Um, what is he waiting for?"

But Max saw that Stu was looking around the bus.

27

"He's looking for revenants," explained the boy.

"Considering he's unarmed, that's not a bad policy," said Lovecraft. He peered through the gate to the large cobblestone courtyard, which looked like the bailey of a castle. "I'm surprised that the police aren't already here."

Seeing that it was safe, Stu opened the larger front gate and swung it open to let in the bus.

Max glanced at the top of the gate, which did not look that tall to him.

"Is this bus going to fit under that gate?" asked Max wearily.

"We'll see," said Lovecraft neutrally. He eased the bus forward. Luckily, it passed within a hair's breadth of clearance. Lovecraft gave a relieved grin. "Piece of cake."

Pulling the bus around the bailey, Lovecraft parked it so that the front pointed back towards the gate. Killed the engine, he pulled open the bus door and stood to look back at the class.

"I'm going to go see what's going on," said Lovecraft. "Stay here for now until we know where we're going."

Tammi looked out the dirty bus windows at the gothic walls which surrounded them.

"No problem," she squeaked.

But Max smiled at her. "Believe me; I'll take thick walls —even creepy ones—any day of the week."

"Okay," said the Substitute Teacher loudly to get everyone's attention. "I need someone to close the door behind me."

28

"I'd be happy to close the door," said Tammi quickly. She jumped up and dove into the driver's seat. Grabbing the door handle, she yanked the door shut.

Lovecraft gave a tiny chuckle. "You have to let me out first."

With an embarrassed smile, Tammi opened the door again.

Lovecraft stepped out of the bus, and Max and Patrick jumped down to follow.

Once they were all clear, Tammi quickly closed the bus door.

Beside Lovecraft, Max and Patrick fell into pace beside him. The three-headed towards Stu, who was closing the front gate.

Lovecraft murmured to the boys. "I'm pretty sure I didn't invite you two along."

"I know Stu; that's the name of the caretaker, by the way," explained Patrick. "After the jail closed, he was put in charge."

Before Lovecraft could reply, they reached Stu, who fixed them all with a beady glare.

"Welcome to Hellboys," said Stu.

"What?" asked Max in surprise.

"He's joking," said Lovecraft to Max, and then he glanced back to Stu with a stern look. "Right?"

"Oh yes, joking," muttered Stu. "No one takes ol' Stu seriously, but I've seen what I've seen, an' none of it's good, especially the man with the noose—now there's a nasty one

—but those things in the halls, they say they're shadows, but old Stu knows different 'cause..."

Lovecraft tried to interject. "Sir?"

"...I've seen the things that I've seen," continued Stu defensively. "'Course, I should've run a long time ago, but in this economy what can a man do, especially with a good-paying job, and I gotta eat, so I can't turn down good money, even if the blasted place is..."

"SIR?" snapped Lovecraft.

"Well, you don't have to snap at me and get all dismissive," said Stu indignantly.

"I'm not dismissing you," replied Lovecraft, straining to keep his voice calm. He nodded at the boys. "But they're already on edge, having just been evacuated from the school. Could you please keep the doom and gloom down to a minimum?"

Patrick looked at Lovecraft.

"He's actually like this most of the time," explained Patrick with a kind but amused tone. He turned back to the caretaker. "Hi, sir."

With surprise, Stu suddenly noticed the boy.

"Oh, Patrick?" asked Stu. "What're you doing here?"

"Running from revenants," said Patrick blithely. "How're you doing, sir?"

"Good," said Stu. "So, you finally got your wish?"

"Kinda," said Patrick. "Wish it was under better circumstances."

"Wish?" asked Lovecraft in confusion. "What wish?"

30

"This young fellow's been trying to get in here for years now," said Stu.

"And...why?" asked Lovecraft.

"He wants to chase after ghosts," said Stu.

"Ghosts," said Lovecraft in a soft voice. His chest tightened like a fist.

"He asked to run around here," said Stu, and he smiled indulgently to Patrick. "Isn't that right?"

"Actually," huffed Patrick, with as much authority as a teenage boy can muster. "I want to conduct a serious investigation of this site."

"You *want* to go after ghosts?" asked Lovecraft incredulously. "That's...that's..."

"Investigate," repeated Patrick. "Some investigators have gotten some outstanding evidence, but no one's ever done a full investigation of the entire facility, including the tunnels?"

"There're tunnels under here?" asked Max, who looked down at the cobblestones.

"The buildings are connected via a tunnel system, but I've been having trouble getting a complete map of them," said Patrick.

Stu fixed Patrick with a stern look. "And I'm not letting you into any tunnels. You stay away from the laundry room. Anyway, it's going to be bad enough with all these people here." He gave a sad moan. "They've been so quiet lately."

"Who has?" asked Max, but Stu did not seem to hear

31

him and continued on.

"Now these people are gonna rile them up like hornets," muttered Stu. "Rile them up until it boils over, and I tol' them not to put anyone in here, but they wouldn't listen to ol' Stu, 'cause..."

A young woman, Florence, suddenly ran up to the gate.

"Can you help us?" she asked breathlessly.

"Yes," said Lovecraft, a little too quickly.

"The TV said to come here, but my Dad's out of town, and my grandmother can't move well," said Florence. "I could move her a little, but I can't get her down the stairs easily."

"It's okay, I'm coming," said Lovecraft. He looked at Stu. "Can you open the small gate?"

"Sure! I can do lots of stuff," murmured Stu. "Man of many talents. Can play the organ."

Stu opened the smaller door in the gate, and Lovecraft went through, shadowed by Max.

Patrick stayed right where he was. He was only interested in people that had non-corporeal bodies. Besides, it was dangerous out there.

While Florence vibrated with tension, Lovecraft looked at Max.

"Who invited you?" asked Lovecraft.

"You might need me," replied Max casually.

"Or you might get gnawed on," said Lovecraft.

"Haven't yet," grinned Max.

"Hurry," said Florence, and she started across the street. Max followed her with a shrug of his shoulders.

"She's right," said the boy. "We gotta hurry."

Lovecraft growled. "All right, but the first sign of trouble, you run back to jail."

"Right, sure," said Max offhandedly, and he paced beside Florence.

The Substitute Teacher said to the empty air where Max had been. "You're not listening."

Lovecraft took off across the street. He followed Florence and the boy towards a little cream-colored house with a wheelchair ramp.

Florence was a slim young woman in a skirt with rose vine tattoos running up and down the outside of her legs. She opened the door and stepped into a tiny but fiercely clean home. As Lovecraft and Max came in behind her, Florence yelled up the stairs.

"Grandma!" cried Florence. "I'm back!"

Florence ran up the stairs as a voice came down.

"Are we screwed?" asked an old woman from above.

"No, grandma," replied Florence. "I brought help."

"That was fast," exclaimed the old woman, Maddie, in surprise.

Lovecraft and Max followed Florence up the stairs to a small bedroom. Maddie lay on her bed in her Sunday-Go-To-Meeting clothes, and Florence gaped at her grandmother in shock.

"You changed?" asked Florence. "How'd you change?"

"I'm not going God-knows-where in my nightgown," harrumphed Maddie.

Lovecraft noted a wheelchair in the corner of the room.

"Max, bring down the wheelchair, and I'll carry Ms...?" asked Lovecraft of the grandmother.

"Conners dear," said Maddie with a little purr. "But, you can call me Maddie."

"Pleased to meet you," said Lovecraft neutrally as he bent over to pick her up. As he lifted her, Maddie wrapped her arms around and leaned her mouth toward Lovecraft's ear.

"Pleased to meet you too hot stuff," whispered Maddie.

Lovecraft instantly blushed. He carefully moved through the door with her. One of Maddie's fingers traced a muscle on his upper back.

"So, you got a girlfriend?" asked Maddie.

"Um, yes...actually I do," stammered Lovecraft.

"Pity. What a...," started Maddie in sadness when there was a crash from downstairs. The broken glass shattered onto the kitchen tile.

"That better not be the new China," said Maddie in a malevolent voice.

"Everyone hurry!" hissed Lovecraft as he moved down the stairs quickly. He slid out into the living room, which was clear for now.

Max was trying to manhandle the wheelchair down the stairs but accidentally whacked one of the walls in his haste.

"Careful," snapped Maddie.

"Sorry," whispered Max in reply with an embarrassed grimace. He tried to move more carefully, but that just slowed his progress. Lovecraft could now hear noises beyond the living room to the kitchen.

"Maybe we shouldn't worry about the walls," whispered Lovecraft in an urgent voice.

"Easy for you to say," said Maddie with a flat iron in her voice.

A revenant shuffled past the doorway to the living room, but it was looking away towards the back of the house.

"Hurry, hurry, hurry!" whispered Lovecraft to Max.

The boy reached the bottom of the stairs and aimed the wheelchair towards the door. The revenant was looking away as Lovecraft carefully shifted Maddie so that one of his arms was free. The fingers of his freed hand across the top rail of a wooden chair.

"Almost...," whispered Max as he moved the wheelchair through the doorway and onto the porch.

The revenant turned and locked eyes on Lovecraft and Maddie. It shambled quickly towards them. Florence gave an involuntary cry. Grabbing the top rail of the chair, Lovecraft swung it up like a lion tamer.

"Everyone out!" cried Lovecraft as he used the chair legs to push the revenant back. The creature snapped its teeth and reached over the chair for Lovecraft and Maddie. Florence escaped through the door, and Max turned the wheelchair around to point the seat back inside the house.

"Wheelchair ready!" called out Max.

Lovecraft shoved the revenant back with the wooden

chair. As it stumbled back, Lovecraft twisted left. He put down the wooden chair and turned towards the wheelchair.

Pulling Maddie free of him, he settled her gently into the wheelchair. But Lovecraft kept turning so that he once again faced the revenant. He picked up the chair and used it to drive the creature back across the living room.

The revenant tripped over the edge of a glass coffee table. Luckily, the creature fell beside it instead of going through it. It tried to rise up, though.

Lovecraft smashed the chair down on its head, which broke both the furniture and its skull. The revenant did not get back up.

Dropping the remains of the chair, Lovecraft ran to the door and found Maddie glaring at him.

"My chair!" she snapped. Lovecraft spun her wheelchair around and pushed her down the ramp.

"I'll buy you a new one," said Lovecraft as they bounced towards the street. After a moment of consideration, Maddie shrugged.

"Meh," she declared as the Substitute Teacher carefully levered her over the curb and onto the street. "It was kind of ugly."

Suddenly, Maddie pointed her Lee Press-On nails towards the jail. "Now mush!"

Lovecraft gave a grin as he pushed her swiftly across the street.

"We got a Z at eight and one at ten o'clock," called out Max, running behind with Florence. More revenants appeared from between the cookie-cutter houses.

One revenant, wearing a Snoopy T-Shirt, was walking towards the front gate quickly.

Maddie noticed and waved. "Hello, Mrs. Henderson!"

The revenant changed direction and started walking more quickly towards them.

"Please don't encourage them," said Lovecraft in Maddie's ear.

Out of the small gate, the Substitute Teacher saw a sheriff's deputy run out. But the deputy stopped in horror at the sight of Mrs. Henderson, the revenant. Lovecraft turned to Max.

"Take over," ordered Lovecraft. "Get the ladies inside!"

"Will do," replied Max.

Lovecraft jumped aside as Maddie looked up in surprise.

Smoothly, Max grabbed the handles of the wheelchair and pushed her through the small gate, followed by Florence.

Lovecraft stopped next to the deputy.

With a hollow voice, the deputy said. "Tha...that's Gail Henderson, my Mom's friend."

"No. No, it's not," said Lovecraft gently. "Not anymore."

The deputy hesitated. Mrs. Henderson was getting closer, but Lovecraft knew from experience that if he took away the deputy's gun now, he'd be useless from now on.

"This is hard, Lord knows it's hard," urged Lovecraft. "But, there is no cure. You're not doing anyone any favors, especially not her."

Scrunching up his face, the deputy fired his gun. Mrs. Henderson's head snapped back, and she flopped over backward. Lovecraft waited a moment as the deputy stared at the dead person he had created.

Finally, Lovecraft put his hand out to lower the deputy's weapon.

Shaking, the deputy leaned over and tossed his cookies. Lovecraft just stood there and patted the poor man's back.

"Come on," said Lovecraft gently as he led the deputy back into the prison. When Stu slammed the small gate shut, the deputy jumped.

Quickly, another revenant reached the gate as Stu backed up. It grasped through the bars.

"Unrgh," it moaned.

Past the gate, more revenants were coming.

Curiously, Patrick stepped closer to look at the one revenant.

"Careful," said Lovecraft and Stu in tandem.

"I will," assured Patrick, staring at the red halos around the creature's irises. He said, mostly to himself. "I wonder what they see?"

"Let's not find out," said Stu quickly. The caretaker grabbed Patrick's backpack and hauled the boy back.

Spotting a squad car, Lovecraft steered the deputy towards it. He needed to keep the lawman occupied. Max ran up but slowed to keep pace beside the Substitute Teacher and the deputy as they walked.

Lovecraft asked of the deputy. "What's your name?"

"Crafty Downs," said the deputy, but then he saw the puzzled look on Lovecraft's face. The deputy shrugged. He continued with the practiced ease of someone who has had to explain their name their whole life. "My parents didn't get around to naming me at first, and apparently, I had a knack for getting out of my crib. So, my father started calling me Crafty, and...wait, who are you?"

Lovecraft introduced himself and Max. Crafty looked down at the boy and then back at Lovecraft.

"Your apprentice?" smirked the deputy.

"Zombie bait," replied Lovecraft in a mock-serious tone.

"Hey!" retorted Max, but he could not suppress his smile.

"When I got here," said Crafty. "That strange guy by the gate said you were helping someone. I was going to come and help."

"I appreciate that," said Lovecraft sincerely. "You know, I worked as a deputy for a while. I know most weapons. Hell, the gun range was the best part of the training."

Crafty grinned. "Yeah! That was my favorite part too."

"What weapons do you have in your squad car?" asked Lovecraft. "Or, do we have to hit those things with sticks?"

Crafty grinned like a magician about to do a trick. "Let me show you *the trunk*."

Jogging over to the car door, Crafty leaned in and popped the trunk. It rose like a lid of a treasure chest.

Lovecraft gave an appreciative whistle. The inside of the trunk was filled with handguns, rifles, and several edged weapons.

"Well now, that's a good start," said Lovecraft. "Do you know when the rest will get here?"

Crafty looked confused. "I thought this was all we got."

"Huh. Well then, could you tell me when the sheriff arrives?" asked Lovecraft.

Max's face lit up, and he reached for a massive rifle.

"Dibs on that one," called out the boy.

Lovecraft lightly smacked the kid's hand, who let out a yelp.

"Not this time!" declared the Substitute Teacher.

"Ow! That's not fair!" replied Max as he stepped back. The smack on the hand had not hurt, so much as surprised him.

"Has anyone ever trained you to use a gun?" asked Lovecraft seriously. "I mean, like proper training, on a range."

"Well, no," admitted Max. "But I've used one...you know, before. In Toledo."

"That's not good enough," replied Lovecraft.

"You don't want to have to do what I just did," said Crafty grimly as he looked at the boy. The deputy's eyes started to unfocus. "I mean, she went down so..."

Max nodded sympathetically. "The first revenant is always the hardest."

"HEY!" cried out Stu from the gate. "We got more buses coming!"

Lovecraft turned to Max. "I've got an important job for you to do."

"What?" asked Max suspiciously.

"Can you find a way up onto that wall?" asked Lovecraft nodding to the outer wall of the jail. "There might be a walkway on top of the main wall, overlooking the gate."

Max looked around and saw a doorway in the outer wall of the jail.

"Sure," said Max.

Lovecraft took out his flashlight and handed it reverently to the boy.

"Take my Klarus flashlight," said Lovecraft solemnly. "But, I want it back. I bought that myself from Thinkgeek, back when it was alive."

"Yeah, yeah," said Max dismissively.

"And, if you don't see anything right away," added Lovecraft. "Don't worry about it. Just, don't get lost— especially in this place."

"I'll be fine," grinned Max. The boy turned and ran towards the door.

"Hopefully, we all will," muttered Lovecraft.

"What'd you say?" asked Crafty.

But Lovecraft just smiled genially.

"Nothing," he replied. He looked down at the trunk of weapons, and his eyes lit up. "Hey! You've got a Gurkha knife!"

"I gotta what?" asked Crafty in confusion. Lovecraft

lifted a massive knife in a black sheath. The Substitute Teacher unsheathed it and held up the large, curved blade, built for chopping. Crafty just whistled.

"Made famous by the Gurkhas Regiments, who the British enlisted from Nepal," explained Lovecraft as he sheathed the knife. He strapped it to his left hip.

"So, it's like a curved machete," said Crafty, trying to fit the idea into his worldview.

"Exactly," agreed Lovecraft. "Now, let's see what else is here."

After a quick appraisal, Lovecraft slung an MP5 submachine gun over his head so that it hung across his chest. Lastly, Lovecraft reverently picked up a Model 94 Winchester Takedown repeating rifle.

"You know your guns," said Crafty in awe, and Lovecraft looked at him in concern.

"I didn't grab anything you wanted?" asked Lovecraft quickly. "I mean, it is your squad car."

"Nope," said Crafty as he reached in for an AK-47. "This should do me nicely."

"Okay, now we need to remove those revenants from the gate fast," said Lovecraft.

"People could just run them down," suggested Crafty.

Lovecraft made a wavering noise. "Um, most people freak out if they hit a dog. Now imagine having to run over Aunt Gertie."

"Oh," was all Crafty said.

"And we don't want those cars to squish them into the

gate because...eew," said Lovecraft in disgust. He pointed to a hook on a metal pole at the back of the trunk. "Oh. Grab that Z-stick too."

"Z, like Z for Zombie?" asked Crafty.

"Yep," said Lovecraft. "Once a revenant is down, we can use that to drag the body away from the gate safely."

Each man grabbed a box of ammo and walked towards the gate.

"And be careful to shoot through the bars," said Lovecraft as he dropped a box of ammo for the Winchester into his coat pocket. "We don't want any ricochets."

"Got it," nodded Crafty as they reached the gate.

Lovecraft leveled his rifle and fired at the revenants beyond.

# 7

Max stepped into a dimly lit hall, inside the outer wall of the jail. As his eyes adjusted to the gloom, he looked around. Squinting down the hall, he saw someone farther down, but the boy could only make out a silhouette.

"Hey! Do you know where to find the stairs? I need to get up on top of the wall?" called out Max.

But the figure just went around a corner without a word.

Max huffed. "Jerk."

Turning in the opposite direction, Max moved forward,

but the corridor was sparsely lit. He switched on the Klarus flashlight at its highest setting—and immediately, the corridor lit up, like on a bright, sunny day.

"That helped," muttered Max happily.

The boy spotted some stairs. Taking them up, he emerged into the sunlight. He was on a walkway set on top of the wall, just like a castle's battlements.

There was a row of several yellow buses waiting—like nervous animals—outside the jail. A line of cars and SUVs followed these.

Below, he heard talking outside the jail and then the sound of a hook hitting meat. Max looked over the edge of the battlements. Deputy Crafty—with a pale face—dragged off the now very dead revenants.

Standing guard over the deputy, Lovecraft scanned the area. Max looked up and saw more cars coming in the distance. He leaned over the wall near Lovecraft.

"More cars coming!" called out Max.

Lovecraft waved. "Good job, kid. Come back down."

Max disappeared up above as the Substitute Teacher looked back out past the buses. Crafty walked over, breathing heavily from the exertion.

"Done," he declared.

"Thank you," said Lovecraft sincerely. "Let's get these people in."

Waving at Stu to open the main gate, the school buses rolled into the jail's bailey. Bringing up the convoy's rear was a news van declaring that Channel 2 News was the best in the state.  Emblazoned on the side was a picture of anchor Rick Hurston with the words "Courage.  Strength." under him.

The news van stopped halfway through the gate, and the passenger window rolled down.  Rick Hurston, without makeup or airbrushing, leaned out.  He looked worn, haggard, and—quite frankly—a little chubby.

"What the hell are you doing?" demanded Hurston. Past him in the driver's seat, Hurston's camerawoman—a black woman called Icewater—looked forward with a neutral expression.

"Sir, could you please move forward?" asked Lovecraft nicely.  "We're trying to clear the gate."

"There are kids here!  And you're shooting around wildly and dragging people off with a hook?" shouted Hurston.  His face became blotchy with anger, and his voice had a manic tone.

"It was the only way to clear the gate," responded Lovecraft calmly.  "Which needs to stay clear so, if you could please move forward."

Lovecraft looked around.  In the distance, he saw a new crop of revenants coming out from between the houses. They turned like a tide towards the jail.

"Couldn't you have waited until the kids were not here?" asked Hurston.

"But the kids were already here," reasoned Lovecraft. "And so were the revenants.  Move out of the gate."

"You should subdue those poor people," huffed Hurston indignantly.  "Have you tried tying them up instead of shooting them like dogs?"

"Um, Lovecraft," said Crafty, who was staring nervously at the coming revenants.

"Even with special equipment—which we don't have—it is extremely dangerous to capture revenants alive," explained Lovecraft quickly, and he turned a hard, flinty look on the Reporter. The Substitute Teacher shifted his rifle to point it right at Hurston's forehead. "Now move your goddamn vehicle!"

Hurston's lip quivered. "You wouldn't."

The Camerawoman's eyes darted over and saw Lovecraft.

"All I care about is the safety of the kids inside," said Lovecraft in a flat tone.

Before Hurston could respond, the Camerawoman pulled the van into the bailey.

"Goddamn it! What're you doing?" demanded Hurston of Icewater.

But the Camerawoman just kept her eyes forward.

"Now it looks like I was scared of him," snarled Hurston, but it fell into a whine.

"You know where I've worked," said Icewater finally in a calm, neutral tone.

"Sure, you've filmed all over the world," shrugged Hurston as she parked.

"Afghanistan, Libya, Iraq," said Icewater. "And I knew that look. You were about to die. Our producer would blame me. He'd make me clean up the van. Also, you'd be dead."

# 8

As the van pulled away, Crafty tried to laugh the tension away.

"Wow," grinned Crafty a little maniacally as they stepped back through the gate.

Behind them, Stu began to close it.

"You sure fooled him," continued the Deputy. "Heck, even I thought you were going to shoot 'em."

"I was," replied Lovecraft calmly as the gate clanged shut. Crafty's mouth opened and closed in shock. Lovecraft continued as he looked Crafty square in the eye. "All that matters right now is the safety of those kids."

Crafty blinked, and then he pulled himself together. A moment later, another revenant reached the gate, moaning sadly. Lovecraft glanced over.

"I'm going to go up on the wall and see if I can't take out the revenants before they clog up that gate again. Can you cover the gate down here?"

"S...sure," said Crafty.

"Good," said Lovecraft, who turned and strode away. Max ran up and paced along.

"We going up?" asked Max.

"Lead the way," nodded Lovecraft.

Max took Lovecraft into the dark hall snapping on the light.

"It's right this way," said Max, speaking like a tour guide.

Inside the jail walls, the air was cool as they walked to the stone stairs leading up. Max led Lovecraft up to an old door, which opened with only a slight creak.

They stepped out onto a walkway on top of the wall. Lovecraft leaned over the edge of the battlements and whistled.

"Good job," said Lovecraft, and he held out his hand to the boy.

Max—who had already pocketed the flashlight—looked up at him innocently.

"What?" asked Max.

"Fork it over," said Lovecraft with a wry grin.

"I lost it?" suggested Max.

"Fork," repeated Lovecraft.

Max gave a melodramatic sigh and handed over the flashlight.

Lovecraft put it away and looked out over the city. In the distance, he saw a raging fire near the hospital.

Lovecraft's face fell. "And now they start."

"What starts?" asked Max.

"The fires," said Lovecraft. "During an outbreak, fires often run out of control, at least until they run out of food."

"Yeah," said the boy in a hollow voice. "I remember that

48

now. We were lucky. None of the buildings near us went up. But afterward, I heard stories. People retreating from the revenants, but with each retreat, getting closer and closer to the fire until they were standing right in front of it."

"Oh, that's right," winced Lovecraft. "Sorry, kid, I forgot who I was talking to."

Lovecraft turned to the boy and patted the gray stones that made up the jail.

"But for us," said the Substitute Teacher. "We should be fine."

"True," agreed the boy, and he gave a little hopeful smile. Max twisted and pointed West. "Oh! More school buses."

"Thank God," said Lovecraft for several reasons, but he put a voice to one of them. "We certainly haven't seen enough to account for all the kids yet."

Lovecraft set the box of bullets for the repeating rifle on the edge of the battlements.

In front of the lead school bus, a revenant in a torn suit tried awkwardly to step out in front of the bus. Lovecraft lifted his rifle and fired. The bullet tipped revenant backward, and it tumbled back down a small hill.

Max patted Lovecraft's right shoulder. "There's another one. Z at 2 o'clock!"

Becoming a spotter for Lovecraft, Max helped him slow the tide of revenants. More buses and cars arrived, which were heralded to safety into the jail by Crafty and Stu.

Suddenly, Max heard a screech of tires from the north.

The boy saw that a car had stopped down a side street to avoid running over a dead revenant.

"What are they doing?" moaned Max out loud.

"Who?" asked Lovecraft, and then he followed Max's gaze. They only saw the car from the passenger side, and the driver was obscured.

"Drive! Just get out of there!" said Max with exasperation.

The car backed up, but it bumped into a curb. The driver moved the vehicle forward but stopped again before they ran over another dead body. The vehicle turned awkwardly towards the original body.

"I think they're trying," said Lovecraft, who saw more revenants appearing. He lifted his rifle and fired, dropping two. But the others had cover from trees or houses.

Futilely, Max called out to the driver, even though they could not possibly hear.

"Come on, hurry! What's taking so long?"

"Bad driver?" suggested Lovecraft.

More revenants were closing in on the car. Lovecraft ran down the wall to get a better shot, but he still had limited visibility.

"What's he doing now?" cried Max in exasperation. The driver's door opened, and the person jumped out of the car. "Oh, no, no no no! Stay in your car."

The driver, a young man in a blue suit jacket, went up to the dead revenant and grabbed its feet to drag it out of the way. Behind the driver, a revenant bore down on him.

Lovecraft fired at the revenant, killing it instantly. But the driver jumped at the sound of the rifle shot. He looked around, confused.

"Go! Go faster!" shouted Max, but again, they were too far for the driver to hear.

The driver grabbed the body's feet and pulled it aside. He began to run back to his car when another revenant jumped out at him. The revenant pushed the driver against the car's left side and out of Lovecraft's sight.

"Damn it!" cried Lovecraft. He paced back and forth when the driver jumped up.

"There he is!" cried Max. Lovecraft lifted his rifle to fire when the revenant appeared behind the driver. The monster tore into the side of the driver's throat, and they both sank slowly out of sight.

"Oh no," whispered Max. "No."

The boy deflated. His mouth opened and closed vainly, but no sound came out.

"I agree," said Lovecraft softly.

Taking a deep breath, the Substitute raised his rifle and went back to work.

# 9

Lovecraft shifted his feet. He and Max had been up on the wall for a good two hours now. Scanning the nearby streets, he did not see any more vehicles. Leaning over the battlements, he spotted Crafty below.

"I don't see any more vehicles," called out Lovecraft. "I'm packing it in up here."

The Substitute Teacher looked over at Max. "Ready?"

Max laughed grimly. "When I got up this morning, I thought the worst thing about my day was going to be a math test."

"Had days like that," smiled Lovecraft gently. "Whole weeks even."

"How did you get through?" asked Max.

"Adam, he works from Downstairs at the Office, has a mantra, 'Calm people live, tense people die,'" said Lovecraft solemnly. "So, we stay calm."

"Is...is it easy?" asked Max.

"Some days are easier than others," admitted Lovecraft. "Now..."

"HEY! HEY Lovecraft!" cried Crafty from below. Moving to the edge, Lovecraft looked down again.

"What's up?" asked Lovecraft.

"We got a broken down bus that's still in town," called out Crafty.

"Damn it," swore Lovecraft, and he tore down the stairs, followed by Max. They ran out into the bailey to find Crafty there. "Where's the bus?"

"It's over by McSub's," said Crafty.

"And where the hell is that?" asked Lovecraft.

"I'll direct you there," said Max.

"You will?" asked Lovecraft. "Who even said you were coming along?"

"You did," said Max. "When you found out you needed a navigator."

"There are these things called maps," said Lovecraft. "And I don't care if they get torn apart by zombies. You're staying here."

"But...," started Max.

"What I need you to do is to empty our bus. Maybe take the kids over to the other school buses," said Lovecraft.

"I could be more help out there," insisted Max.

"It's one thing to have you help me in here," said Lovecraft. "And I've appreciated your help!—but I need to know that my students are safe too."

Max opened his mouth to speak but then stopped. "Damn it. Okay."

Reluctantly, the boy ran towards bus #7.

"Kid's crazy," muttered Crafty.

"Yeah, but it's a good kind of crazy," smirked Lovecraft proudly. He did not want to point out that the boy had more experience under his belt when it came to revenants than the deputy. Instead, he turned to Crafty. "If you hold down the fort here, I'll get the school bus."

"I feel kinda weird letting you go out there alone," said Crafty guiltily.

Lovecraft glanced and saw Max leading the students away from bus #7.

"The jail is the most important place to guard right now," explained Lovecraft truthfully. "We don't want to send out the only police officer we have right now on what may be a suicide mission."

Crafty's eyes grew big. Sensing the importance of his role, the deputy puffed out his chest a little. Also, he realized that he did not want to go back out there. The broken-down bus could easily be a lost cause.

"I hadn't thought of it like that," said Crafty at last.

"Also, you might want to see if anyone else is qualified to carry a firearm," said Lovecraft.

"Good idea," said Crafty. Lovecraft turned towards bus #7 when the High School Principal ran up to him and engulfed the Substitute Teacher in a massive bear hug.

# 10

By the time Max reached bus #7, Tammi already had the door had opened. The boy jumped up into the aisle to address everyone.

"They're taking this bus out," said Max, quickly. There was no small-talk in a place like this. The small talk got people dead. "We got a broken down bus out there, and they need this bus to go get them. Can everyone get out now?"

"Out there?" asked Missy with a tremble in her voice.

"It's safe within these walls," assured Max.

"You gotta be crazy if you think we're going out there. And a little guy like you can't *make* me go," snapped Craig. He put a protective hand on Missy's shoulder and stood up to face Max.

It was a display that might have garnered a different response, even that very morning.

There was only one problem. The bully didn't have a clue of what the boy was really going through.

Colossally unimpressed, Max said. "Okay! If you want to stay here, that's cool. But *this* bus *is* going out there." Max pointed out past the big iron gate. "And, anyone who doesn't want to be on it, come with me!"

Max jumped out of the bus. For a moment, no one moved, and then Simp got up. He started forward when Craig grabbed his arm.

"Where're you going?" demanded Craig.

"Not back out there," shrugged Simp. "At least, not until it's safe."

Ignoring the bully's glare, Simp pulled his arm free of Craig and walked out of the bus. After a moment, more students came out. Even Missy pulled away from Craig and left.

Eventually, Craig was forced to admit that he needed to leave as well. As the bully stepped off the bus, Max started to lead the students towards the other school buses.

"How're you doing?" asked Tammi of Max as they walked.

"I'm good," said Max automatically.

"I'm surprised you didn't try to go back on the bus," said Tammi.

"Who says I'm not?" asked Max slyly.

"You can't go back out there!" exclaimed Tammi.

"I'm with Mr. Lovecraft," said Max. "And I've seen him shoot. I'll be relatively safe with him."

"Still, it's crazy," said Tammi urgently. "Why do it?"

Max did not answer right away.

Tammi put her head down. "Sorry, I'm prying. Mom says I do that a lot. I'm just glad they're out of town this week. I just...I can't imagine going out there."

They reached the other school buses. He looked around and saw that everyone was here, including all the bullies. In the distance, he saw Lovecraft talking with the school principal. The Substitute was going to be stuck there for a while.

Max turned to Tammi, who was probably his only real friend and said. "I just can't stand here and do nothing. Because it's scary out there."

Tammi blinked at him in confusion. "But, shouldn't that stop you from going out?"

"After...after Toledo, I had nightmares. I still have nightmares every once in a while," admitted Max. "If I'm working, I don't have to think about where I am—again! Especially when I could be helping."

"And you made it out of Toledo," sighed Tammi. She spoke softly, trying to reassure herself, not only of Max's safety but of her own.

"I wish we had had a jail last time," laughed Max, but it was rueful.

Tammi shivered.

"You okay?" asked Max.

"Just cold," said Tammi. "I forgot my coat at school."

Max took off his Detroit Tigers jacket and laid it over her shoulders.

"You don't have to," said Tammi quickly.

"Just a loan," said Max good-naturedly, and then he smiled. "I'll be back soon."

"You better," huffed Tammi.

# 11

Lovecraft finally extracted himself from the principal, who was a hugger and gushing over his future rescue of bus #9.

The Substitute Teacher hated that. Even if he got to the bus, there was no assurance that everyone was still alive. Or that he could get them all back to the jail safely.

Jumping into bus #7, Lovecraft started it up without stalling. He grinned at that minor victory. Looking in his side mirror, he saw his students milling around the other buses. In the middle, he briefly saw a silver Detroit Tigers coat.

Satisfied, Lovecraft drove the bus slowly forward as Stu

and Patrick opened the main gate. Moving out onto the street, he managed not to look back as the gate closed.

After a quick consult with his map, Lovecraft took the bus back down into the city. It was not the first dead town he had driven through, but the stillness still gave him the willies.

Maybe it's good that I'm not used to this, he suggested to himself as he stopped at a T-intersection. He opened the map again when he paused. It was not so much a single noise but a gut feeling.

Lovecraft hit the turn signal and started to veer left.

"You're going the wrong way," called out a voice from the back.

"Busted," muttered Lovecraft. Despite himself, though, he flashed a quick grin as he stopped the bus.

"Um, this is the bus' talking GPS," said the voice. "Please turn right."

Lovecraft just sat there.

Finally, Max got up. Slowly, he trudged up to the front like a condemned man.

Without looking back, Lovecraft just pointed at the first seat on the right.

"Sit," said Lovecraft.

"But...," said Max.

Lovecraft slowly turned and gave the boy a flinty look.

Max sat down quickly.

Shaking his head, Lovecraft turned the bus right.

"Next time, I'm going to handcuff you," said Lovecraft, but without any heat. Oddly, a small part of him was happy to have the resourceful kid along.

Max leaned over the rail and looked out the front window as they moved onto Main Street. They passed a car wrapped around a telephone pole. A dark swath of dried blood painted the grey road.

"It's eerie," said Max quietly.

"Let's get this over with quickly," said Lovecraft earnestly as they passed the darkened storefronts.

"There's the bus!" said Max, a little loudly. He wanted to get back to the jail. On any other day, he would have thought that strange, but not today.

Lovecraft slowed the bus to a crawl. The yellow school bus was indeed in front of McSub's. The bus was gently rocking from the press of bodies around it. Revenants were massed on the upper right side as if they knew that the door was there but could not open it. Instead, they pawed like drunks.

"I don't have that much ammo," said Lovecraft slowly.

"We could run them over," suggested Max, though he hated the thought.

"Dangerous. Broken bones are sharp," mused Lovecraft. "Heard a story of someone who was trying to flee an outbreak. He attempted to drive over a mob of revenants in his SUV. A shattered tibia punctured one of their tires, and...well, it didn't go well."

"And I really don't want to walk back to the jail," murmured Max, but then his eyes brightened. He slapped

59

the rail. "Airlock!"

"What?" asked Lovecraft.

"The bus doors open inward," said Max quickly. "We move this bus right up against the other one and open the doors. That way, everyone can pass through safely." He hesitated. "But, we'll have to drive over a few revenants first."

"If we go slow, we might be okay," suggested Lovecraft. He smiled at the kid. "Damn good idea."

Lovecraft slowly moved forward, watching the side of the other bus. He reached the mob of zombies first.

The revenant's attention was squarely on the other bus, so they did not move as Lovecraft's vehicle crept up on them. He stopped just shy of the outermost revenant, but it did not move. It did not even seem to notice him.

Lovecraft looked over at Max.

"You may not want to watch this," suggested the Substitute Teacher.

Max took a deep breath and spoke in a resolute voice. "If you have to watch, I can too."

Lovecraft studied the boy's face for a moment but then nodded slowly.

"Okay," he said.

The Substitute Teacher turned back to the revenants. Easing up on the brake pedal, the bus began to roll forward. The front bumped into a revenant in a fast-food uniform and caused it to stumble into several other creatures. A few wandered aside, but most stayed focused on the other bus.

Lovecraft spoke a final warning to Max. "Here we go."

Pushing the bus forward, Lovecraft knocked over the first group of zombies. The front tires bounced up while the back tires dug into the road. Lovecraft slowly closed onto the crippled bus.

There were no cries beneath them as the bus ground forward. Lovecraft made a minor correction so that he was flush with the stationary bus. He stopped when both doors were even with each other.

Lovecraft could see the teacher, Chris Rayton, through the other door. There was only a small gap between the buses. When both doors were open, Rayton grinned in relief at them.

"Thank God you're here," cried Rayton.

"We were in the neighborhood," shrugged Lovecraft. "Come over, but mind the gap!"

"No problem," said Rayton. He looked back into bus #9. "Okay, everyone, let's go! Carefully."

The students appeared one by one, looking shaken and scared. The first one jumped over the gap with no trouble. Soon, more crossed over into Lovecraft's bus. Max leaned over the stairs of bus #7, ready to lend a hand.

"Head to the back of the bus so that we can get everyone in," called out Lovecraft as the students shuffled to the back. Some looked okay, but others needed to be led to their new seat.

A sharp cry came from the stairwell.

A young girl, Layla, was dragged to the ground. A revenant was trying to pull her jean skirt through the gap between the buses. She had barely had time to cry out when Lovecraft leaped out of the driver's seat. He drew the big curved Gurka knife at his hip.

Dropping into a crouch over the Layla, Lovecraft hacked the revenant's hand off. The young girl let out a squeak. Taking her hand, Lovecraft helped her up and pulled her into the safety of bus #7. He stopped her from going deep in.

"Pardon me," he said as he took the hem of Layla's skirt. He quickly pried the revenant's hand off and smiled up at her. "It's going to be okay."

Layla tried to nod to him, but she was still in shock and shaking visibly. Max stepped forward and gently took her arm.

"Come sit here," murmured Max as he set her down next to him. Layla sat down in a daze, and Max began to speak gently to comfort her. "I know where you've been. It *is* going to be okay."

Lovecraft walked back to the gap as Max continued to console the girl. The Substitute Teacher dropped the severed hand between the busses and kicked the revenant's flailing limb back down. He looked at those left on the other bus.

"Come on," said Lovecraft with assurance. "I'll keep you safe."

When the last student—and the bus driver Randy—were safely on board, Rayton's runner frame easily jumped across the gap with a chuckle of relief.

"Thanks again," grinned Rayton.

"Let's get back to the jail first," said Lovecraft, and he sheathed the Gurkha knife.

"Um, what if we just...you know, kept on going?" asked Rayton.

Curiously, Lovecraft looked at the teacher.

"Would it be safer for us to just drive out of town," suggested Rayton. "I saw some buses that looked like they were doing just that."

"I understand," said Lovecraft. "But I think it's too risky —too many unknowns. First, we don't have a lot of gas. Second, I don't want to get out right now to pump more gas. Third, we don't know how big the outbreak is. The kids are safer in the jail behind those thick walls."

"Well, that's the odd phrase of the day," laughed Rayton, and then he nodded. "Okay. Just needed to make sure."

Lovecraft turned to the driver, Randy, who had just sat down. "Actually, could I talk to you?"

Randy gave a confused frown, but then he stepped up to the front.

"Um," started Lovecraft. "can you drive the bus back to the jail?"

"You got here," said Randy puzzled.

"Barely," said Lovecraft. "I'm not a bus driver, and getting everyone back safely is more important than my pride."

"Oh," nodded Randy. "I can do that."

"Sorry, you're going to have to back out over the run over revenants," said Lovecraft.

"Anything to get us somewhere safe," said Randy, and his voice almost broke. "I thought we were done for."

Lovecraft stepped down in the well by the door and held on as Randy started to back up. He tried not to look down, but it was hard to avoid the mashed zombies, some of which were still reaching out spastically. He was happy that it had been a long time since the continental breakfast at the hotel.

Pulling around the remaining revenants, Randy headed back to Fallen Oaks jail.

# 12

Max and Lovecraft stood quickly aside. Led by Layla, all the students barrelled out of the bus. Ambling along, Rayton followed them like a sheepdog.

The bailey of the jail was almost filled now with cars and buses. Some people sat in their vehicles while others congregated in little groups near their parked cars, like tailgaters at a football game. In the center of the bailey, there appeared to be a heated discussion. Lovecraft could see the news Reporter, Hurston, amongst the people there.

Before he could move, an older man and woman suddenly ran up to them. Lovecraft tensed—ready to defend the boy—but then he saw that the man was nearly in tears.

The older man engulfed Max in a hug.

"Um, hello, Mr. and Mrs. Jonesson," gasped Max from the tight embrace. He saw Lovecraft's questioning look. "This is Jerome and Hannah Jonesson, who live next door to my grandmother and me."

"Oh! Oh my God, it's...," bawled out Jerome, and he began to cry. "We tried. We really did."

"What?" asked Max with a hollow voice. The boy pulled himself away from Jerome, who took out an old, crusty hanky and blew his nose noisily.

Lovecraft found that he was more worried about that dubious handkerchief than anything else. He resisted the urge to pull the boy away from it.

"It's about Doris," said Hannah over Jerome's blubbering. She was concerned, but not overly so.

"Where's my grandmother?" asked Max, and his voice grew small and still.

"I'm sorry," said Hannah.

Max stood there frozen in place.

"We...we tried, but it was too late," sputtered Jerome.

"She had already been bitten when we found her," explained Hannah.

"Oh God," wailed Jerome, and he covered his mouth with that suspicious-looking handkerchief.

"Okay," said Max after a moment. "Well, thank you for trying to help her."

"I'm sorry, dear," said Hannah.

Max just nodded. "As Father Gene kept saying, 'First, let's just get through this all in one piece.'"

The boy turned towards the heated discussion at the center of the bailey.

The shouting from the middle of the courtyard had grown more pronounced. Hurston and some other man were arguing while the Camerawoman filmed it all.

"We should find out what that's all about," said Max as he squared his shoulders.

"You don't have to," said Hannah. "You could..." And there was just the slightest hesitation in her voice. "...come with us."

"Thanks, but I'm okay," said Max, and then he turned to Lovecraft. He spoke in a clipped, professional tone to the Substitute Teacher. "We should check that out."

Max marched off towards the bailey center, and Lovecraft looked back at the couple with a bemused smile.

"Don't worry," said Lovecraft. "I'll keep an eye on him."

Lovecraft could not help but note that Hannah and Jerome looked more than a little relieved. However, he did not know if that was because they had given their bad news or did not want to be burdened with the boy.

For his part, the Substitute Teacher followed Max dutifully.

"Father Gene?" asked Lovecraft when he had caught up with him.

"We were in Toledo together," was all the boy said in a tight voice.

And Lovecraft did not push. However, the Substitute Teacher did take a small tin out of his suitcase. He pried open the lid and scooped out some cream.

"What's that?" asked Max.

"Don't you moisturize?" replied Lovecraft blithely as he put some on his face.

Once they drew closer, the argument grew more audible. The Reporter, Hurston, had cleaned himself up. His chin was now baby smooth, and he wore a crisp blue suit.

"What was going through your mind when you agreed to all this Councilman Tibbons?" asked Hurston of a burly black man whose beard had grown unkempt.

"What do you mean?" rumbled the burly man, Councilman Tibbons. Glancing at the camera, he self-consciously pulled at his beard to try and straighten it out.

"You're on the city council," insisted Hurston aggressively.

The camerawoman, Icewater, had set herself a few paces back to capture Hurston's good side. The Reporter puffed up for the camera and waved his free hand, a little melodramatically thought Lovecraft.

"You MUST have agreed to all this!" said Hurston.

Tibbons, however, was staring at the Reporter as if the man were mentally challenged.

"Maybe you haven't noticed at the city council meetings," said Tibbons, and he forced a patient tone through his gritted teeth. "But, I've been out with back surgery for the last three months, which is why I have the beard. And I'm feeling much better, thank you for asking."

"They would have told you anyhow," insisted Hurston.

Tibbons chuckled without humor. "They wouldn't have told me crap. I was the only one from my party on the council, and they hated my guts."

"It was your radical agenda," said Hurston smoothly.

"Radical?" exclaimed Tibbons. "I suggested we make sure to set aside money for school books before we thought about building a new football stadium for the high school."

"That's important for the local economy," said Hurston.

"Bull! I mean, sure, someone's going to make money, but it will not be the 'local economy,'" said Tibbons as he added in the air quotes.

"We need a new stadium, though!" added Craig, proudly wearing his letter jacket for football.

"Not as much as you need a good education," replied Tibbons.

"Right," scoffed Craig.

"Most people don't get to play for the NFL. And, more than half of all NFL players that do, are broke by 50," said Tibbons. "With a good education, you won't be one of them."

"But, the NFL pays millions," sputtered Craig, who was having serious trouble with this idea.

"I don't mind helping your athletics—really I don't!—but your mind is more important to me," said Tibbons.

Craig fell into thoughtful silence for once.

"I thought that City Hall was supposed to be the rally point," interjected Lovecraft.

"That's what I thought too," said Tibbons as he turned to

Lovecraft. Icewater moved the camera to frame both of them. "That is until I opened that envelope that the city council sent me. Glad I looked at it, or I'd have driven there."

"And where are the rest of the City Council and the mayor?" asked the school teacher, Rayton, as he joined in on the discussion.

"Aren't they all here?" asked Tibbons in surprise.

"We haven't seen them," said Stu, the caretaker, who had wandered up with Patrick to watch the show.

"Well, we can't stay here!" declared Hurston. "This place is...it's...

"Now, two very nice ladies have worked hard this past month to make this place pleasant," said Stu in a strident voice.

"Pleasant?" laughed Hurston bitterly. He shook his hand at the jail infirmary. "You're joking. Who can sleep here."

"There's always the cells," quipped Lovecraft.

Hurston huffed with indignation.

"You should've seen it before, " said Stu. "With all the spiders."

"Spiders?" asked Hurston, and his voice became tight with fear.

"Those ladies—Ms. Rita and Ms. Consuela are their names—worked very hard to fight them off," said Stu. "There was a whole mess of spiders, but they got this place cleaned up and even put fresh sheets on the beds."

"Where are they now?" asked Lovecraft.

"I...I don't know," muttered Stu with concern in his voice. "They left when they were done. Just shot out the gate. They would not stop holding their rosaries the whole time. I mean, I tried to convince them to stay on, but all they muttered was 'fantasa' or 'fantastic.' Something like that."

"*Fantasma?*" asked Lovecraft wearily.

"That's it," said Stu, snapping his fingers. "They'd mutter that, an' you know what, they even tried to get me to come with them."

"What's *Fantasma?*" asked Max.

"That's not important," said Lovecraft quickly.

"It's terrorists, isn't it," bellowed Hurston.

"What?" asked Lovecraft with disbelief.

"They're behind the revenants, aren't they," said Hurston. "Al Qaeda on some jihadi."

"It's Jihad, and no, it's not terrorists," said Lovecraft.

"How do you know," said Hurston dismissively. "Could be them spreading the disease."

"Because the disease—the R-virus, or reanimatus esuriit virus to exact—is natural," said Lovecraft.

"How the hell can those people out there be natural," sneered Hurston with derision.

"It's true," said Rayton stepping up. "The CDC has proven that it's a naturally occurring disease."

"What's the CDC?" asked Max of Lovecraft.

"Center for Disease Control," replied Lovecraft. "They study—well—disease."

"Well, they should know then," shrugged Max.

"That's just what the government wants you to believe," said Hurston.

Lovecraft threw his hands in the air.

"Of all the journalists, we had to get you," muttered Lovecraft. "Where's Edward R. Murrow when we need him?"

"Who?" asked Hurston in confusion.

But Lovecraft did notice a small smile flit across Icewater's face.

"Never mind," said the Substitute Teacher, trying to keep his voice even. "No one is behind this disease."

"I don't believe that," said Hurston.

"The CDC has already done a lot of studies on what is commonly known as the R-Virus," said Rayton, falling comfortably into his role as a science teacher. "The 'R' stands for revenant because I think the CDC was too embarrassed or felt it was unprofessional to call them 'zombies.'"

"And how do you know about this?" asked Tibbons curiously.

"I did a paper on the virus for my Masters at Central Michigan," said Rayton. "The CDC, Stanford, John Hopkins, and Michigan State have poured over the virus, and they did not find any signs of human engineering."

"But, for it to be natural...?" questioned Hurston. "That's

71

hard to swallow."

"Smallpox, Measles, and the Spanish Flu are all-natural, and they've killed at least 550 million people in our history," said Rayton.

"And Ebola makes you bleed from every part of your body," added Lovecraft with amusement.

"I like to tell my students," smiled Rayton. "Mother Nature can be mean, and don't you forget it."

"More importantly," said Lovecraft with finality. "We need to get these people inside." He looked at Stu. "Is there any food?"

"Of course, lots of food," sniffed Stu, as though he were offended by the question. However, then he stopped and shrugged. "I haven't tried it, though, but we'll do that soon enough. I am getting hungry."

"The food had better be good," said Hurston.

"At least it's food," insisted Lovecraft.

"Easy for you to say," sneered Hurston.

"I'm in a jail that is soon to be surrounded by revenants," said Lovecraft flatly. "I'll take my victories where I can get them."

"And who are you anyhow?" asked Hurston indignantly.

"Substitute teacher for the high school. History," said Lovecraft, and he turned to look at Tibbons. "Sir, as a member of the City Council, could you and the caretaker of this facility, Stu, lead everyone inside."

"You make it sound like we're staying here," snapped Hurston.

There was a sad moan from the gate as a revenant pawed through the bars.

"You're welcome to leave anytime you want," said Lovecraft waving a hand absently at the gate.

"Come on, everybody," called out Tibbons as he stepped towards the infirmary. The double doors were already open, showing clean sheets on the mattresses. "Let's see what Stu—and those nice ladies—have set up for us."

Tibbons walked towards the infirmary with quiet authority. After a moment, Rayton motioned for all the students to follow him, and he walked towards the infirmary as well. Tibbons was soon ushering people inside, except for a few stragglers like Craig, Missy, and Hurston.

"I'm hungry," announced Missy. She turned to go into the infirmary, and Craig followed her dutifully.

Hurston, seeing that his audience was leaving, turned to the camera. He gave a bright, confident smile.

"Well, let's go see what our temporary living quarters are like," said Hurston to the camera. He marched quickly to the infirmary, followed by the Camerawoman.

Lovecraft turned to Crafty before the deputy went in.

"We should leave someone on the gate in case anyone else comes," said Lovecraft.

Crafty eyed the revenants at the gate. "People are not going to want to stand out there for long."

"We could do three-hour shifts," suggested Lovecraft. "I can take one this evening."

73

"I can do a couple as well," said Crafty.

"Do you have any walkie-talkies?" asked Lovecraft.

"In the trunk," said Crafty, and they went back to his squad car. The deputy opened the trunk and handed one to Lovecraft.

"I better get a walkie-talkie for the Councilman as well," said Lovecraft. As Crafty handed an extra one to him, the deputy looked thoughtful.

Max cut in with a whine. "I really can use a gun. I shot one a couple of times. I even saved Father Gene."

Lovecraft smiled proudly. "I believe you." He thought for a moment. "Okay, here's the deal. You can't have a gun now..."

"But...," started Max, and Lovecraft just raised a hand for pause.

The boy quieted.

"But if we have time—and ammo is not an issue—I will teach you how to handle a firearm correctly," said Lovecraft.

"Really?" asked Max excitedly.

"And—only *IF* that goes well—you can carry a gun," said Lovecraft.

"Okay," agreed Max.

Crafty piped up. "About guard duty, I know Brick has some experience with firearms."

"Brick?" asked Lovecraft.

"Oh," said Crafty. "His real name is Beauregard or

something like that."

"Ah, that makes sense," nodded Lovecraft.

"Yeah," agreed Crafty. "And when you see him...well, anyhow, not sure if he was law enforcement or military. But I'll see if he can help."

"Thanks," said Lovecraft sincerely. "And, anyone else who has any military or police experience would be great. Tibbons looks like he might be a good man to talk to."

"Sure," said Crafty. "I'll do that."

"And call me if you need anything. But right now, I want to see our digs for the night," said Lovecraft, and he and Max headed into the infirmary.

Crafty, for his part, went back to the front gate.

The infirmary was a large room, which had been hastily subdivided with a wall through the middle during a tuberculosis outbreak. Each of those halves were now further subdivided by rows of opaque privacy curtains on rollers. But, the sheets on the bed were indeed crisp and clean.

People had hopped onto beds to stake their claim for the night.

But Lovecraft was distracted by the skylights set above. They did let in a lot of natural light.

Out of the corner of his eye, he noticed Stu and Patrick by the door. They were talking animatedly. Patrick was fiddling with his cell phone.

"...but if I can get some evidence," said Patrick excitedly. "It could validate some of the claims about this place."

"Just don't talk too much about this," said Stu in a calm voice. "We should be fine here. But people are already edgy as is. And I don't want them to worry about this too."

"Worry about what?" asked Lovecraft as he and Max walked up.

"Nothing," said Stu before Patrick could speak. "How can I help you?"

Patrick looked miffed at being shut down, but he kept silent.

Lovecraft pointed up. "Skylights?"

"Oh, the fellow who designed this place wanted skylights in the infirmary," said Stu.

"Because the natural light would be good for the patients?" suggested Lovecraft hopefully.

However, Stu looked embarrassed. "Umm, actually, it was so that their souls could easily leave when they died."

"He must've been a fun guy," said Lovecraft drily.

They took their leave of Stu and Patrick, and the two went returned immediately to their hushed conference.

"Are we worried about them?" whispered Max once they were out of earshot.

"I think we're good for now," replied Lovecraft. "If there was an immediate problem, I think Stu would tell us."

"Okay," said Max, but he seemed less than convinced.

In the second room of the infirmary, Lovecraft noticed Icewater filming the Reporter who had cornered the Councilman again. Hurston was pelting Tibbons with questions.

"Where are they?" demanded Hurston.

"How should I know?" asked Tibbons, who shouldered his way past Hurston. The Councilman moved around the infirmary, trying to get away from the Reporter.

"I'm just having trouble buying this whole back surgery thing," said Hurston. "*Some people* might wonder if it's just a smokescreen."

Tibbons stopped and whirled around to face the Reporter.

"Do you want to see the scar?" asked Tibbons as he started to untuck his shirt in the back.

"God no!" cried Hurston as he took a step back.

"Then shut your cake hole!" snapped Tibbons. He took a second and calmed himself. "Maybe you're just going to have to take that one on faith."

"All I'm saying is that they should be here," said Hurston.

"Mr. Tibbons!" called out Lovecraft from across the room. "Can I have a word?"

"Sure!" said Tibbons to Lovecraft. He spoke brusquely to Hurston. "Excuse me."

Quickly, Tibbons walked away from the Reporter.

"Where are you going?" demanded Hurston to the Councilman's back. "We haven't finished our talk!"

As Tibbons reached the Substitute Teacher, Lovecraft nodded towards the front door of the infirmary.

"Councilman, let's step this way," said the Substitute Teacher loudly.

Lovecraft, Max, and Tibbons walked back through the first section of the infirmary and then out the front door.

Safely outside, the Councilman's shoulders lost some of the tension that had been building up. Stu and Patrick, who had watched them all walk past, followed them.

Tibbons leaned against the wall of the infirmary facing Lovecraft.

"Thank you," said Tibbons sincerely to the Substitute Teacher.

"Don't mention it," shrugged Lovecraft. He handed Tibbons the extra walkie-talkie. "And, I brought you a present."

"As long as that reporter doesn't have one too," chuckled Tibbons.

"Is he still peppering you with questions?" asked Stu.

"He was wondering where the Mayor—and the rest of the council—were," nodded Tibbons.

"Well, that is a good question," said Lovecraft carefully.

"And I wish I had an answer for him," sighed Tibbons. "But, they aren't answering any of my calls..." The Councilman stopped, and then he added. "Not that they ever did before."

"Well, they're definitely not here," said Stu. "I saw everyone who came through the gate."

"And you'd know it if they were here," laughed Tibbons without humor. "Especially the mayor."

"How?" asked Lovecraft.

"His ever-present trophy wife. I think this is #3:

Tiffany," said Tibbons. "Her laugh can peel the paint right off a wall."

Stu grimaced. "It's pretty bad."

"And they would be hogging the camera," added Tibbons.

"I could see that," said Stu.

"So, things were bad between you and the council?" asked Lovecraft to Tibbons.

"Well, there was no love lost between us," said Tibbons. "I grew up downwind of the factories, and most of them came from Cedar Hill. They saw my election as an aberration."

"Maybe it just seemed like that," suggested Lovecraft gently.

"No, Mayor Crow told me right to my face that my election was an example of a flawed system," said Tibbons. "*And* I beat the other guy by twelve points, so it wasn't even a close race."

"So, they're jerks," said Lovecraft.

"Well, Mayor Crow, and his people from Cedar Hill, are jerks, but the others on the council are just toadies," said Tibbons.

"And you wouldn't play their reindeer games," smiled Lovecraft.

"Had a job to do," shrugged Tibbons.

"I wonder where they are, if not here," mused Stu. "Maybe City Hall?"

"Or up in Cedar Hill," said Tibbons. "It is a gated

community." The Councilman sighed. "Oddly enough, I hope they're safe. I don't like'em, but I hope they're safe."

Stu agreed. "I hope they don't get got."

"Well, they'd probably be too tough to chew on anyhow," said Tibbons with a guilty laugh.

But Max froze as Tibbons and Stu began to joke about how distasteful the city council was. Noticing that, Lovecraft spoke up.

"Well, the kid and I are going to have a look around," said Lovecraft. He looked at Stu. "Do you have an extra set of keys for the jail?"

Patrick looked worriedly at Stu, and Lovecraft spotted it. But Stu did not flinch.

"Sure, it should be safe enough during the day," said Stu, as if he were speaking to both Patrick and Lovecraft. "Why do you want to look around, though?"

"I just want to stretch my legs, and it wouldn't hurt to check out the place," said Lovecraft.

"Those gates are pretty thick," said Stu nodding at the front of the jail.

"And Thank God for that," said Lovecraft sincerely. "But —just in case—I'd like to have a fall-back point. I promise I won't mess with anything."

"Okay," said Stu eventually.

Lovecraft turned to Tibbons next. "And the deputy could use some help. We should have people at the front gate, in case someone shows up. Could you speak with him?"

As Tibbons went to the front gate, Stu led Lovecraft, Max, and Patrick into the central part of the jail. They entered through an old wooden door inlaid with metal. Moving down a few corridors, Stu arrived at his office. It was neat and orderly, in contrast with his unkempt personal appearance. The Caretaker took an extra set of keys from the drawer, but he did not hand them to Lovecraft right away.

"Just be careful. This place is ancient," said Stu first.

"I won't disturb anything," promised Lovecraft.

Stu looked concerned. "You think something will go wrong?"

"No," said Lovecraft cautiously. "Not necessarily. But I want to err on the side of caution."

"But...shouldn't the deputy be doing this?" asked Stu.

"Probably," admitted Lovecraft. "But, at the same time, he's young and probably hasn't done more in his career than handed out speeding tickets."

"And you've seen more? Where do you normally substitute teach at?" asked Stu.

Lovecraft laughed. "I've spent some time in some scary places." But then his face got serious. "Right now, though, my only job is keeping the kids safe."

Stu harrumphed. "I guess it probably wouldn't be a bad idea if someone else had the other set. Just in case."

"Don't worry," said Lovecraft. "I'll take care of your jail. I swear."

Stu sniffed but handed over the keys. "You better. And

the second this is all over, you hand in those keys."

"I promise," said the Substitute Teacher sincerely.

Lovecraft and Max left Stu and Patrick, who immediately went into a huddle, whispering furiously.

Patrick looked somewhat concerned about something.

When they were out of earshot, Max asked. "Are we still not worried?"

"Maybe a little," admitted Lovecraft. "But Stu seems like a good egg, as my grandmother used to say. If Stu were anxious, he wouldn't have let us wander off."

"For that matter," said Max. "Why are we going into this dark and spooky jail?"

"Well, I did need to stretch my legs before dinner," said Lovecraft. "And, while I don't want to be wandering around abandoned jails, I do want to get a feel for this place."

Lovecraft opened the metal gate leading to Fallen Oak's general population. The gate was just big enough for two men to squeeze through shoulder to shoulder.

Just inside the gate, Lovecraft stopped and swung the black metal gate back and forth a few times. It moved quickly without a whisper.

"What?" asked Max.

"Just expected it to have more squeak, you know, for a big, spooky door," shrugged Lovecraft.

"Are you disappointed?" asked Max.

"Kinda," admitted the Substitute.

Beyond the gate were rows of open cells on the right-hand side. A set of stairs were located at either end of the cells. As they walked in, he did not notice that Max was lost in thought.

Lovecraft's attention was captured by the view above. "Wow."

The general population stretched up to four stories. Each floor had a walkway beyond the cell, which ended in a railing. Between each floor was a mesh of wire that went straight across from the walkway and was bolted into the concrete wall opposite.

Max blurted out, suddenly and fiercely. "You don't need to protect me, you know."

"What?"

"When they talk about revenants eating people," said Max.

Surprised, Lovecraft looked at the young man for a moment. But then the Substitute Teacher nodded solemnly.

"Duly noted," said Lovecraft. He thought back to the conversation. "Truth be told, I was getting tired of hearing them whine on anyhow. Humor can be beneficial for getting through tough times, but I was not up for that type of ghoulish talk right now."

"Agreed," said Max with a little smile.

"Have you ever been to this building before?" asked Lovecraft.

"Not in here," said Max. "But I remember visiting the jail when I was younger. I didn't want to go in."

83

"I don't blame your past self," said Lovecraft. "My present self doesn't want to be here either."

"But, at the same time," said Max thoughtfully. "It was the only time I got to see my father."

"When you say he was in Fallen Oaks," started Lovecraft as he tried to find the words. "You don't mean as a guard, do you."

Max's eyes fell to the cement floor.

"Oh," said Lovecraft.

"He...he did something foolish," said Max.

"It's okay," insisted Lovecraft gently. "You don't need to talk about it."

"No, it's okay," said Max. "The day they hung his partner was the day that the last riot broke out, and...." The boy faltered. "Well, he didn't make it out."

"You know, it looks like there are still names next to the cells. What was his name?"

"Cole Chow," said Max carefully. "Why?"

Something in the shadows perked up at that name. Something that wore a severed noose around its neck and now looked at the boy with acute interest.

"If you want, we can go looking for his cell," said Lovecraft.

"Not right now," said Max, but he was thoughtful.

Lovecraft smiled gently at that. "Why don't we just explore then?"

And some of the tension fell from Max's shoulders.

"Okay," said the young man. He looked at the general population and then at all the floors above them. "Why is there wire mesh between the floors?"

"I was wondering that myself," replied Lovecraft.

They walked deeper into the general population. The air was musty with a sour tang. Each cell was open, showing a bed fixed to the wall and a lidless toilet. There were still old mattresses on the beds, but they had an unhealthy tan parlor.

Beyond the general population, there was another section of cells, but these all had ancient wooden doors.

In this next section, they stopped by the first door on the left. Max got up on his tiptoes to look through a slot in the door, which was cut at eye level for an adult.

"Wonder what these were for?" mused Max as he stepped back. Lovecraft opened the first door. The rooms were similar to the general population cells, except that opposite the bed and the toilet was a little desk fixed to the wall.

"Solitary confinement?" suggested Lovecraft.

"Maybe," said Max.

By silent agreement, they did not open all the doors and kept on moving.

The next room was tiled a dreadful green, and it had big metal drawers at one end. Max walked towards them.

"What're those?" asked Max out loud, and he reached out to open a drawer.

"Morgue drawers," said Lovecraft, and Max's hand froze

an inch from the handle.

"You're kidding," replied Max.

But Lovecraft just smiled and waggled his eyebrows. Max snatched his hand back and moved quickly away from the morgue drawers.

"Eww, " cried Max. "Why're they here?"

"I don't know, but if they have a hospital, there must have been a morgue," said Lovecraft. "I wonder why it's over here, though."

"Do we want to know?" asked Max.

Lovecraft stopped while he pondered the question. Quickly, he decided. "No, not really. Why don't we keep moving."

"Good idea," agreed Max quickly. They turned and headed around a corner, which led to the laundry room. Passing through a wooden door, they looked at all the industrial laundry equipment.

"Good news!" said Lovecraft happily. "If we're here long enough, we'll at least have clean clothes."

Then he spied something odd in the far corner. A bronze metal hatch in the corner that had been set into the floor. He opened his mouth to comment on it.

Something swept through the jail like a blast of air. It first shut the gate out of general population with a slam, but then it tore through the building towards the laundry room. It was heralded by a roar, which was at a distant, almost inaudible register.

The door to the laundry room slammed shut behind

them. Lovecraft and Max froze and then slowly turned to look back at the door. Lovecraft's right hand was shaking at his hip. He quickly balled his hand into a tight fist to stop the tremors.

"What...was that?" whispered Max.

"The wind?" suggested Lovecraft hopefully.

"We're indoors," said Max.

"I know," replied Lovecraft in a small voice.

"I think we should go back," said Max.

"Good idea," agreed Lovecraft.

The Substitute Teacher reached out tentatively for the door, and it opened with a grinding squeal. Lovecraft winced, but he kept on opening it. There was no one else around.

Lovecraft and Max quickly walked around the corner, through the morgue, and into the next section. Seeing the gate leading out to the jail offices, their pace quickened.

They were a little over halfway across general population when they heard someone shout something above them. Lovecraft caught a glimpse of someone falling. Before they had time to stop and turn, a body hit the cement with a bone-crunching thud.

They both jumped out of their skins. But Lovecraft still had the presence of mind to step between the boy and what was sure to be a gruesome sight.

But the floor behind them was empty.

Lovecraft's heart raced, and Max grabbed his arm.

"We need to go!" said the boy breathlessly.

Lovecraft and Max ran to the locked gate. The boy rattled it.

"Damn it!" snarled Max.

Lovecraft pulled out the keyring, selected a key, and tried it in the lock. But it was the wrong key.

Deep in the jail, they heard a whisper.

"Hurry," hissed Max.

Lovecraft was trying more keys when Max suddenly biffed him on the shoulder.

"I'm going as fast as I can," snapped Lovecraft.

"There's someone back there," whispered Max. The boy had turned, and he was looking down the length of general population. His face was as pale as the moonlight.

Lovecraft froze and then carefully looked over his shoulder. Past the opposite doorway out of the general population, something in the shadows was in the shape of a man.

"It could be a trick of the light," he suggested, but it sounded weak, even to him. He turned back and started going through the keyring even more quickly.

"It's moving," said Max. The shape moved out into general population, but the shadows seemed to follow it. Shrouded in darkness, the figure moved closer. It was whispering something.

Unconsciously, Max found himself straining to try and hear. He felt his mind fogging over. Something dangled around the shape's neck.

The door unlocked, and Lovecraft whipped it open. He

grabbed Max and dragged the boy through the gate.

The unexpected, physical motion snapped Max out of the trance which he had been falling into. Turning around, Max got his feet going in the right direction to run out of the jail. Lovecraft let the boy go as he slammed the door shut. They took off at a dead run towards the exit.

Stu and Patrick were still in the office when the two-shot by.

"Maybe we should've gone with them," muttered Stu.

Bursting out into the sunlight, Lovecraft instantly felt better. He huffed and puffed—desperate for breath—as he looked to reassure himself that Max was still there.

The kid was bent over, trying to get his breath back, but he was safe and sound. Looking up, Lovecraft was surprised to see Deputy Downs standing by the gate. Crafty watched them with concern.

"You okay there?" asked the deputy carefully.

Lovecraft cleared his throat, realizing that this might look odd. And he did not want to talk about what they had just seen. For that matter, he was not sure what they had just seen.

Instead, Lovecraft said smoothly. "We were racing to see who could reach the outside door first. Poor kid didn't have a chance."

"Hah," barked Max as he played along. "You're slow, even for an old man."

Crafty blinked in puzzlement.

"Has anyone else showed up?" asked Lovecraft,

changing the subject quickly.

"Not yet," said Crafty. "I'm wondering how many more will show up."

Lovecraft looked out at the gate. There were almost a dozen revenants there. Beyond the gate, the town looked still.

"I think we've seen most of them," said Lovecraft, a little sadly. "The rest are probably hunkered down, hoping this will all blow over soon."

"God help them," whispered Crafty.

"Amen," agreed Lovecraft fervently.

Crafty looked back at the revenants beyond the gate. "Should I shoot them?"

Lovecraft just shook his head. "At this point, we'd just be wasting ammo."

"Good," replied Crafty, and he relaxed a little.

"You okay for now?" asked Lovecraft.

"Sure," said Crafty. "I'm good for a few more hours. Anyhow, I'm too tense to rest right now."

"I hear that," chuckled Lovecraft companionly. He and Max said their goodbyes and wandered back towards the infirmary.

"We don't have to go back in that jail again?" asked Max after a moment. "Do we?"

"Hopefully never again...Ever!" said Lovecraft, fervently and honestly. He suddenly stopped and looked across the bailey, which was filled with vehicles.

90

"What?" asked Max worriedly.

"Someone's still in their car over there," said Lovecraft.

"Maybe they feel safer," suggested Max.

"Maybe," murmured Lovecraft.

In an old yellow car, there sat an older man with a priest's collar. He was still gripping the steering wheel with white knuckles.

"That's Reverend Jennings," supplied Max. "Grandma likes him." The boy paused, realizing how that had sounded. "Not 'likes' like that, but he's a nice guy." The boy paused and then added sadly. "I wonder if he'll do a memorial for her."

Lovecraft patted the boy on the shoulder as Max sighed.

"It's gonna be okay," said Lovecraft.

"Sure," said Max, but he did not seem convinced.

Brow furrowing, Lovecraft grabbed the boy's shoulders and whipped the kid around.

"What!?!" asked Max in surprise.

The Substitute Teacher looked the boy square in the eye, dead serious.

"It's *going* to be okay," repeated Lovecraft. "You *will* get through this."

The conviction in Lovecraft's eyes put some wind back into the boy's sails. Max straightened his shoulders.

"Okay," the boy said again, but this time with more resolution.

"Now, let's see what's up with the padre," said Lovecraft.

91

"The who?" asked Max.

"The reverend," amended Lovecraft as they walked over to the yellow car.

The windows of the reverend's car were all rolled up, so Lovecraft gently tapped on one. The reverend jumped, looking around in surprise.

"Sorry," said Lovecraft with a wince.

The reverend looked first at Lovecraft but then at the rifle that the Substitute Teacher carried. Seeing the look, Lovecraft carefully put his rifle on the hood of the next car. That done, he turned back to the reverend and smiled gently.

"Hi," said Lovecraft. "Are you okay?"

"Sure," said the reverend, who turned to face forward again. Lovecraft looked at Max, who shrugged.

"Can you roll down your window?" asked Lovecraft of Reverend Jennings. The man did not move for a moment, but then he peeled one hand away from the steering wheel. He rolled down the window a crack.

"What?" asked Jennings without turning. His voice was not sharp but terse.

"Are you coming out?" asked Lovecraft. "Dinner will be soon."

"It's the end of the world," replied Jennings.

"Oh, I'm sure the food is much better than that," joked Lovecraft, but the reverend did not even blink. Nervously, Lovecraft turned to Max. "I think the reverend and I need a moment to chat."

"Okay," said Max quickly. The boy was having a rough enough day already, and he did not need fire and brimstone as well.

Lovecraft looked back at the reverend after the boy was out of earshot.

"I'm pretty sure that the world is not ending," said Lovecraft.

"Zechariah 14: 12 'And this shall be the plague with which the Lord will strike all the peoples that wage war against Jerusalem: their flesh will rot while they are still standing on their feet, their eyes will rot in their sockets, and their tongues will rot in their mouths. And on that day a great panic from the Lord shall fall on them so that each will seize the hand of another, and the hand of the one will be raised against the hand of the other'," quoted Jennings as his eyes took on a fiery glow.

"And God promised not to flood the Earth again after Noah," said Lovecraft.

"That was water," said Jennings.

"I don't think God's that petty. He's not going to play semantics like that," said Lovecraft. "He promised not to wipe us out again."

"It's the End Times," declared Jennings. He gave a little sigh. "And we must not have been saved."

"It's not the end times," said Lovecraft kindly. "It's just a revenant outbreak."

"The dead are walking the Earth, and you say that it is nothing?" asked the reverend.

"Okay, it's nothing," conceded Lovecraft. "But, it's not

exactly the first time that this has happened."

"This is the final time," said Jennings.

"Sadly, this isn't going to be the last time this happens either," said Lovecraft with a solemn voice.

"See, we're all going to die," said Jennings.

"I understand that you're scared," urged Lovecraft. "I'm scared too. But right now, there are people in there that need your help." Lovecraft loosened the knot of his tie and reached under his collar. He took out a small steel cross and held it up. "Now, more than ever, they need to know that they are *not* alone."

But Jennings just sighed and rolled up the window. The reverend slowly put his head on the steering wheel and closed his eyes.

Lovecraft let the cross fall against his royal blue tie. He looked up at the heavens for a moment, and he used that time to quench the frustration burning inside of him.

Once he had calmed down, he reached into one of his many small pockets, hidden inside his coat. He pulled out a small device.

Lovecraft jammed the device into the door lock and twisted. The lock popped up, and the reverend looked up in surprise.

"What the...?" asked Jennings, but Lovecraft was staring at the little device.

"Hot dog!" he exclaimed excitedly.

Lovecraft opened the door, smacked the lock down, and shut the car door again. He then proceeded to unlock the car door again.

"That's awesome!" he grinned.

"How did you do that?" asked Jennings, and Lovecraft held up the device.

"It's called a Hot Pick," said Lovecraft.

"But how...?" sputtered Jennings.

"Hey! I don't ask. But for some reason, it only works on cars," shrugged Lovecraft as he put the Hot Pick away and made a mental note to tell Kari how well it had worked. That was part of the deal. Kari and the boys Downstairs did not bore him with the technobabble, and he field-tested all of their gadgets.

"But who...," said Jennings.

"We don't have time for that," said Lovecraft, and his face grew serious. Since Jennings was not wearing his seatbelt, the Substitute Teacher grabbed the reverend by the coat and hauled him out of the car.

"Get your hands off me," cried the reverend in horror.

"I tried to do this the nice way," said Lovecraft. "But I've run out of patience."

"Let me go!" said Jennings.

"No!" said Lovecraft firmly. "Not 'til you pull yourself together!"

"I'm not falling apart," countered Jennings. "I'm just stating the obvious."

"No! You're wallowing in self-pity. And honestly, if you were anyone else, I'd let it slide. But right now, I need you," said Lovecraft.

95

"I can't do anything," said Jennings.

"You can go into that infirmary—where there are a lot of scared people!—and tell them that all hope is NOT lost," said Lovecraft.

"But all this...," said Jennings. "It's Revelations!"

"Revelations is a parable saying—in essence—'shit happens'," said Lovecraft. "Lord knows bad things happen, but if you have faith, and you stay strong, Jesus is going to ride over that hill on a white horse leading the cavalry to save our asses." Lovecraft reached into the car without letting go and grabbed a well-worn Bible on the passenger seat. Then he smacked it against the reverend's chest, who grabbed it unconsciously. "Until then, I need you to stay strong and remind them that help is on the way."

"It is?" asked Jennings, and his face brightened a bit.

"The National Guard should have mobilized by now," said Lovecraft. "They are going to have to work their way towards us. But, we should be safe here. God willing."

After a moment, the reverend nodded and then gave a weak smile. "God willing."

"Is everything alright here?" asked a paramedic sharply as she hurried on over. She looked pointedly at Lovecraft, who was still holding the reverend's coat. The Substitute let go and stood back.

The reverend smiled warmly at the paramedic and said. "Everything's fine. We were just having a theological discussion." Reverend Jennings' voice had a rich, calming tone that made everything sound like it would be all right.

"A rather heated one—admittedly—but, still just theology."

"Oh, okay," said the paramedic wearily. She was a thin woman in a pale blue paramedic uniform. Her sandy brown hair was pulled away from her youthful face. "I was just checking."

"He had some persuasive arguments for an old man like me," said the reverend. "Ms. Belinda Boyle, isn't it?"

"Yessir," said the paramedic, Belinda Boyle, quickly.

Jennings walked up to the paramedic, Boyle. "And how're you doing, Belinda?"

"I'm holding," said Boyle. "Me and my partner Zeke were away from the hospital when things..." She tried to speak. "I tried to save Zeke, but he went too far from the ambulance. I told him not to, but he didn't listen. And by the time I got to him, I...there was nothing...Oh God, I barely got this far..."

Boyle lost her words, and Jennings patted her sympathetically on the shoulder.

"I know. Sometimes people stray too far," said Jennings. "I will say a prayer for Zeke and all the others. But right now, stay strong, and we *will* get through this."

"Oh...okay," said Boyle, straightening up. She seemed a little lighter as if a burden had been lifted.

"Now, I want to check out our temporary digs," said Reverend Jennings, and he looked over at Lovecraft. "Thank God we have nice, strong walls."

"Amen, reverend," replied Lovecraft as he tucked his cross back under his shirt.

Jennings turned and went to the infirmary. In the crook of his arm, he held the Good Book like a shield.

Boyle was suddenly uncertain as she turned to Lovecraft. She reached up and pulled back a stray hair, which had escaped her ponytail.

"Um, sorry," said Boyle. "I just thought..."

"It's okay," said Lovecraft quickly, but then he noticed her ride. "Oh! I'm glad you brought an ambulance!"

"Well, I was in the neighborhood," said Boyle with a sad, little laugh. "We were told to come straight here, instead of...well, going back to the hospital."

"I haven't gotten a chance to see what medical supplies we have on hand here," said Lovecraft.

"Mr. Tibbons had asked me to look into it," said Boyle. "That's where I was going."

"Can we walk with you?" asked Lovecraft, nodding at Max, who had trotted on over.

"Your assistant?" asked Boyle as she nodded at the kid.

"Boy Wonder," said Lovecraft, and they all introduced each other.

"It should probably help that this was formerly an infirmary," suggested Lovecraft as they walked into the building.

"I don't know," said Boyle uncertainly. "Haven't seen the inside of any prison hospitals, outside of movies."

"Don't mind me," said Lovecraft with a relaxed smile. "I'm just trying to stay positive."

Boyle gave a wry smile. "Can't fault you for that."

"I can," grinned Max mischievously.

They went through the two large rooms of the infirmary, which had been set up for sleeping. As they followed, the paramedic and Lovecraft noticed that she had short pink hair underneath Boyle's dark blue baseball cap. For some reason, that amused him, but he didn't think it would be polite to mention.

"Can an EMT have pink hair?" asked Max a little loudly.

Lovecraft turned to correct the boy. "Hey, kid…"

But Boyle piped up. "As long as you dress and act professionally, it's not a problem. And I'm a paramedic."

"What's the difference," asked Max.

"More schooling. I can give a patient an IV line," said Boyle, and then she gave a little smile. "And more money."

"More money is always good," nodded Lovecraft.

Past the second infirmary room was a corridor that had a door to their immediate right. Further down the corridor, they saw that the kitchen cooks were preparing food, and off of that was a dining hall.

Max gingerly sniffed the air.

"Well, it smells good," said the boy cautiously.

"As long as it's edible," said Lovecraft.

They moved through the door on their right. It was a doctor's waiting room complete with old vinyl couches in a disturbing, esoteric blue. Branching off from the waiting room were old medical offices and examination rooms. Inside Examination Room #5 were boxes marked "Medical Supplies."

"Hopefully, it's not 500,000 tongue depressors," joked Boyle.

"Why are there cereal boxes in here?" asked Max.

Lovecraft and Boyle turned to follow the boy's gaze. Examination Room #1 was filled with generic dry cereal.

"That's odd," said Boyle.

"Feed a cold? That type of thing?" suggested Lovecraft when a cook appeared in the doorway.

"Ah, there you are," said the cook. "My name's Marta. I'm in charge of the kitchen. And you're probably wondering about the cereal."

"More curious than anything else," admitted Lovecraft.

"Sorry about that," said the head cook, Marta. She was a slender woman with a nervous grin. "When the guys came in to drop off the food, they put these boxes in here."

"Because the kitchen is soooo far away," suggested Lovecraft with playful sarcasm.

"Well, that's the other problem," said Marta. "Outside of the pantry and the walk-in fridge, there's no room. I don't know how they stored food when the jail was running at full capacity. We probably only have a fourth of the supplies, and we're really struggling for room. Anyhow, gotta go."

And just like that, Marta disappeared. Boyle looked at Lovecraft, who shrugged.

"At least we got Frosted Flakes or its second-cousin-twice-removed," he said with a smirk.

"Tony the Tree Frog?" joked Max.

100

"Something like that," replied Lovecraft with amusement.

Boyle turned to the medical supplies. They opened the first box to find a box full of adhesive strips and bandages.

"Looking good," murmured Lovecraft, and they started to open all the boxes setting aside necessary materials on an examination table. Lovecraft found an invoice and handed it to Max. "Do you know how to detail receive?"

"Umm...," started Max.

"It's easy," smiled Lovecraft. "Let me show you."

# 13

It took a while to really dig through the boxes. Boyle suddenly stood up with a grin.

"Found it!" cried Boyle.

"What is it?" asked Lovecraft.

"A surgical kit...," started Boyle. Her voice trailed off as she opened the kit. After a moment, she looked back up again. "This is neat. It comes with needles, thread, syringes, and local anesthetics."

Max gave a shiver at this. "Yikes. Just the thought."

"At least we have anesthetics," said Lovecraft.

"Still, yikes!" said Max.

"Hopefully we won't need any of this," said Lovecraft.

"But, I'd rather have too much than not enough."

"Dinner!" chimed a voice from near the kitchen.

"Ohhh!" started Max, and he moved to turn towards the door.

"I'd wait a moment," warned Lovecraft, and the boy turned to look quizzically back at the Substitute Teacher.

"What do you...," began Max when he heard the rumble of feet. The corridor was suddenly jam-packed with people rushing towards the cafeteria.

"We *might* just want to wait a little bit," suggested Lovecraft.

Max sighed. "I guess I'm not that hungry."

"I want to get some supplies from the ambulance," suggested Boyle.

"Sounds good," said Lovecraft.

As soon as traffic had lessened, Lovecraft, Boyle, and Max went back out into the sleeping rooms. Deputy Crafty ran from outside.

"Chow time!" he cried merrily, barreling past them.

"I wonder who's at the gate," mused Lovecraft off-handedly.

They kept moving through the sleeping rooms. A few others were waiting for the traffic to die down, like Tibbons and Hurston. Hurston had stopped pestering Tibbons for the moment, but they sat on either side of the room like a pair of cats watching each other.

Lovecraft took one step outside, and a bullet zipped past him. Without thinking, he pushed Max to the ground. The boy was utterly baffled as he hit the ground hard. Lovecraft went to one knee and looked around. He saw Boyle hunkered down behind an SUV.

"What the heck?" demanded the paramedic.

"I don't know," replied Lovecraft as Max tried to get up, but the Substitute Teacher pushed him back down. He glared down at the boy. "Stay down."

Max saw the steely look in Lovecraft's eyes and decided not to press the issue. Satisfied that the boy would stay put, Lovecraft slid across the ground towards the SUV. Gunfire and hollering were coming from the front gate.

"See anything?" asked Lovecraft of Boyle.

"No. Someone by the gate," said Boyle. She flinched as a bullet shattered a car window near them.

"Can you keep an eye on this?" asked Lovecraft as he handed Boyle his rifle.

"What do you want me to do?" asked Boyle as she timidly held the rifle.

"Stay here. I just don't want the kid having a rifle in the middle of this," said Lovecraft.

"Hey!" barked Max from the ground.

But Lovecraft ignored the boy.

"Wait here," said Lovecraft, and he disappeared in amongst the cars.

"Sure, whatever you say," said Boyle as she ducked again.

Quickly, Lovecraft moved between the vehicles towards the chaos. He lifted his MP5 submachine gun just in case of trouble. Closer, he saw three men shooting revenants through the front gate, and the idiots were having a grand old time. A bullet hit one of the metal bars, bounced off, and ricocheted into a car.

"Stop shooting!" shouted Lovecraft, but the yahoos did not hear him over their own whooping and hollering. He moved closer. Once again, he tried to scream, but to no avail.

For a hot second, Lovecraft considered shooting them—just on principle—but then he saw the deputy's car nearby. Scooting over to it, he used the Hot Pick to open the trunk and then glanced inside for a workaround.

A bullet whistled past the car, and Lovecraft ducked. He started to take out his cellphone when there was a sudden silence. Glancing up, he saw that the men were reloading.

"That's awesome!" cried Brick happily.

"Didja see the one that I got," replied Smithie. "Nearly took its head off."

"I think I got two at once," grinned a young, fresh-faced guy, Tic.

"No way!" cried Smithie.

"Really!" insisted the young man, Tic.

"Hey!" cried Lovecraft as he stood up. They looked over at him in surprise. "Stop shooting! Your bullets are ricocheting all over the place."

"What did he say?" asked Brick.

A nasty smile came across Smithie's pinched face.

"He said shoot more!" he laughed and then started

shooting again. Quickly, the other two joined in. Lovecraft dropped down again.

"Damn idiots," growled Lovecraft as he leaned against the bumper of the police car. He did not dare stick his head up to look in the trunk.

Lifting his cell phone, he took a picture of the open trunk.

Examining the picture, he saw just what he needed. He groped around the right side of the trunk and grabbed a can of tear gas.

Letting go of his MP5, he pulled the pin and tossed the can. Even as the canister lobbed over the cars, he saw Tic's head jerk to one side, and the man crumpled to the ground.

But the can bounced across the cobbles of the bailey, zipped in between the bars of the front gate, and rolled harmlessly into the crowd of revenants outside.

"Are you kidding me?" growled Lovecraft. Grabbing another canister, he threw another can of gas, which rolled right into the midst of the idiots. The tear gas billowed out, covering Brick and Smithie. Tic was still nowhere to be seen. Brick appeared from the cloud of tear gas, coughing and choking.

Springing up, Lovecraft ran forward, slid across the hood of a car, and knocked Brick down with one punch. Smithie emerged from the gas. Grabbing the AK-47 from Brick's hands, Lovecraft flipped it around and drove the butt of the rifle into Smithie's stomach.

Both men lay on the ground crying as he kicked Smithie's gun under a car. Lovecraft stepped back from the gas, blinking tears.

"Okay, it's clear!" cried Lovecraft over his shoulder. As he looked away for a moment, Brick grabbed the muzzle of the gun.

"Give it back," moaned Brick.

Lovecraft just booted Brick in the face; not terribly hard, but hard enough to get his point across.

The paramedic ran up. Boyle was still holding onto Lovecraft's rifle gingerly.

"Here!" said the paramedic quickly, and she thrust the rifle back at Lovecraft. As he took his rifle, Boyle saw the tear gas and began to cough. "What the..."

"Tear gas—though I don't know why they put that in a Revenant Kit—but I'm not going to complain," explained Lovecraft. "Oh, and there's one down in that cloud."

"Well, pull him out!" ordered Boyle.

Surprised, Lovecraft looked at the seemingly soft-spoken paramedic, but she was in full-on medic mode. Boyle was already checking Smithie for injuries.

"Right," said Lovecraft as he juggled weapons. After a moment's hesitation, he took the bullets from the AK-47 and dropped the neutered weapon onto a car.

Plunging into the cloud of tear gas, he went for Tic. Lovecraft's eyes hurt as he strained to look for the fallen man.

In front of him, a shape appeared on the ground. He grabbed one arm and pulled the man out of the cloud, which was thankfully dissipating.

Setting Tic down next to Smithie, Lovecraft walked away to get some fresh air. He wiped his eyes to clear away the tears.

"Oh shit," said Max. The boy had stopped a few feet away from the Substitute.

Lovecraft reluctantly followed Max's gaze and saw the bullet hole in the side of Tic's head. The idiot just stared up at the sky with empty eyes with a face that barely looked old enough to shave.

"Well, that's just great," snarled Boyle as she noticed Tic's body. She glared up at Lovecraft.

"What? I didn't do that," said Lovecraft defensively.

"This gas is hard to work near," complained Boyle.

"You'd rather I'd have shot'em?" asked Lovecraft as he tried to keep his temper.

Boyle scrunched up her face, but then she shrugged. "Sorry. I'm just pissed."

"It's okay," said Lovecraft. He took a deep breath and released his growing frustration, as he had been trained to do. "Maybe if I'd gotten there sooner."

"Maybe if they hadn't been idiots, to begin with," countered Boyle.

"True," smiled Lovecraft without humor.

"What the hell is going on out here?" called out Tibbons, who Hurston and Icewater were shadowing.

"I'm curious about that myself," replied Lovecraft.

Hurston and Tibbons stopped near Max, and they recoiled at the sight of Tic's dead body.

107

To his credit, Hurston stepped in front of Max to shield him from the sight. This did not endear him to Max, who stepped to one side so he could still see everything. Besides, the boy had seen bodies before.

"We were walking out here when a bullet nearly hit us," explained Boyle. She saw Icewater crouch on the hood of a car to shoot everything from a higher angle.

"Were they fighting with each other?" asked Hurston hurriedly. "Couldn't take the pressure of being locked up in here?"

"They've only been here a few hours," said Boyle, dismissing the idea immediately.

"Besides, they were shooting at the revenants outside," said Lovecraft. "Poorly shooting, I might add since the bullets kept ricocheting off the bars."

Tibbons waved at the fallen man, Tic. "Is that what happened here?"

"I think so," said Lovecraft. "I tried to stop them."

"Not very well," sniffed Hurston.

Lovecraft threw up his hands. "Why is everyone complaining that I didn't shoot them?"

"I didn't say that," sputtered Hurston. "But there must have been a better way."

"I did the best I could with what I had," said Lovecraft, and he noticed Brick and Smithie trying to crawl away in opposite directions. He moved over to Brick and knelt on the man's back, pressing him down.

"Get off me!" growled Brick.

Pulling a zip tie from another inner pocket, Lovecraft snagged Brick's hands and fastened them behind the man's back. Jumping up, Lovecraft went and hogtied Smithie as well. Once that was done, Lovecraft turned to the crowd of people.

"What do we do with them?" asked Boyle. Her eyes blazed with anger, but it was focused on Brick and Smithie this time.

"Right now, I'm tempted to throw them over the wall," said Lovecraft honestly.

"You can't do that!" cried Smithie.

"Shut up," said Lovecraft casually. "I said I was tempted, not that I was going to do it."

"So, what do we do?" asked Tibbons.

Max held up his head.

The bemused Substitute Teacher gestured at the boy. "Mr. Max?"

"Well, we are in a jail," suggested the boy.

# 14

Lovecraft frog-marched Brick into a jail cell in general population and gave him a little shove. As Brick stumbled forward, the Substitute Teacher slammed the door shut.

"What the hell?" growled Brick.

The man turned around and ran over to the door. His

shoulders slammed into the bars. He glared at Lovecraft with red-rimmed, watery eyes from the tear gas. Now, the Substitute teacher could see why he was called that name. His head gave the odd appearance of being rectangular with an almost flat face.

"You can't put me in here," snarled Brick.

"Remember, I was the one who was tempted to throw you over the wall," reminded Lovecraft.

"I have rights," said Brick

"Which is why you're in here," said Lovecraft patiently. "Now turn around, and I'll cut your zip-tie."

"What if I don't want to?" asked Brick petulantly.

Lovecraft shrugged and turned to go.

"Wait! Wait!" cried Brick as he hastily turned around and presented his wrists. Lovecraft turned back and used his folding knife to cut the zip-tie.

Once freed, Brick jumped away from the bars and started rubbing his wrists. He glared at Lovecraft, but the Substitute Teacher just turned back to Max.

Since there was no chance of a firefight, the boy was standing a little ways away with Lovecraft's rifle.

"You make a good caddie," said Lovecraft as he took the gun.

Max held out his hand.

Lovecraft looked at the open palm. "What?"

"Aren't you supposed to tip your caddie?" asked Max.

Lovecraft grinned. "At the end of the game."

110

Crafty walked into the jail, a little sluggish from his meal.

"Someone said something was going on in here?" said the deputy amiably.

Crafty stopped when he saw the men behind bars. Tic's body was already in the morgue. He turned to see Tibbons' stormy look.

"What happened?" asked the Deputy as his face fell.

# 15

Not long after, Lovecraft picked up a chunk of vaguely mashed potatoes and examined it. He was sitting next to Max while Stu, Tibbons, Hurston, and Icewater sat across. The Camerawoman had even put her camera down for the first time in hours. But it was set on the table pointing down at all of them, so Lovecraft suspected that it was still running.

They had come to the cafeteria after Tibbons had finished chewing out the deputy. Lovecraft had felt a vague pang of sympathy, though. This was not the first time that some yahoo had gotten their hands on a gun, nor the last. That line of thought got him wondering—once again!— where the sheriff was hiding.

But then his stomach grumbled testily and demanded that he get back to work. He cautiously turned the potatoes on his fork.

Lovecraft asked the table at large. "Did I mention that I have a superpower?"

"What?" asked Max curiously.

"Right," sneered Hurston with a roll of his eyes.

"Which kind?" asked Tibbons with amusement.

"Don't egg him on," ordered Hurston of Tibbons, but the Councilman just ignored the Reporter.

"It's not a big one, but handy," said Lovecraft. "You see, I can eat anything."

"Like anything, including Lima beans," asked Max. "Or anything, like tin cans and bricks."

"Or even frog's legs and monkey brains?" suggested Icewater jovially. She blithely ignored the withering glare that Hurston gave her.

"More the monkey brain variety, though I haven't tested it on that," explained Lovecraft. "You see, my palette can take Sushi, raw eggs, and bits of an animal that most people...well, they'd rather starve first."

"Not much of a superpower," sniffed Hurston snidely.

"Well, it's not invulnerability...," admitted Lovecraft.

"Eating anything could be a great power," mused Icewater. "I mean, he's like Anthony Bourdain. He can go anywhere in the world and sit down to dinner without blinking at the food."

"Even if it's staring back," added Max with a smirk.

"That would be horrible," said Hurston with a shudder.

"I don't know, I could've used that power a time or two

when I was overseas," suggested Icewater.

"See, small but super," said Lovecraft pointing his potato-laden-fork at Hurston.

"Man has a point," nodded Tibbons. "That would be handy. Remember when the first President Bush threw up on the Japanese prime minister at dinner. That superpower would've helped him."

"Was that the food or something else?" asked Icewater curiously. And it bugged her that she could not remember this little bit of trivia.

"Don't remember," shrugged Tibbons. "But I'm just saying."

"Anyhow! My point is that," said Lovecraft as he waved the lumpy potatoes on his fork for emphasis. "I have the authority to say that this food is unpalatable."

"Hey!" said Stu. "The cooks worked hard on making dinner..." But he faltered when he looked forlornly at his plate. "I mean, I know it's not great..."

Lovecraft raised his hands in surrender. "I don't think it's the cook's fault. It may be their great skill that has gotten me this far into the meal. No, it's something else."

"What's wrong?" asked Tibbons.

"As you know," said Lovecraft. "There was a revenant outbreak in D.C. recently..."

"How would you notice?" grinned Stu.

Lovecraft ignored the stale joke. "It was a small one— well, smaller than Toledo—but after that, FEMA..."

"Who?" interrupted Hurston.

113

"The Federal Emergency Management Agency," answered Max.

Lovecraft looked in surprise at the boy, but it made sense that he would have met them after Toledo.

Max gave a little shrug. "They're nice people."

"Right," agreed Lovecraft. "Well, FEMA marked cities close to outbreaks that might be likely vectors for the next outbreak of the disease."

"What does that have to do with us?" asked Hurston.

"Your town was recently given twenty-million-dollars to prepare for the worst," said Lovecraft. "And *these* are not twenty-million-dollar potatoes."

"Twenty million? You're kidding," asked Tibbons in surprise, and then he glared at the potatoes of dubious origin.

"I figure they spent some on food and the mailing to tell residents where to go in case of emergency," said Lovecraft. "And the two people to clean here, and a few to cook..."

"And all those guns," added Hurston.

"That trunk doesn't have that many guns or that much ammo, even before those idiots had gotten their hands on it," said Lovecraft. "Which begs the question, where did the money go?"

Tibbons glared at Hurston. "And before you look at me, I still don't know."

"I...I...," stammered Hurston impotently.

"And this would have happened in the last three months," added Lovecraft.

114

"While I was at home watching my way through the Netflix catalog," said Tibbons.

"That is what you said before," murmured Hurston, as if he still did not quite believe it.

Tibbons just focused on Lovecraft.

"So, if they didn't spend the money here," wondered Tibbons. "Where did they spend it?"

"That's the, well now probably $19.5-million-dollar question," sighed Lovecraft. "But, I guess that's also a question for another day."

"True," said Tibbons. "Right now, we just need to get through the next few days."

"What if that isn't good enough?" asked Hurston, who had a sharp edge to his voice.

"It's going to have to be," shrugged Lovecraft. "We're here." He paused to glance at the boy. "As Max's friend Father Gene said, 'First, let's just get through this all in one piece.'"

And Max gave a warm smile at that.

Lovecraft continued. "Now pass the ketchup. The myth is that Americans can eat anything with ketchup. And it's my patriotic duty—nay privilege!—to test if that myth is busted or confirmed."

# 16

Sitting on the edge of a single bed, Max's face warped as he tried to stifle a yawn.

Lovecraft, who stood nearby, pretended not to notice.

"I don' wanna go to bed," whined Max.

"Try," said Lovecraft. It was nearly ten o'clock, dark outside, and he was needed for guard duty at the top of the hour.

They had left deputy Crafty on duty at the gate for several hours. While Lovecraft thought the deputy had messed up, it was not fair to leave him out there all night long. At least not alone.

"What if I don't want to go to bed?" asked Max. The boy stuck out his jaw in defiance.

"Then you're no good to me tomorrow," said Lovecraft. "And I'm going to need your help. Which means I need you well-rested."

"Huh. I guess I could just lay here," conceded Max. "You know, to conserve my energy."

"That's all I ask," said Lovecraft.

As Max laid down, Lovecraft walked back through the infirmary. They had found a spare bed for the boy in the second half of the infirmary. The lights had dimmed at 9:30 pm to encourage people to sleep. Besides, there was not much else to do in jail.

No one had cared enough to leave a tv or even a radio. As such, most people were starting to lay down.

There was a small knot of people gathered around Reverend Jennings. He was telling upbeat biblical stories with great zest and large dramatic gestures. As Lovecraft passed, Jennings smiled at him. The Substitute Teacher gave him a little salute as he went by.

Lovecraft walked through the first part of the infirmary and out the door.

Happily, no one was shooting this time.

The air had a nice chill to it. It was almost pleasant, except for the fact that monsters surrounded him and in an ancient, decrepit—possibly haunted—jail. But other than that, kind of nice.

Threading his way through the parked vehicles, the Substitute walked towards the gate.

"Hey Downs!" called out Lovecraft. "It's me!" He grinned. "Don't shoot!"

There was no answer.

Slowing, Lovecraft approached the gate. Near it, a camping lantern sat on a car's hood, which partially illuminated the revenants beyond the gate. But there was no deputy.

"Crafty?" called out Lovecraft while he looked around. There was no sign of anyone. But near the gate was the door to the offices, and beyond that, the spooky jail.

Pushing aside the memories of this afternoon, he reluctantly walked inside. Through the darkened offices, he followed the empty corridor around several bends. To add to his joy, none of the hallway lights were working either.

Reaching the gate into the general population, he shook it, but it was still locked. Neither Tibbons nor he had not wanted anyone wandering into the jail accidentally.

"Hey!" called out Brick. "Is someone there?"

The Substitute Teacher could not quite see into the cells that Brick and Smithie were in from the doorway.

"I'm here," responded Lovecraft.

"See!" said Smithie in a petulant tone. That nasty grin widened. "You were probably just hearing him."

"I don't know, man," replied Brick uneasily.

"What's wrong?" asked Lovecraft.

"There are some weird noises in here," said Brick worriedly. "Like real weird."

"But you two are okay?" asked Lovecraft, who was suddenly worried himself.

"We're fine," growled Smithie. "Except that some jerk put us in a jail cell."

Satisfied that the two of them were safe for now, Lovecraft returned to the bailey. After a quick circuit of the nearest vehicles, he found himself back by the gate.

Peering out through the gate, he saw the revenants gazing back at him with their white eyes.

"You haven't seen the deputy, have you?" he asked the creatures.

But they just moaned sadly in response.

"Well, thanks anyway," he told them.

Lovecraft took out his walkie-talkie.

"Councilman? You there?"

After a moment, Tibbons came over the walkie-talkie. "I'm here."

"Have you seen the deputy?" asked Lovecraft.

"He's not at the gate?" asked Tibbons in surprise.

"Nope."

"He seemed green to me, but...not the sort to run off."

Lovecraft sighed. "We were pretty hard on him."

"True," agreed Tibbons soberly. "But even so, he looked like he wanted to make it right, you know. Not like he was pissed at having gotten caught."

"I agree," replied Lovecraft. "That's what I thought too."

"Then, where could he have wandered off to?"

"...dragged up...," came a voice over the radio.

"What?" asked Tibbons and Lovecraft together.

"I thought that was you," said Tibbons.

"Not me," said Lovecraft.

"What was that?" asked Tibbons.

"Crossed wires maybe?" suggested Lovecraft. He was starting to feel really creeped out, and being out in the dark, surrounded by revenants, was not helping. His positive vibes were quickly eroding.

Resolutely, he straightened. "Well, I'm here now."

"I wonder if we really need someone at the gate," suggested Tibbons.

Lovecraft shook his head as if Tibbons were there. "If

anyone tries to drive up to the gate, we'd never hear their car horn back in the infirmary. I still think it's a good idea to have someone here for the next day. Now, after that..."

"God, I hope we're not here that long," moaned Tibbons softly.

"Agreed," said Lovecraft.

"Did you see how much ammo was left after those yahoos got through with it?" asked Tibbons.

"Yeah, they burned through a lot of it. Those AK-47s are clubs now," sighed Lovecraft. "But we still have these stone walls."

"True," agreed the Councilman.

"Well, I'll yell if anything weird...," started Lovecraft, but then he amended. "Or at least, weirder happens."

"Do that, and Stu and I'll look for the deputy," said Tibbons.

Lovecraft shut off the connection. Cradling his rifle across his chest, he leaned against the front of the car.

Despite the lantern's light, he did not notice the claw marks that went down and then back up the brick wall to his right.

One of the revenants moaned sadly by the gate.

The Substitute Teacher nodded in sympathy. "I hear you, brother."

# 17

Lovecraft heard a noise behind him, and his chest tightened. Something was back behind the cars. He slid his hand along his rifle and looked away from the lamplight to let his pupils open. Jumping away from the light, Lovecraft aimed the rifle over the roof of the car and right at Max's head.

"Don't shoot!" squeaked Max as his hands flew up in surrender.

"Do you wanna get shot, kid?" snapped Lovecraft angrily as he swung the barrel upwards.

"How did you know it was me?" asked Max.

"I didn't!" growled Lovecraft with acid in his voice. "Hence the reason I asked you if you wanted to get perforated." But then his tone softened. "And you should be in bed."

"I'm not a kid," said Max.

Lovecraft just gave the boy a long, hard look.

Finally, Max sighed in exasperation.

"Fine. I had a bad dream," admitted Max.

Lovecraft nodded, and then he walked back to the front of the car. He patted the hood on the other side of the camping lantern.

"Talking about it helps," suggested Lovecraft.

"What if I don't want to talk about it?" asked Max wearily.

"Then I'd appreciate the company," said Lovecraft as he

121

nodded toward the revenants. "They're not so chatty."

One of the revenants moaned, almost as if in protest.

Lovecraft leaned against the front of the car as his heart settled down. After a moment, Max appeared out of the corner of his eye. The boy jumped up onto the hood and sat cross-legged. For a time, they just waited in silence, watching the revenants.

Finally, Lovecraft blurted out. "Okay, spill the beans already. I can tell you want to talk about it!"

One of the revenants made a sad noise.

"See, even they want to hear about it!"

Max chuckled at that. "Okay, but it was weird."

"I'm pretty at home with all types of wyrd."

# 18

Max looked around the whitewashed room. He could hear people moving above by the creaking of the wooden floorboards. That was when he noticed the trapdoor in the ceiling.

"You were convicted of the brutal murder of Candace Smith during an armed robbery. Do you have any last words Hugh Dustin?" asked a voice upstairs.

"I told her not to move," was the only reply, and it was said in a smug tone.

The trapdoor opened, and a man in scarlet clothes

dropped through on a noose. Dustin came to a sudden stop as the rope pulled tautly, but his neck did not break. Max watched in terror as Dustin slowly started to strangle to death.

Turning to the door, Max found it closed. He grabbed the handle. It rattled but would not turn. He took several deep breaths to steady himself. Forcing himself, he looked back towards the man, but Dustin was gone. The severed rope hung through the open trapdoor.

The door jerked open, and Max stumbled back. Dustin came in through the door, the severed end of the noose swinging across his scarlet shirt. His black-nailed fingers grabbed for the boy.

# 19

In horror, Lovecraft looked over at the boy as his story ended.

"Goddamn! That's a bad one," exclaimed Lovecraft with a deep-in-the-bones shiver. "I never liked ghost stories."

"Sorry," said Max.

"No, I don't mean it like that," amended Lovecraft quickly. "I just meant that...ghost stories, in general, creep me out, and having a dream like that...Yikes!"

Max gestured at the revenants outside the gate. "And they don't give you nightmares?"

"Not really," said Lovecraft thoughtfully. "I mean,

they're just people with a disease."

"So, they're just sick?" mused Max, and he rolled the idea around in his head. But the sight of revenants still scared the pants off of him. "I don't know."

"I mean, it's a weird disease, no doubt," admitted Lovecraft. "But it's just a virus that affects the person by shutting down the higher functions of the brain. And it's transmitted by a bloodborne pathogen."

"Meaning it's transmitted by blood?" asked Max tenuously.

"Exactly. And that's just medicine. You can take precautions to avoid getting infected, just like any other disease. And I'm still not convinced that Ebola isn't scarier."

"What's Ebola again?"

"Makes you bleed from every orifice," said Lovecraft.

"Every?"

"Every."

"Yikes, I see your point."

Max stared out at the revenants for a moment.

Lovecraft was trying to enjoy the night air and not think about the long shadows around them. He tried to counter the ghostly thoughts with the more comfortable idea of hemorrhaging from every orifice. It was times like this that he reflected on how wyrd his life was.

"I saw a bunch of zombie films with my Mom," said Max at last.

"Cool, Mom," smiled Lovecraft.

"She was...," started Max, but then he hesitated. "Now, I don't enjoy them."

"Understandable," nodded Lovecraft.

"But, that's just movies," huffed Max. "That's not going to help you out here."

"You might be surprised," said Lovecraft, and he looked at the boy out of the corner of his eye. "What's the one thing you don't want a zombie to do to you?"

Max hesitated for a moment.

"It's almost too easy an answer to be right," added Lovecraft.

"Um, to bite you?" asked Max hesitantly.

"Exactly!" said Lovecraft. "And how fast do they move in movies?"

"Um, not that fast," suggested Max, and then his brows furrowed together. "Wait? Are you saying that the movies..."

"Not all of them," interjected Lovecraft. "But, let's just say that certain government agencies wanted to disseminate..."

"What?"

"To give out important information to everyone," continued Lovecraft smoothly.

"Zombie films were just instructional films?" asked Max.

"At first," said Lovecraft. "There's been revenant outbreaks for over a hundred years. And there was a short-lived—but bad one—in the Bronx a year before 'Night of the Living Dead' came out."

"Bullshit," blurted out Max.

"Don't swear," chastised Lovecraft absently. "But the outbreaks were historically smaller, and that was before everyone carried a camera in their pocket."

"So, this has happened before Toledo and Phoenix," suggested Max.

"I can neither confirm nor deny that," said Lovecraft. "And if you tell anyone, I'll have to deny it."

Max thought about this for a moment, but then he nodded. "Fair enough."

They looked back at the revenants, who moaned softly.

"So, what now?" asked Max after a while.

"We wait for reinforcements," said Lovecraft.

# 20

"Help is coming!" cried a voice behind them. They turned to see Tibbons waving an empty hand. The burly man was steering his generous belly through the hedgerows of vehicles.

"Earlier than expected, but I won't complain," said Lovecraft.

Tibbons walked up to them and then gestured towards Max.

"I see that you had help."

"The kid did all the hard work," said Lovecraft with a low drawl. "I just stood around and looked pretty."

Tibbons gave a bark of laughter. "Well, I'm here now, and..."

A long, painful howl split through the night air. Lovecraft shouldered his rifle but did not see anything. Outside the gate, the revenants just moaned, as usual.

"What the hell was that?" asked Tibbons as he looked around.

"I don't know," said Lovecraft, and he glanced back at the boy. But Max—poised to spring off the hood—just shrugged.

"I've never heard a revenant make that sound before," said Max.

"If that was a revenant," suggested Tibbons.

"What else could it be?" wondered Lovecraft.

"I don't know," said Tibbons. "But, is it our worry?"

"Well...," started Lovecraft, but he stopped as he mulled this over. He was hesitant to leave now.

"If you can stand a little while longer, we'll see if we hear it again," suggested Tibbons. They all agreed, and Max settled back onto the hood of the car,

But there were no more strange noises.

Lovecraft let out a short but hearty chuckle.

"What?" asked Tibbons in concern.

"I was thinking that I haven't heard any strange noises," said Lovecraft, and then he nodded his chin at the revenants beyond the gate. "But I don't consider their noises strange. And that struck me as funny."

Tibbons' mouth quirked up. "Hah. That is funny."

"Still creepy," said Max wretchedly.

"It is still creepy, kid," agreed Lovecraft.

After ten minutes, the Councilman looked at Lovecraft. "They made some chili in the kitchen, and it's actually pretty good. Well, edible. Why don't you two get some?"

"I don't know," said Lovecraft, despite what his stomach was saying. He had not had much at dinner.

"Have you ever met any revenant that can get through that?" asked Tibbons seriously as he waved at the gate.

"No," said Lovecraft reluctantly.

"Then I'll call on my walkie if anything interesting happens," finished Tibbons with a stern tone. "Now you two get some shuteye." Then a bright smile grew across his dark, weathered face. "Because I need you two well-rested tomorrow, or you're no good to me."

Lovecraft chuckled warmly. "You heard me talking to the kid earlier."

"Yes, I did, and you had a good point," said Tibbons. "Now get."

"Yes, sir," smiled Lovecraft, and Max hopped off the hood of the car.

Lovecraft started to turn away but hesitated. He looked back at Tibbons. "Hey, any sign of the deputy?"

"Not yet," said Tibbons. "But even in the daylight, there are probably a lot of places to hole up around here."

"Huh," grunted Lovecraft. "It just doesn't make sense."

"Does anything about this day make sense?" asked Tibbons.

"No...I guess not," admitted Lovecraft reluctantly. "Call if you see or even hear anything."

"Beat it," grumbled Tibbons with a smirk.

Lovecraft walked towards the infirmary with Max.

"So, what is the plan...really?" asked Max, after they were out of earshot.

"Food, and then bed," said Lovecraft.

"No exploring?" asked Max, a little sadly.

"Food. Bed" repeated Lovecraft with resolve.

Max hesitated for a moment, but then he tried a different tack.

"I'm not sure I ever want to sleep again...ever," said the boy.

"Time's like this, you sleep when you can and eat when you can. That's why food, then sleep," said Lovecraft finally. "If I kept sleeping pills on me, I'd give you one to help you sleep."

"That's okay," said Max. "I don't want to be that out of it."

"Good point," agreed Lovecraft.

They walked into the first part of the infirmary and closed the door quietly behind them. Most people were asleep by now. Walking through the second part of the infirmary, they moved past the doctor's rooms and into the cafeteria. There was a small knot of people at one table, but the Substitute Teacher was more interested in what he smelled.

"What is that?" asked Lovecraft as he sniffed the air like a big dog. He followed the scent to a big pot of chili and some cornbread. Lovecraft grinned in gastronomic euphoria. He and Max each got a bowl of chili and some cornbread. Then they headed over to a table of people, which included Tammi and Craig.

"Hi, Max!" chirped Tammi eagerly. "Where've you been? Did you have trouble sleeping too?"

Max stammered for a moment.

"Pulling guard duty," said Lovecraft in a macho growl.

"Bull," snapped Craig as he rolled his eyes.

"Really?" asked Tammi in interest.

"I was at the main gate," confirmed Max.

"Cool," said Tammi.

Craig looked surprised at this, and then he became sullen.

Before Tammi could ask more, Lovecraft spoke. "Did I hear something about bad dreams?"

Max tensed, but no one except Lovecraft seemed to notice.

"Yeah," said Tammi softly as she looked down.

"I'm just too wired to sleep," said Craig quickly.

"Of course," replied Lovecraft in a neutral tone, but Tammi chimed in.

130

"I saw you twisting and turning in bed," she scolded.

"I was dreaming of a Sports Illustrated Swimsuit shoot that...," started Craig quickly.

"That's good," interrupted Lovecraft swiftly. "I'm eating here."

While Lovecraft tucked into his chili, Max poked at his meal.

"What kind of dreams were you having?" asked Max of Tammi, and it made the girl pause.

"It...," she started to say but then stopped.

Suddenly, remembering how reluctant he was to speak earlier, Max quickly spoke up. "You don't have to share."

"It's...it's okay. It was about this old man with a rusty chain around his ankle," she replied, and the memory of it made her shrink deeper into herself.

"Lucky," shuddered Turk. "I was trapped in a cell during a prison riot by some guys who were paid to kill me. Something about if he went, he wanted you to go too.' And then they started stabbing me."

"For me, it was things coming down from the skylights," moaned the driver of bus #9, Randy.

"I don't like this place," said Tammi.

"Well, we shouldn't be here too long," said Max reassuringly.

# 21

Again, Max was sitting on the edge of his bed. His hands fidgeted nervously while Lovecraft brought a chair over and set it quietly next to the bed. The Substitute first removed his MP5 submachine gun and hung it on the footboard of Max's bed. Then he added his satchel.

Bone tired, Lovecraft sank gratefully down onto the chair. Fiddling with his Gurkha knife, he got it to hang down from his waist, and then he laid his rifle across his lap with a happy sigh.

"Feels good just to sit down," murmured Lovecraft.

Max did not say anything. The Substitute looked up at him.

"You okay?" asked Lovecraft.

"I can't believe that my Grandma's gone," whispered the boy. "She probably won't even get a grave. They burned the bodies in Toledo. They threw them into an incinerator and then buried all their ashes together. There was supposed to be a stone marker for the grave with people's names on it, but it got stalled in the state legislature. Some politicians thought it was too expensive for a bunch of zombies."

The boy looked so sad and alone, even in this infirmary full of people.

Lovecraft watched the boy thoughtfully. He started to speak, but then he stopped as he looked for the right words. Finally—unable to get his verbal ducks in a row—he decided to stagger forward regardless.

"I understand...more than you know," said Lovecraft. "But you'll get through this."

Max gave a sad little laugh. "How can you be so sure?"

Lovecraft wrestled with his orders for a moment longer. But then he came to a decision.

"I did," he said softly.

"What?" asked Max in surprise.

"I...," started the Substitute Teacher, but then he paused and looked up at the clear night sky through the skylights. After a moment, he began again. "What I'm about to tell you, I'm not supposed to talk about."

"By who?" asked the boy.

"You have to promise to keep this between us," said Lovecraft, and then he gave the boy a solemn look.

"Sure," shrugged Max offhandedly.

"No. I need you actually to promise," said Lovecraft, and Max suddenly realized the gravity of this promise.

"I promise not to breathe a word of it," said Max solemnly.

Lovecraft nodded after a moment.

"Okay," said Lovecraft. "When I was, well...about your age, I lost my family. If you want to be accurate, I lost my whole town."

"You're kidding," said Max, but the substitute just looked the boy squarely in the eye. Lovecraft did not try to hide any of the old wounds there.

When Max spoke, it was quietly and carefully. "What

133

happened?"

"I've already said too much," said Lovecraft with a shake of his head. "But, I can tell you that it was a situation like this. Not revenants. Monsters though. Nasty little buggers."

"How did you...," began the boy, but he could not find a way to finish the sentence.

"Not die?" supplied Lovecraft. "Luck, mostly. And afterward, too."

"What do you mean?" asked Max.

"I didn't have any extended family left, so it was just me," said Lovecraft. "Luckily, I got a scholarship to a boarding school in Virginia."

"Hah, I'm not going to get one of those with my grades," chuckled Max darkly. He yawned as he laid down, but he felt better. "But, if you made it through, I can too."

Max tried to keep his eyes open, but they betrayed him and closed.

Lovecraft carefully put his feet up on the bed's metal footboard and shifted his rear until he was comfortable. It was not long before the boy's eyes raced under closed lids. Content, Lovecraft closed his own eyes.

# 22

A boy of fourteen huddled in a storm drain. He was too

exhausted to be scared anymore. Now, he almost felt numb.

Something began to approach, and the boy gripped a sharp piece of metal. The thing stepped in front of the storm drain blocking out the morning sun.

The white boy leaped out and stabbed with the metal. Only a quick hand managed to deflect the pointy steel, but the boy collided with the man dressed in grey. They both fell back into the water.

Suddenly, the boy realized that the man was not one of those monsters with horrible grins on their faces. He jumped off the man who stood quickly in the chilly water.

"Yo...you're not one of them?" exclaimed the boy in surprise as the man straightened his royal blue tie.

"What was your first clue," grinned the man as he helped the boy up.

"Who...who're you?" asked the boy wearily.

"Name's Agent Zane," replied the man with the big mustache and a wry grin. "And who're you, kid?"

# 23

Lovecraft's eyes snapped open. He listened to the dark but heard nothing more.

Max was still asleep. A quick look around showed that no one else had stirred. But the Substitute Teacher had heard something.

Standing, Lovecraft laid the strap of his satchel over one shoulder and then the strap for the MP5 submachine gun over the other. He held the Winchester rifle loosely as he walked to the main aisle.

The Substitute Teacher walked into the first part of the infirmary but froze just inside the door. His eyes roamed over a quiet scene, which was covered in way too many shadows.

After a long moment, one of those shadows rippled on the right. Something was lowering itself from the ceiling. Time seemed to slow. Lovecraft caught the shape of it in a splash of light. The thing—which would be later dubbed a 'runner'—was lowering itself by its tail from broken skylights. It had a long, winding head that bobbed up and down as it surveyed a group of sleeping teens.

The thing slowed to pause right above one of his students, Simp. With a dread chill, Lovecraft realized that the creature had once been a person, but no more.

The runner's head snapped up to glare at Lovecraft and hissed in warning. That hiss showed off dozens of pointed teeth. Shifting his rifle gently, Lovecraft rested the stock firmly against his shoulder and slid his finger to the trigger.

Tibbons burst through the door. He veered and hit the lights, which left his bloody handprint smeared across the panel.

The room immediately flooded with searing light.

The runner and Lovecraft both winced.

"We're under attack!" shouted Tibbons in alarm.

The runner was coiled over. Simp let out a shriek and quickly lowered itself towards the youth. Lovecraft swung up his rifle and fired. The bullet tore through the runner's brain, and the creature stilled. Teens around Simp jumped up and scattered. Above, the dead runner's tail started to lose its grip.

But Lovecraft saw that Simp—frozen in terror and surprise—was still on his cot looking at the thing above.

Lovecraft shot forward and jumped over an occupied bed while dropping his rifle. The runner's tail let loose above, and the body plunged. Lovecraft dove and grabbed Simp, who cried out. Bowling his student over, he pulled Simp out of the way as the creature's corpse smashed the folding cot flat as a pancake.

Hitting the ground hard, Lovecraft rolled to a stop on his back.

"Sorry about that," said Lovecraft. "My fault."

The Substitute moved away from Simp, who scrambled to his feet.

"Wha...What...?" was all Simp could manage.

"Sorry. I don't know," said Lovecraft as he got up quickly.

The Substitute Teacher looked over at Tibbons, whose shirt was stained with blood. Before the Councilman could speak, the skylights above exploded. People screamed as glass shards showered down. More runners appeared at the skylights.

Hooking their long tails above, they descended quickly towards the floor. Lovecraft gripped the MP5 submachine gun and wondered vaguely where his rifle was. He fired the MP5 into the back of the closest runner.

Everyone started panicking, but they did not know which way to run. While people leaped up from their beds, the runners hit the ground on all fours and scuttled like crabs. The privacy curtains on rollers further blocked his line of sight. The Substitute looked around, trying to get a clear shot at the creatures.

Lovecraft bellowed out. "Everyone! To the main jail."

The Substitute Teacher pushed Simp towards the front door of the infirmary, and Lovecraft tried to get other people to follow his student. Simp got to the front door and stepped outside with a few others, but they milled around in confusion.

Dodging between people, Lovecraft tried to get a clear shot at a nearby runner. He jumped left and gunned the runner down. But it was too late for the man under it.

Hurston wandered by with a glazed look in his eyes. The anchor's microphone was in his hand.

Lovecraft grabbed him by the upper arm.

"Take everyone to the jail," ordered the Substitute.

"Wha...?" asked Hurston in bewilderment. "Where?"

Max leaped out of the mass of people and skidded to a halt in front of Lovecraft.

"What the actual hell?" asked Max.

Lovecraft let go of Hurston, who just stood there like a stunned rabbit. Digging out the jail keys, Lovecraft tossed them to Max.

"Can you get everyone to general population?" asked Lovecraft.

"Sure, but...," started Max, but he faltered. "General population?"

"I know, kid," shrugged Lovecraft helplessly. "But, there are bars everywhere."

Max nodded if a tad reluctantly. "O...okay!"

"And take this," said Lovecraft. He pushed Hurston towards the boy. "I'll follow and grab Tibbons if no one else has. Now go!"

"Got it, general population!" repeated Max, and he grabbed Hurston's arm. The boy guided the Reporter towards the front door while shouting over the din. "Follow me! I'll take you to safety! Follow me!"

Gratefully, Lovecraft saw Patrick and Stu follow the boy. Craig also ran out in a panic with Missy.

Shoving aside his sharp concern for the boy, Lovecraft moved towards the edge of the crowd. A runner was trying to snap its teeth at Florence's ankle, but she booted hard in the face.

"Get away!" she cried.

Lovecraft ran up and fired a short burst from the MP5 into the back of the monster's head. He looked up at Florence.

"Look for the kid with the Tiger's coat!" said Lovecraft. He waved Florence towards the front door, and the young woman pushed her grandmother ahead of her.

Another runner appeared on the edge of the crowd, and

Lovecraft fired. But the bullet just grazed its leg. The thing ducked behind an overturned bed. Lovecraft saw his rifle lying nearby. He leaped over and scooped it up as the MP5 dangled across his body.

Someone let out a high-pitched scream from across the room.

"Help!" cried Turk. Lovecraft caught a glimpse of the big man through the stragglers running out of the infirmary. Lifting his rifle, he waited for a clear shot and prayed he would not be too late.

Something growled next to him. Blindly, he kicked out with his boot, and he was rewarded with a short yip.

A gap opened in the crowd. Turk had been thrown to the ground, and the runner leaned over him. Its jaws opened.

Lovecraft fired. The bullet shattered a tooth in the thing's mouth and then blew out the back of its skull. Turk shrieked as the thing wavered. But he had the presence of mind to move aside before it fell. Scrambling to his feet, he ran for the infirmary door.

The growl by his knee came back. From such a close distance, Lovecraft could feel the vibration in his back teeth.

"Aw crap," muttered the Substitute. The runner near his leg leaped and knocked him over. He slammed down so hard on his back, his teeth rattled.

# 24

Shoving aside his worry for Mr. Lovecraft, Max ran out
into the bailey with Mr. Hurston. The kid saw Simp there.
He was at the edge of the parked vehicles with a group of
people who were arguing.

"I don't think you should," said Simp.

The principal of the school glared at the football player.

"If you paid better attention in school, *Mr. Simpton*, you'd
know the quickest way between two points is a straight
line," huffed the principal, and he pointed across the
hedgerows of vehicles to the entrance of the jail.

"He would know best," added Mrs. Hannah Jonesson
with a condescending voice. "You kids today never listen
to your elders."

"Are you..!" started Max in anger, and then he called out.
"Never go near a vehicle without looking under it first!
And there are too many to check. Run around the outside
of the Goddamn cars!"

The principal twisted with anger.

"There's no need to swear!" he retorted.

"Exactly!" agreed Hannah.

"The hell there isn't," said Max. And he turned to look
at every one. "This way! Follow me! We have a safe
place!"

The kid started to drag Hurston around the cars.

Simp looked at the principal but nodded toward Max. "I
trust him."

141

The principal shouted after Simp, who ran to follow Max. The rest soon followed, except for the principal, Hannah, and a reticent Jerome. They went into the maze of vehicles and were never seen again.

Max led the ragtag group of refugees to the door, which led to the jail offices.

Some of the refugees slowed down as the kid opened the door.

"But...," started Rayton as he glanced up at the ancient walls of the four-story jail.

"No time!" said Max. He drove everyone inside, through the darkened corridors, and to the door leading to general population.

As the boy tried to find the right key, the group muttered behind him. Max knew he needed to find the right key quickly, or the group would stampede like frightened animals.

"This is safe?" asked Turk in disbelief.

"Thick walls and a big iron gate!" said Max. "I used to dream about having an advantage like that." He blinked. "Used to dream."

Rayton was about to ask the boy what he was talking about when Max suddenly unlocked the gate.

"Now, please, get the hell inside!" said the boy.

# 25

In the infirmary, the runner snapped at Lovecraft.

Pushing the rifle up between them, he jammed it into the creature's mouth. The runner's jaws tried to bite down on the weapon, but it could not get purchase.

Lovecraft grinned.

"Is that the best you got?" he growled.

Something chittered by his ear. He saw a second runner flashing those big pointy teeth at him. It lunged to chew off his face.

Letting out an involuntary yipe, Lovecraft twisted the rifle around, even though it was still in the first runner's mouth. He fired and killed the second runner instantly.

But the rifle produced such a loud noise that he and the first runner were rattled for a split second. Lovecraft blinked, and he tried to ignore the ringing in his left ear. He was about to turn his attention to the first runner when a third one grabbed his ankle.

"Can't everyone just wait their turn?" barked Lovecraft in annoyance. With one hand, he kept the rifle in the first runner's mouth, and with the other, grabbed his MP5 submachine gun. A burst from the MP5 killed the runner on top of him.

As Lovecraft dragged the rifle out of its mouth, though, he saw that there was still a tooth embedded in the Winchester's wood. The runner at his foot was worrying his ankle, but it hadn't gotten through the special fiber of his pants. Distantly, Lovecraft knew that his ankle was

143

going to hurt in the morning.

Lovecraft aimed the MP5 at the third runner, but the weapon's clip was empty, so he let it go.

Swinging the rifle like a Louisville Slugger, he hit the third runner in the head. It went cross-eyed from the blow and backed away quickly. Dragging himself out from under the first runner, Lovecraft saw the rifle was now at an unnatural angle. It was an ex-rifle now. Poor thing, he thought as he looked up.

Ex-rifle under one arm, he put a fresh clip in the MP5 and then let it hang by its strap.

Most of the living people were out, which left him with monsters and corpses. The runners slowly looked up from their kills.

Backing gingerly towards the door, he grinned.

"Maybe we could talk this out over a nice steak," suggested Lovecraft.

One of the runners growled with a low harmonic.

"Sushi then?" asked Lovecraft weakly.

"Maybe, they're vegans," chuckled a voice near him. He glanced at Tibbons, who was still sitting against the wall. There was a line of drying blood leading to him from the light switches, but Tibbons stubbornly held onto his MP5 submachine gun.

"What are you still hanging around for?" chided Lovecraft. He carefully knelt so that he would not take his eyes off the remaining runners. He helped Tibbons stand.

"The party's in general population now," he said.

"Well, what're we waiting around for?" asked Tibbons with his gravelly voice. "An engraved invitation."

One of the runners jumped at them. Lovecraft slugged it with the dead rifle and knocked it aside. He dropped the rifle as the other runners started to follow. Moving out the front door, he lifted the MP5 and sprayed the room.

Out in the bailey, Lovecraft grimaced as he tried to walk Tibbons towards the door to general population. It looked too far away. He jumped at the sound of gunfire.

A runner scrambled away from Tibbons' smoking MP5.

"We need to go faster," commented Tibbons. His teeth were gritted from pain and annoyance.

"No kidding!" said Lovecraft.

Boyle leaped out of the door of the Infirmary and over a runner. She hit the ground and ran over to Lovecraft and Tibbons.

"What're you two still doing here?" asked Boyle archly.

"Not running fast enough, it seems," said Tibbons.

Boyle put a shoulder under Tibbons' other arm.

"I got'em," said Boyle.

"Sure?" asked Lovecraft.

"Just get us there safely," said Boyle, and it was somewhere between a plea and an order.

Lovecraft let go of Tibbons and shouldered his MP5. He saw something darting in between cars, but he could not get a bead on it. The runners were keeping low and out of sight behind the vehicles in the bailey.

"Enough games," growled Lovecraft. He leaped up onto a car's hood and immediately fired at a nearby runner. It just managed to getaway. A few more shots, and the runners were now giving them a healthy distance. It was exceptionally beneficial for the monsters due to potential lead poisoning.

"You've gotta be kidding me?" exclaimed Boyle.

Lovecraft shot a glance at Boyle, but then he followed the paramedic's gaze.

"The hell?" added Lovecraft.

On top of the news van, the camerawoman, Icewater, filmed the evacuation while chewing Bubblicious bubblegum.

Lovecraft started hopping cars until he reached the van. Running up the hood, he leaped up onto the roof. Lovecraft stopped next to Icewater, but he spotted a runner.

The Substitute Teacher twisted quickly and put a bullet in its back. It made a pitiful noise. Lovecraft fired again and put it out of its misery.

"Nice shot," commented Icewater with a calm voice.

"Thank you," replied Lovecraft sincerely, and he turned to look at the Camerawoman. "Do you want to run away now?"

"Not really," admitted Icewater. She would have shrugged, but that would have spoiled her shot. "I'm trying to get a good picture of these things."

Lovecraft saw the creatures getting closer.

"We need to...," started Lovecraft when there was a

tremendous crash from the gate. Something in the dark, like a runaway semi, had just hit it hard. "What the hell!?!"

"Maybe, it is time to go," conceded Icewater.

Something hit the gate again.

Lovecraft looked from the van to the gate. There was a path through the other vehicles. It was big, but it was there.

"Key's still in the van?" asked Lovecraft.

"Yeah," said Icewater. "What're you..."

"Hold on!" said Lovecraft as he leaped down to the ground. He jumped up into the driver's seat just as a runner's teeth snapped from beneath the vehicle, trying to pull him under.

Lovecraft started the van. Icewater crouched down as the van jerked backward, ran over the runner underneath. The drive scraped the sides of other cars. The Camerawoman filmed as they drove up to the gate, and then the Substitute Teacher braced the back of the van against it.

Through the bars, Icewater filmed something big outside the gate. It leaned back and hit the gate again with a massive fist.

"Let's get outta here!" cried Lovecraft. He exited the vehicle and fired a couple of shots at the oncoming runners. The creatures skidded to a stop and then ran for cover.

As the Camerawoman jumped down, she and Lovecraft moved quickly towards the door to the jail. But Lovecraft halted when he saw that the back of the ambulance was open. Tibbons was leaning against the open door covering Boyle, who was inside.

"What're you guys still doing here?" cried out Lovecraft in exasperation.

"We're going to need medical supplies," said Boyle.

"For us, if we don't get going!" growled Lovecraft urgently. He reached in and tugged a little on her sleeve. Boyle jumped out, carrying a bag, which was leaking supplies.

"Inside!" urged Lovecraft.

Boyle once again helped Councilman Tibbons up while Icewater filmed everything. Lovecraft shooed them all through the wooden door and into the offices for the jail. Moving fast, they turned the last corner, and Lovecraft was relieved to see the kid at the far end of the corridor.

"What took you so long?" grinned Max in relief when they got close enough.

"Quiet Falcon," replied Lovecraft good-naturedly.

"Who?"

"Just get in there," ordered Lovecraft. He herded the kid through the gate and into general population after Boyle, Tibbons, and Icewater. Lovecraft waited for a moment, but he did not hear any pursuit. He backed into general population slowly as Max closed the metal gate shut.

Turning, Lovecraft saw Boyle taking Tibbons left, over to the gray wall, opposite the jail cells. The wounded had been set together near some exposed pipes in the concrete wall. To his credit, Tibbons did not cry out when he was set against the wall.

"What's that pounding sound?" asked Max worriedly. They could hear whatever-it-was beating on the gate outside, even through the news van and in the general population.

"Something wicked this way comes," said Lovecraft softly.

"What?"

"Nevermind."

Hurston, who had his wits again, saw Icewater filming and walked over to her.

"Thank God you made it," said Hurston sincerely. "I was worried when I didn't see you in here."

"Still not as bad as Afghanistan," shrugged Icewater, and then she added with a wry grin. "And still cooler to boot."

Hurston turned to look at Lovecraft, and the Reporter's pleasant look disappeared.

"What the hell was that?" snapped Hurston.

"What was what?" asked Lovecraft in surprise.

"What was all that out there? And, what are those...things?"

"I don't know."

"How can you not know?"

"I mean, I've never seen them before."

"Me neither," added Max helpfully, but Hurston gave the kid a condescending look.

"Please stay out of this son," said Hurston. "This is grown-up talk."

"Excuse me!" snapped Lovecraft. Hurston turned back to look at the Substitute Teacher in surprise. The Substitute glared at the Reporter. "Is this your first Revenant outbreak?"

"I reported on Toledo and D.C.," sniffed Hurston as he drew himself up.

"Was that during or after?" asked Lovecraft with precise words.

"Well...after...," admitted Hurston and Lovecraft broke in swiftly before the Reporter could continue.

"Right!" snapped Lovecraft. "This is the kid's second outbreak! So from now on, he's a subject-matter-expert for me, and I expect him to be treated as such."

"Um, okay," said Hurston, but he gained his footing quickly. "So, now we're talking about a new form of Revenant."

"At least one," said Lovecraft.

"What do you mean?" asked the Reporter.

There was a crash from the front gate, and then came the screeching sound of tortured metal as something gave. A rumble followed this as the news van was moved.

But then silence.

"That's not good," said Max.

"What was that?" asked Hurston.

"That was the front gate," said Lovecraft.

"You're kidding?" exclaimed Hurston. "I mean, those gates were really, really thick."

"Yes, they were," said Lovecraft, and he turned to look at the people who had made it into the general population. It seemed like such a small group to him. Boyle was tending to the wounded.

Max stepped close to Lovecraft, but the kid did not look the Substitute Teacher in the eye.

"I tried to save more," said Max softly. Only Lovecraft could hear as the kid's voice almost broke. "I'm...I'm sorry."

"Not your fault, kid. Not. Your. Fault," said Lovecraft as he patted the kid's shoulder comfortingly, and some of the tension eased away. "Who could've guessed that those things were out there."

"What do we do now?" asked Max, and the kid sounded a little lost.

"What we've been doing. Protect those that are left," said Lovecraft firmly, and after a moment, Max nodded solemnly. The Substitute's face scrunched up, and he gave a humorless smile. "Looks like we're not the only one getting back to work."

"What?" asked Max, and then he followed Lovecraft's gaze.

Hurston had completed primping himself and now turned to face Icewater's camera. The Reporter spoke with a dark, solemn tone.

"We are refugees here. Our town's good people had been safe in Fallen Oaks Infirmary when something— something new!—attacked. It climbed up over the very walls that protected us. Outside, new forms of revenants have appeared: both terrifying and fascinating. And they have taken countless lives with them. Yours truly struggled to save as many as he could, but sadly..." Hurston looked

151

choked up for a moment. "...Not all could be saved."

Lovecraft saw someone's hand wave beyond the Reporter.

"Come on," said Lovecraft to the kid. "That much sugar —and bullshit—isn't good for a kid your age. And I'm going to bust something if I don't laugh out loud soon."

They walked over to Brick and Smithie in their cells.

"What the hell is happening out there?" asked Brick.

"There's some kind of new revenants out there," explained Lovecraft.

"You're joking," exclaimed Brick, and he rattled the cell door. "Well, let us outta here."

"Not yet," said Lovecraft. He and Max turned and walked over to Tibbons. They found Boyle putting a field dressing on the Councilman's left arm. Tibbons looked up at Lovecraft weakly.

"You gonna survive?" asked Lovecraft with genuine concern.

"Don't care," smiled Tibbons. "Whatever this young lady gave me...it's keeping the pain at bay."

Boyle finished her work and got Tibbon's attention.

"I need you to stay here for right now," ordered Boyle.

"Not sure I could stand up, even if I wanted to," murmured Tibbons happily.

"Good," said Boyle crisply. "Then don't test that theory."

"Yes, Ma'am," said Tibbons.

Boyle stood up and stripped off her bloody gloves. She

shoved them into an empty plastic bag that now doubled as a wastebasket. Picking up her bag of medical supplies, she motioned for Lovecraft to follow as she moved on to the next person.

"He's okay for the moment," reported Boyle to Lovecraft. But then, her voice took a flinty edge. "But we don't have a surgical kit to suture up the lacerations. I was trying to find it when you pulled me out of the ambulance."

"Sorry," said Lovecraft sincerely. "But I didn't want us to get eaten."

Boyle quit moving, and she swung around to glare at Lovecraft. The paramedic was about to say something nasty, but then she stopped herself. She was just frustrated at the sharp turn of events, and there was no reason to take it out on him.

"Okay," admitted Boyle at last. "I can see that." Then she gave a little laugh. "And I do appreciate that."

"Was this all from the creatures?" asked Lovecraft.

"Falling glass too," said Boyle.

"Where are the sutures in the ambulance?" asked Max thoughtfully.

"That's the problem," admitted Boyle. "They're not where they're supposed to be. Either we were out because we did have many calls about lacerations before I got here. Or, my partner Zeke must've put them somewhere wrong. He is..." She stopped. Her voice grew melancholy as she remembered her fallen partner. "...He was always doing that. The big jerk."

Lovecraft leveled a severe look at Max. "And we're not

153

going to go out there and rummage around hoping to find it. Not with those things out there."

"What?" asked Max innocently.

Lovecraft turned back to Boyle. "Wasn't there a surgical kit in the infirmary?"

"Sure," said Boyle. "It was in the green tote, but isn't that even farther?"

"It is," replied Lovecraft thoughtfully. "But at least we know right where it is."

"And that will help us, how?" asked Boyle, who looked unsure.

"I have no idea," admitted Lovecraft.

"Well, we're going to need a surgical kit, or a hospital, sooner rather than later," said Boyle.

"Got it," nodded Lovecraft.

"I have patients to tend to," she said, but not unkindly. Boyle left them to finish her work.

Kneeling in front of a man, Boyle peeled off a makeshift bandage from Rayton's hand. She took out a bottle of Hydrogen Peroxide but looked up at the science teacher first.

"This is going to hurt a bit," said Boyle.

"O...okay," said Rayton. The paramedic poured the Hydrogen Peroxide onto the wound, and Rayton hissed as the wound bubbled.

"Hopefully, this will stop any infection," said Boyle as she professionally finished cleaning and bandaging the wound.

Lovecraft and Max kept going. They soon stopped by Stu and Patrick, who were once again in a quiet consultation.

"Excuse me?" asked Lovecraft of Stu. The Substitute pointed to the wire mesh, which ran from each floor and secured into the wall opposite. "Why?"

"Oh, the wire...," started Stu.

"That's so no one gets pushed over, " interjected Patrick.

"What?" asked Lovecraft.

"The railing of the balcony was built too close to the cells," explained Stu. "Prisoners could stick out their arms and then push a guard over the railing."

"Splat!" added Patrick.

"Yikes," grimaced Max.

"It was pretty horrible," nodded Stu.

Just then, Tammi walked past, holding her cell phone up. She stopped just beyond them and waved it at the barred windows, high above.

Lovecraft paused, and Tammi saw the Substitute Teacher's questioning look.

"I can't get a signal," she explained.

"Maybe I can," suggested Patrick helpfully. He dug into his backpack for his phone and turned it on. After a moment, his face turned into a frown. "That's odd. I'm not getting a signal either."

"This is a brand new phone," moaned Tammi. "My Dad got it for me *because* it had the best reception."

"Is everything alright?" asked Lydia from Bus #9 as she walked up.

"Does your cell phone work?" asked Tammi.

"Should," replied Lydia, but she soon found that she did not get any reception either.

Shortly, a small crowd had formed as more people tried their phones. With a self-important huff, Hurston marched up and shouldered his way to the center of attention.

"What's going on here?" demanded Hurston. He turned a little to make sure that Icewater's camera had his best side.

"No one's phone is getting any reception," moaned Tammi.

"Someone's phone must work," said Hurston with a condescending tone. He pulled out his phone. "*Now*, this is a state-of-the-art phone called the Bright. It was not cheap, of course."

"Oooooh. I read those. There are only a few on the market right now," whispered Patrick in awe.

With a smile full of capped teeth, Hurston turned on his phone, which chirped happily.

"Now, we'll just...," started Hurston, but he stopped abruptly. "What the hell?"

Lifting his phone to the barred windows above, Hurston desperately looked for a signal.

"God damn it," growled Hurston. "How can *I* not get a signal?"

"It's this old building," explained Stu. "Hard to get a

signal in here. I was giving a tour to some city officials a while back. You see, they had the dumb idea to turn the jail into a tourist trap."

"You're kidding," said Patrick in shock.

"I know, I know," said Stu quickly. "So, the funny thing was, one of the councilmen spent the whole tour on his phone until we got in here. And then..." Stu just finished with a raspberry noise. "It's these walls. They just eat up the signal."

"Well then, what're we supposed to do?" snapped Hurston.

"Go outside?" replied Stu with a smile.

Hurston looked like he was ready to explode when Lovecraft cut in.

"Max? Do you have that piece of paper with the emergency number on it?" asked Lovecraft.

"Um, yeah, sure," said Max as he reached into his pocket. He pulled out a wad of papers and started to dig through them.

The kid noticed the look on Lovecraft's face.

"Don't judge me," grumbled Max.

Lovecraft just smiled, and he held up his hands in supplication. Max peeled off a sheet with their evacuation information and handed it to Lovecraft.

The Substitute took out his phone and put on his reading glasses.

"Your phone's not going to work if my three thousand dollar phone didn't work," sneered Hurston.

Lovecraft snapped open his phone and dialed. It started ringing, and Hurston looked like he had swallowed a bullfrog.

An electronic voice came over the phone.

"Name and city of birth," it requested.

"Henry P. Lovecraft, and I was born in East Lansing, Michigan," replied Lovecraft.

"Stop pretending," scoffed Hurston.

Lovecraft just shushed the Reporter.

"Why does it want to know where you were born?" asked Patrick curiously.

Lovecraft shrugged with a little smile. "FEMA needs customer data for a better shopping experience? I don't know."

An older woman came on the phone. "Twain here."

"This is Henry Lovecraft in Soundsville, Michigan," said Lovecraft.

"Hey Lovecraft," replied Twain happily. "You alive?"

"Yes, there are survivors," said Lovecraft.

"Are there civilians listening?" asked Twain carefully.

"Yes," replied Lovecraft.

"Okay," said Twain. "Well, good to hear from you. Agent Swift is en route with backup, but it's going to be at least two days. Where are you? City Hall, right?"

"We're in Fallen Oaks Penitentiary."

"What? As in...jail?"

"Yes, as in jail."

"What the hell are you doing there? Our records said City Hall was supposed to be the rally point."

"I don't know why they have us here, but we're trapped."

"Are there more than the usual amount of revenants?"

"There are not a huge amount of revenants, but some of them have changed, evolved."

"What? How?" asked Twain.

"I don't know how, but there are two new kinds, other than the run-of-the-mill moaning type."

"Describe."

The Substitute Teacher paused for a moment to collect his thoughts.

"One is a fast mover. It appears to climb walls..." he started, but then he stopped.

Lovecraft's breath hitched. "The deputy..."

"What did you say?" asked Twain.

"There was a deputy here that disappeared," said Lovecraft. "Those things can climb walls. I wonder if they took him."

"What do they look like?" asked Twain.

"They have powerful back tails—which they can hang from—and scuttle across the ground like crabs," said Lovecraft.

"I'll tell Swift to bring the melted butter."

"Very funny. They actually can run pretty fast."

159

"Okay, so we have 'runners.' What else do we have?"

"The others are bigger. We haven't seen them yet, but it looks like they broke down the gate to the jail."

"You're kidding me."

"Bring guns, a lot of them. And maybe something bigger, like a .50 cal. We also need a med unit. We have injured here."

"Okay, I'll tell Swift. She's been asking after you. When are you going to make an honest woman out of her?"

"Sorry, your connection died there for a second. Must be interference."

Twain laughed. "Okay, sweetie, you take care. And I just found some blueprints for the jail...sending them to your phone right now. Godspeed."

"Thanks."

Lovecraft ended the call. Hurston looked at it with a mixture of jealousy and bewilderment. Then he looked at his phone and—with a sour face—shoved it away.

"Crappy phone," muttered Hurston darkly.

Before anyone could ask any more questions, a rending screech came from the gate. They turned and saw a runner there reaching through the bars to grasp at them.

"Shoot it! Shoot it!" shrieked Hurston, but Lovecraft was already moving.

Shouldering his weapon, Lovecraft moved up to it, followed by Max, Hurston, and Icewater. But the Substitute stopped just outside of the thing's grasp and paused.

"Well, what're you waiting for?" screamed Hurston.

Lovecraft looked back at the Camerawoman.

"Here's your chance. Can you get a good shot of this guy?"

Icewater looked at him curiously, but then she nodded. "Happily."

Lovecraft turned back to the creature. Its features had started human, but the face was now widened and flattened. Clumps of permed hair still clung to the back of its head.

"What happened to you?" he asked softly.

The runner hissed at him as the Camerawoman filmed it.

"Got a good shot of it," reported Icewater.

Lovecraft fired and put two bullets in its head. It slumped down as he walked over.

Kneeling, he whispered to the creature. "Sorry about that."

"What was that?" asked Hurston behind him.

Lovecraft stood quickly, and he turned to look back at everyone. "Nothing. We need to step back and hope they didn't hear it."

But there was an answering roar outside.

"Oh God," quivered Hurston. "They're coming."

Several slow-mover revenants moved jerkily around the corner. They shuffled towards the gate.

"Shoot them! Shoot them!" ordered Hurston.

Lovecraft rolled his eyes. "What are you? A Looney Tunes cartoon? "

161

Hurston grabbed the Substitute's arm. "Kill them now!"

Glaring down at the hand on his arm, Lovecraft said. "You like that hand?"

Hurston suddenly got nervous and took it off.

Turning back to the gate, Lovecraft watched as more revenants arrived. The first one made it to the gate and pressed up against it. It reached through, but Lovecraft was safe, just out of reach.

"Why don't you shoot them?" demanded Hurston with a hint of panic.

"They're not going to get in right now," said Lovecraft, without looking back. "I'm not worried about them."

Then there was a commotion behind the wave of revenants. The hallway was not lit, and something big was moving through them, like a whale amongst minnows. It strode forward and just bumped the other revenants aside as if it did not notice them.

"That, on the other hand...," started Lovecraft, but he let his voice trail off. He could not quite see it.

"What is it?" gasped Huston.

Lovecraft took a high-intensity glowstick from his suitcase and cracked it. The Substitute Teacher threw it through the bars and into the dimly lit corridor. It illuminated the press of bodies, and out of that group came a considerable bruiser. Bone white armor-plating covered its head and chest.

The armor on its face covered its eyes, so it shuffled forward blindly towards the gate until it thunked into it.

"Max!" cried Lovecraft. "I need you to make sure all your classmates are in the cells. Everyone should get in there, Now!"

"Got it!" replied Max, and he ran off to move everyone to the cells. However, the kid stopped in the middle of the herding everyone.

"What about the wounded?" he asked of Lovecraft. But, by the grey wall, the paramedic answered.

"They can't be moved," called out Boyle, who was in the middle of bandaging an arm. "Not far, at least."

"We have to risk it then," said Lovecraft. He noticed that the people were so frightened that they were following Max willingly. Even the bully, Craig, let himself be guided, along with his girlfriend, Missy.

Max helped Florence get Maddie and her wheelchair into one of the cells.

Boyle finished bandaging an arm and suddenly realized what Lovecraft was going to do. She moved over and used her body to shield a young patient.

"What're you up to?" asked Hurston to Lovecraft. "They've already seen that we're here."

But Icewater was backing up and using the zoom to get a good view of the action still.

"Ricochet," was all that the Camerawoman said.

"What?" asked Hurston as he watched Icewater retreat.

"That's a lot of armor plating," nodded Lovecraft towards the bruiser. "Please go into the cells."

"I'll do no such thing," huffed Hurston.

"Suit yourself," shrugged Lovecraft.

The bruiser reached out and tentatively touched the bars. Then it took a fighting stance and pulled back its fist to punch the gate.

"Clear!" called Max as he ducked into Cell #5.

Lovecraft fired twice at the bruiser's head, but the bullets hit the armor-plating and then ricocheted back down the corridor towards the offices. One revenant, who had standing behind the big one, did not even seem to notice that its chest had been ventilated.

"Glad we got the kids away," murmured Icewater.

"What just happened?" demanded Hurston.

The bruiser hit the gate hard, but the bars held fast. It pulled back its fist to hit the gate again. Lovecraft fired one shot at a soft spot between the armor, but the bullet just disappeared into its body. The creature barely even paused. The facial armor hung just below the chin.

Lovecraft noticed that it had neck armor as well. There were only small gaps in the armor between the face, throat, chest, and shoulders.

It's breathing. Maybe if I could get a rope between the neck and chin armor, thought Lovecraft quickly. But he did not want to open the door to test out that theory.

Lovecraft hopped forward and pushed the MP5 submachine gun through the bars of the gate. Aiming the barrel at the same spot where he had fired before, he emptied the magazine into its body. The bruiser staggered back as the MP5 clicked empty. But then, with a shake, the monster shrugged it off.

164

"Shoot it! Shoot it more!" cried Hurston.

"Would, if I had any more ammo," said Lovecraft, and he tossed the MP5 aside.

"Oh God," cried Hurston. "Does anyone have any more ammo!"

"Calm down," advised Lovecraft. He pulled his tan satchel to his side.

"How can you say that?" whined Hurston.

The bruiser hit the gate again, and a shower of dust fell from the ceiling. But the metal held fast to the stone.

"The submachine gun was just tickling him anyhow," replied Lovecraft absently.

"Then we're dead," moaned Hurston.

The Substitute Teacher opened his suitcase and reached inside.

"I'm still breathing," growled Lovecraft.

"What're you going to do!" snapped Hurston nastily. "Tickle some him more."

"I was thinking of something a little more final!" explained Lovecraft without explaining.

The Substitute Teacher lifted a handgun out of his satchel. He pulled back the slide and slid a red-tipped bullet into the chamber. In one smooth move, he readied the weapon as the bruiser pulled back its fist again.

"What the...," started Hurston.

Lovecraft fired at the center of the bruiser's face. The bullet not only penetrated but blew out the back of its skull.

The creature teetered for a moment but then fell back, pinning two revenants beneath it. Pulling out a clip with black-tipped bullets, Lovecraft slipped it into his handgun, Rikke.

Firing quickly, he put a bullet into the head of every revenant by the gate. Once done, he fished a hip holster from his pouch and attached it to the side of his belt. Slipping the gun into its holster, he turned back towards general population.

"Oh my God...," started Hurston loudly.

"Shh," admonished Lovecraft. "Keep it down, or you'll attract more."

"That was awesome!" bounced Hurston quietly, and Lovecraft just glared at him. The Substitute Teacher did not even bother to hide his disgust.

"No, it wasn't," hissed Lovecraft. He looked back at the cells and spoke with a loud whisper. "Max! All clear."

The kid poked his head out.

"We good?" asked Max.

"For the moment," replied Lovecraft cautiously.

As Max came out, everyone else began to leave the cells.

"Please! Everyone keep your voice down," said the Substitute Teacher.

"What'd you do?" asked Max. He ran up next to Lovecraft as everyone spoke in hushed tones.

"He took them all out like that!" gushed Hurston, and he snapped his fingers.

"Cool," exclaimed Craig.

Lovecraft shook his head. "I did what I had to do. Poor things didn't have a chance."

"But you fought them all off," said Hurston.

"It was about as manly as hunting a bear tied to a stake," scoffed Lovecraft.

"How did you kill that big guy?" asked Icewater curiously.

The Substitute hesitated before speaking. "A special round."

Max went right up to the bars. He looked at the bodies strewn about before Lovecraft grabbed the back of his Tiger's coat to drag him back.

"Wow," said Max. "That was some special round."

"Round?" asked Tammi.

"Bullet," explained Icewater.

"And you just happened to have it?" asked Hurston suspiciously. "Who are you exactly?"

"Substitute teacher?" suggested Lovecraft.

And even Max looked at him as if to say, 'who the heck do you think you're kidding?'.

"Pretty skilled shooting for a substitute teacher," murmured Hurston.

"Many teachers have had lives before this," said Lovecraft. "Some have been in the Marines."

"Were you ever in the Marines?" asked Maddie from her wheelchair.

"Well, no," admitted Lovecraft, and everyone just kept

167

looking at him. With a sigh, Lovecraft relented. "Okay, I'm not supposed to say, but I'm with Homeland Security."

Lovecraft pulled out a wallet badge and held it open. Those nearby leaned forward to read it.

"'Homeland Security," read Max.

"Henry P. Lovecraft," read Hurston.

"Really?" scoffed Craig, but Lovecraft just shrugged.

"I was wondering about the validity of that name," murmured Patrick as he looked over Max's shoulder. "Especially with the author and all."

"No relation," said the Substitute Teacher absently. He put away the badge and addressed everyone. "Now, we have a few things we need to talk about."

"What part of Homeland Security?" interrupted Hurston.

"I'm part of the Task Force for Urban Search and Rescue," replied Lovecraft. "I was sent here to see if the school was prepared for an evacuation."

"And you carried a gun into my school?" asked Rayton with cold fury in his voice. His uninjured fist balled up at his side.

"Not my choice," said Lovecraft apologetically, and he raised his hands in supplication. "Really, I didn't want to, but I have to keep my sidearm at all times in the field."

"Since when is 'the field' in a classroom?" asked Hurston archly.

"Since I was supposed to be secretly checking out the school," explained Lovecraft patiently.

"What if a student had gotten their hands on your gun?" asked Rayton pointedly.

"Actually, that wouldn't have been possible," said Lovecraft. "I'd even take my bag to the bathroom."

"You had a gun in your purse," sneered Hurston.

"Satchel," corrected Lovecraft.

"Whatever," said Hurston. "How hard can it be to get?"

"Okay," said Lovecraft, and he drew his gun with two fingers so as not to panic anyone. He put it into his satchel and closed the latch.

Holding the satchel out to Hurston, Lovecraft raised an eyebrow.

"Get the gun," said the Substitute Teacher.

Hurston blinked.

"Why me?" he asked nervously.

"You're the one who asked," said Lovecraft in a level voice. "Don't worry; it won't kill you."

"This is about the 'purse' comment, isn't it," said Hurston.

"Yes, yes it is," said Lovecraft. "But, I also want to assure these nice people that I would never, ever endanger their kids. Now, are you going to try and open it, or not?"

The Reporter reached out but suddenly hesitated.

"Come on!" urged Craig, like a spectator in a Roman coliseum.

Hurston—steeled on by the crowd—grabbed for the latch. He was immediately zapped with a sharp electrical

169

shock. The Reporter jumped back, sucking on his fingers.

"Ow!" cried Hurston. "You said it wouldn't hurt."

"I said it wouldn't kill you," corrected Lovecraft. "And better that a student gets zapped than shot. Also again, I was ordered to have my sidearm."

"That's enough," said Tibbons as he leaned up. He glowered at Lovecraft with fierce eyes, but those same eyes showed a hint of amusement. "Stop toying with him like a cat."

"He asked," replied Lovecraft defensively.

"And you made your point," stated Tibbons with parental finality.

Lovecraft fiddled with the latch, which opened as soon as it sensed his fingerprints. Taking out the gun, he put it back in his holster.

"I would never take a chance that a student could stumble across my gun," said Lovecraft, and Rayton nodded, at last, convinced.

"Okay," said Rayton. "Thank you for taking those precautions."

"Gotta protect the kids," shrugged Lovecraft.

"I, for one, am glad that you have all those special little bullets," grinned Hurston.

"Which ones are those?" asked Lovecraft.

"Whatever those red-tipped bullets are. The one that blew that thing's brains clean out," grinned Hurston.

"Oh, those. Those are High Explosive rounds. I have three," said Lovecraft. "Well, two now."

"Two?" asked Hurston. "Are you nuts?"

"I wasn't even going to bring those," huffed Lovecraft. "Most revenants go down when you put a regular bullet through their skulls. The explosive rounds are more for opening a locked door if you don't have time to pick the lock."

"What about those big things?" asked Hurston.

"First time I've ever seen those bruisers," said Lovecraft.

"You should've been more prepared," said Maddie coldly.

"First, the Federal government gave the city 20 million dollars for durable food, medical supplies, *and guns*," explained Lovecraft.

"Where're the guns?" huffed Hurston.

"I don't know," said Lovecraft, and he rolled his eyes. "AND let's not start that discussion again."

"And how can you *only* have two more explosive rounds?" whined Hurston.

"I don't know about you," said Lovecraft. "But I don't like running around with too much explosive ammunition?"

Hurston shut down as he tried to process that thought.

The older woman, Maddie, leaned forward. "You haven't answered my question yet."

"I can't answer for the city government because they're not here," said Lovecraft, and he kept going before Maddie could interject. "And Councilman Tibbons was kept in the dark about all this. I believe that. So, you will find out what happened here after this is all over. People above my pay grade will sort it out, but not until after all this has happened."

"But they sent you," said Maddie.

"As an observer," said Lovecraft. "I don't usually even deal with the Revenants. They're not my specialty."

"What is your specialty?" asked Hurston curiously.

"Easy Bake Oven Ops," said Lovecraft off-handedly, and then he turned back to the rest. "The guy who was supposed to be here had the flu. I was just supposed to come in for a day or two, nose around, and then report back. Had this all not happened, my higher-ups would've already known about the jail by now. And government accountants would've been asking pointed questions about where all the money was.

"So, what do we do now?" asked Maddie, but her voice had lost its edge.

"We endure. We endure and take care of our people," said Lovecraft, and he walked over to one of the cells. He reached in and grabbed an old mattress. Striding over to the wounded, the Substitute experimentally sniffed the mattress. "Not bad."

Lovecraft dropped the mattress next to Tibbons, and then he looked down at the Councilman.

"I'm not that sick," grumbled Tibbons.

"Better this than a concrete floor," shrugged Lovecraft.

Tibbons reluctantly conceded. "You do have a point."

"And better than a cell," added Lovecraft.

Tibbons chuckled. "You do have an excellent point."

Lovecraft reached down and helped Tibbons onto the mattress. Then he turned back to the group.

"We're going to need more mattresses for the wounded," suggested Lovecraft.

After a moment's hesitation, Max moved towards the cells. He was followed by Florence, Rayton, and then more people. They grabbed mattresses and started bringing them back to the wounded.

As Craig was dragging a mattress out of Cell #5, he suddenly stumbled forward.

"Hey!" snapped the bully.

Dropping the mattress, Craig whirled around, ready to fight. But he stopped cold.

There was no one else in the cell.

"What is it?" asked Lovecraft in concern.

"I...," started Craig. Lovecraft walked over, followed by Stu and Patrick.

"What?" asked Lovecraft in a calm, neutral tone. "It's okay. Tell us."

"Someone pushed me," said Craig in a whisper.

"Are you okay?" asked Stu.

Turk, who was nearby, grinned and made a spooky noise. "Oooh, scary."

Others heard this and laughed, even Missy and Simp.

"It's true," snarled Craig, which drew more attention.

"Sure it is," sneered Turk.

173

"Screw you!" snapped Craig.

"That's enough!" said Lovecraft sharply as he looked at everyone.

His words cut through the laughter, which died quickly away.

Lovecraft continued. "We're all tired, hungry, and in here for the duration. But we will get through IF we stick together. In the meantime, everyone stay out of that damn cell."

As the mob went away, Lovecraft heard Stu make a thoughtful, clicking noise.

"Cell #5," he said quietly.

"I'm not surprised," agreed Patrick.

Once the wounded were on mattresses, Lovecraft and Max stopped near Tibbons, and the Substitute crouched down.

"You comfy?" asked Lovecraft.

"As good I can be, under the circumstances," smiled Tibbons weakly. "But we do need to talk soon."

"Agreed," said Lovecraft. "First, though, I'm going to have a look around."

"Aren't we just going to hole up in here?" asked Tibbons wearily.

"Maybe. Hopefully," said Lovecraft. "IF nothing else goes wrong. But, we're going to need water before too long."

"What about food?" asked Tibbons' stomach.

"We can last three weeks without food.." began Lovecraft.

"Three weeks?" hissed Tibbons.

"Don't worry, it's not going to come to that," said Lovecraft firmly.   "But if we're talking about water...then we only have three days."

"You think it'll take them that long to rescue us?" asked Tibbons.

"I don't want to find out," said Lovecraft honestly. "Besides, I'm feeling squirrely.  A walk will do me good."

Lovecraft straightened up and headed towards the other end of general population.  As he walked towards the next section—which he still thought of as solitary confinement— he noticed that Max kept pace with him.

Lovecraft looked at Max out of the corner of his eye.  "I don't remember inviting you."

"You didn't," smiled Max, and he whistled an aimless tune.

Lovecraft just smirked in reply.

The kid eyeballed the Substitute.  "What're we looking for?"

"Drinking water," said Lovecraft as they passed out of general population.

"No, I mean, what are we looking for?" asked Max, but he suddenly stopped walking.

Lovecraft stopped as well and gave a small smile.

"A place to fall back to, if things go badly...," started Lovecraft, but then he amended.  "More badly.  Wait, is

175

'more badly' a real term?" He shook his head. "Anyhow."

Glancing at the cells on the left, Lovecraft looked more closely this time. Each one held a fixed bed and a toilet with a sink above. He walked in and tried the faucet, but it did not even cough. Lovecraft moved from cell to cell, trying faucets.

The Substitute did not notice that Max had glanced right and had frozen in place. But then the kid moved a little closer to a wooden door. He reached out—stopped—but then gently pushed the door inward.

"No *aqua* here," called out Lovecraft from further down. He walked out of the last cell. "Even the toilets look bone dry. I say we keep..."

The Substitute saw Max. The kid was staring through the open door, and he looked absolutely terrified.

Lovecraft shot forward. His fingers brushed the hilt of his Gurkha knife, as much for reassurance than anything else. He stopped by Max.

"What?" asked Lovecraft in a low whisper.

The room beyond had faded white paint. There was a set of stairs on one side leading up and in the middle of the wooden ceiling, a trapdoor. Lovecraft looked from the trapdoor to the cells and back again.

"This is the last stop, isn't it?" said Lovecraft in a hushed tone. "Death Row."

Max nodded slowly. "It's also the room from my dreams. You know, the guy with the noose."

"No shit," said Lovecraft. "Maybe you saw the room when we walked through here before?"

176

Max shook his head. "Door was closed."

"Okay, that's weird," said Lovecraft.

"Let's just get out of here," said the kid fearfully, and he moved towards the laundry room.

But Lovecraft did not budge. His fear and anxiety about this spooky jail blew away. In their place was the vivid memory of a frightened kid who had come out to stand guard with him.

"Not yet," growled Lovecraft, and he stalked forward into the execution room.

"Don't!" hissed the kid, who jumped forward to stop him.

But Lovecraft stomped right in and hooked his thumbs in his belt. He jutted out his chin and bellowed in a loud voice.

"Hey! Dickcheese! Yeah, you with the noose. Don't you go scaring the kid. He's had a bad enough day already."

"Mr. Lovecraft," hissed Max from the door, but he did not dare go in. Lovecraft looked back at him.

"You have to stand up to bullies," explained Lovecraft. "Or they think they can walk all over you."

Suddenly, Lovecraft gave a shiver.

"You okay?" asked Max.

"Yea," said Lovecraft. "Just got cold in here all of a sudden."

"At lunch last week, Patrick said something about how people can feel ghosts by a sudden drop in temperature," said Max nervously.

177

"I don't know about that," shrugged Lovecraft, but he was still too angry to be scared. "Maybe Dickcheese doesn't like to be called names."

"...not my name..." whispered a voice in the room. Both Lovecraft and Max stilled.

"Was that...?" asked the kid.

"Definitely," replied Lovecraft quickly. But then he sniffed aggressively and hitched up his pants.

"No," said the Substitute as he turned back to the— seemingly—empty room. "Your name is Dickcheese until you apologize to the kid."

With a dismissive huff, the Substitute turned and stomped out of the room. He headed straight towards the laundry room.

"Come on, kid," said Lovecraft. "Let's go find some H20."

"Okay," replied Max, with a small smile escaping across his face.

As they walked off, the ghost of Hugh Dustin raged impotently. The severed noose around his neck shook. But they could not hear his threats.

Past the morgue and around the corner, Lovecraft and Max walked down a short corridor to the laundry room.

Inside, the Substitute's eyes darted to one corner. One part of Lovecraft was tempted to check out that colossal bronze hatch set into the floor. But, he decided to save that mystery for later. Then he amended, maybe never.

The Substitute went right over to the first faucet and

twisted it. First, the faucet coughed shakily, but then it began to produce brownish water.

"That's not good," said Max with disgust.

"Wait for it," replied Lovecraft patiently. The faucet coughed again, and fresh water started to pour out. Lovecraft cupped some water in his hand and drank. He grinned. "We struck water! A little well-watery but still good to drink. Now, let's see if there's anything to carry it in."

After a brief search, Max came back with two buckets.

"Found these, and they don't smell of chemicals," said Max. "Dusty, but no chemicals."

In the corridor, a shadow creeper scuttled across the ceiling and disappeared.

Slowly, Lovecraft and Max looked out into the now empty corridor.

"Did you...?" asked Max.

"Oh yeah!" whined Lovecraft. "I don't like this place."

# 26

W ATER!" cried Missy. She ran away from her boyfriend and across general population. Lovecraft was quick to hand her a metal cup, which they had scrounged up. Missy snatched it from him and took some water. Delighted, her eyes rolled back in her head as she drank.

More people came up, and Lovecraft raised a free hand.

"Okay, hold on, everyone," said Lovecraft gently. "I want to get water to the wounded first, and then everyone will get some."

"Where did you find the water?" asked Boyle as she came up.

"There's at least one working faucet in the laundry room," replied Lovecraft.

"Good, I was worried that we'd be drinking out of the toilets soon," grinned Boyle.

"We are saved from that fate," said Lovecraft, and he returned her smile. He and Max set the water buckets next to the wounded. Tibbons smiled as he looked from the buckets to Lovecraft.

"That's a welcome sight," said the Councilman.

"And there's more where that came from," replied Lovecraft.

"Okay!" called out Boyle with authority. "Everyone form a line—Nicely!—so that we can dole out water."

As everyone hastily started to get into line, Stu came up to Lovecraft, followed by Patrick.

"Good news back here too," said Stu. "Four of the toilets down here are working."

"That is good," nodded Lovecraft sincerely. He added more quietly. "I don't think we should have people wandering around upstairs."

"Definitely not," agreed Stu.

And Stu's response was a little too quick for Lovecraft's

180

comfort. The Substitute was tempted to comment on it, but instead, he went with a different tact.

"Excellent," exclaimed Lovecraft. "We got water and indoor plumbing. That will help."

"Any sign of any food, 'cause my belly button is rubbing a hole in my spine?" asked Stu.

"Sorry," said Lovecraft. "Just detergent."

Hurston leaned out of the waterline and bellowed. "What if help doesn't come soon?"

Everyone in line looked between Lovecraft and Hurston.

"Then we improvise," shrugged Lovecraft calmly.

"What do you mean by 'improvise'?" prodded Hurston.

"Means we stay cool and find a way around our problems," said Lovecraft.

Tuck suddenly cried out. "I'm not going to make it. You'd better eat my leg."

"I'd rather eat Hodges," replied Patrick immediately, who had gotten the joke.

"I wish you'd all stop bickering and just eat me," said Tuck with mock seriousness.

Lovecraft just looked at Tuck in confusion, along with everyone else.

"I'd rather you not eat my leg," said Stu, who had missed the reference entirely. "I play the organ at church on Sundays."

Tibbons gave an exasperated sigh. "They're quoting 'Monty Python's Flying Circus.' In poor taste, I might add

181

—funny!—but in poor taste."

"If there's a church left," muttered Stu, who had lost the thread of the conversation. "Lord, I hope they're okay. I hope they didn't go to the church. It's got more windows than walls." He sighed worriedly. "I'll say a prayer for them."

"Can you say one for us too?" asked Lovecraft. He looked up quickly and noticed with sadness that Reverend Jennings was not here either.

"Sure," replied Stu.

"Okay, bad jokes aside," said Lovecraft, raising his voice so that everyone could hear. "There's not going to be anything drastic on the menu. Further, I recommend that no one wanders off."

"Why?" asked Hurston with a predatory look.

"You ask a lot of questions," replied Lovecraft.

"I am a Reporter."

"Fair enough," shrugged Lovecraft. "I don't think that people should wander off because it's not safe."

"Really not safe," added Max.

"Is this building a danger?" asked Hurston, and his voice raised in alarm.

And Lovecraft knew that that type of alarm could snowball quickly.

"Not a danger per se," said Lovecraft quickly.

Hurston sniffed. "I'm not surprised. It's such an old building." He gave a mean little laugh. "This heap'll probably fall before we get rescued."

"YOU TAKE THAT BACK," cried Stu. The man in his oversized brown coat stomped straight over to the Reporter. Hurston took a step back in surprise, but Stu followed him.

"This is a fine old building," continued the Caretaker. "As sturdy as they come. Better than your ramshackle news building, which won't even last sixty years."

"I didn't mean...," stumbled Hurston. "I mean, it is a little old, and..."

"This place housed thousands and thousands of souls that needed penance, and it held up admirably," spat Stu.

Lovecraft called over to Stu with a calming voice.

"Stu. He's an idiot."

"Hey!" cried Hurston, but Lovecraft just glared at him.

"You keep quiet for once," said the Substitute to the Reporter, and then Lovecraft turned back to Stu. "He doesn't see how well this place was built. The time that went into its planning."

"It did take a lot of time," said Stu, and he turned towards the Substitute.

"And you can't expect *That Guy* to understand the historical import of such a place," said Lovecraft.

"Do you know that they had to bring in two architects to help design the place?" asked Stu. Forgetting all about Hurston, the caretaker wandered back over to Lovecraft. "There's a bit of a mystery surrounding the first one. He sort of disappeared..."

"Dennis Neight," said Patrick. "That was the first architect, right?"

183

"That's him," nodded Stu to the young man. "And the other one, well...he wasn't quite well after he finished the design. You know, 'not well' in the head. But, their work is quite impressive."

"Indeed," said Lovecraft. "And since this is a historical building, we need to preserve it, so we don't want people wandering off."

"That's true," agreed Stu.

Lovecraft looked up at everyone. "So—just to be safe—let's all stay in this area for now."

There was a wave of nodding heads to this. Thank God, he thought. They bought it. The line grew cohesive again, and everyone got some water. When the last person had gotten water, Lovecraft eyed the partially filled bucket.

"We're in luck," said the Substitute to Max. "We don't have to run back for water yet."

"Some good news," agreed the kid.

Lovecraft turned and fixed Max with a stern look.

"And don't you go off by yourself to get more water," said the Substitute sternly.

Max gave a little laugh. "You don't have to tell me twice. And I don't want to carry water alone."

"That's true," nodded Lovecraft, but he did not look convinced.

"Seriously," said Max. "I don't want to go back into that laundry room without company. Maybe a whole platoon."

Convinced, Lovecraft gave a little grin. "Me too." He looked around. "Now, time to deal with the next set of problems."

The Substitute motioned to Stu and Patrick. He fixed them with a glare.

"We need to talk," said Lovecraft. "Let's go over here, though."

Stu and Patrick looked at each other in surprise, but then they reluctantly followed. Lovecraft moved over to Tibbons, resting on his mattress.

"Councilman," said Lovecraft. "We need to have a meeting."

"Group or private?" asked Tibbons.

"I think private would be best," said Lovecraft.

"Okay. Then we should move down a ways," said Tibbons, and he started to rise.

But Boyle saw this and came over. "Whoa! Sir, you need to stay at rest."

"Stay?" asked Tibbons playfully. "Stay! Like a good dog."

"Yes, I need you to...," started Boyle. She did not recognize the joke at first, but then it hit her. She came back icily. "No! I didn't mean it like that!"

"I know," smiled Tibbons. "I'm just playing around."

"You're just in no condition to move about," said Boyle as her tone softened. She looked at Lovecraft. "We need to keep my patient stable."

"I understand," said Lovecraft.

"Aren't you just a paramedic?" asked Stu.

"Until someone else arrives who has more experience than me," shrugged Boyle.

"She's our senior medical officer, as far as I'm concerned," added Lovecraft in a firm tone, which carried to everyone in earshot. "I'm deferring to her."

In surprise, Boyle looked at him for a moment. "Thanks. Why does he need to be moved?"

"We need to have a quick meeting *Doctor* Boyle," said Tibbons with genuine delight.

"Which you should attend," added Lovecraft. "But we'd like to have a little privacy."

"Wait!" said Max. "Can't we just...um, drag'em?"

"Should be able to," nodded Lovecraft, and he looked at Boyle, who looked at Tibbons.

"If you'll lay back," said Boyle with authority.

"Not too bumpy," said Tibbons airily, like an emperor arranging transport.

"We'll do our best, your highness," smirked Lovecraft. He and Boyle grabbed the end of the mattress by Tibbons' feet.

After a few false starts—as they tried to get a good grip—they were soon dragging Tibbons. They moved a little ways down, following the outside wall of general population.

"Where're you taking him?" asked Hurston as he walked over. Icewater and her ever-present camera followed him.

"Weekend retreat," said Tibbons to the Reporter, and then he looked at Lovecraft. "This should be far enough."

186

Lovecraft and Boyle set Tibbons so that he was facing away from the wall. Then they plopped down at his feet. Max sat next to Lovecraft, who was huffing a little from the exertion.

"Whew," said Lovecraft to Tibbons. "No pudding for you tonight."

"Don't even joke about that," replied Tibbons with a mock growl.

"What's going on?" asked Hurston.

"Why don't you come into my office?" invited Tibbons, and Lovecraft looked up at him questioningly. The Councilman shrugged. "We might as well keep him in the loop."

Lovecraft thought about this and then nodded a little reluctantly.

"What loop?" asked Hurston.

"We're having a little meeting," said Tibbons.

"We need to talk about where we are," said Lovecraft, and he motioned for Stu and Patrick to come over.

"What do you mean?" asked Hurston, and he sat down opposite Stu and Patrick.

Icewater stood back against the wall filming the whole thing. Spotting this, Lovecraft took out his tin of cream and rubbed a little more of it on his face.

"It's worse than *just* being in a jail, isn't it," said Lovecraft pointedly to Stu and Patrick. "There's something here."

"Duh, revenants outside," snapped Hurston as he waved

187

his hand melodramatically towards the gate into general population.    Lovecraft just looked at Tibbons in exasperation, and the Councilman—in turn—glared at the Reporter.

"Just listen, then you can ask questions," admonished Tibbons.    "Think of it as a press conference."    The Councilman then looked back at the Substitute.    "Mr. Lovecraft."

Lovecraft nodded and turned his attention back to Stu and Patrick, who looked uncomfortable.

"What's happening here?" asked Lovecraft, and his tone left no wiggle-room around it. "And by here, I mean *inside* this jail."

"Well...," started Stu, and then he looked at Patrick.

Lovecraft continued. "I'm not mad. I'm not trying to yell at you. I need to get as many people as I can to Christmas day, alive and in one piece. And I can't protect them if I don't know."

"Um, there's a lot," started Patrick, but he looked down, a little embarrassed."

"Okay then, let's start with this," said Lovecraft. "When we were in class, Patrick knew a lot about this place, *and* he knew you." The Substitute nodded at the caretaker. "Patrick knew the history of this place and its secrets."

"Not all of them," insisted Patrick.

"How about we start with Cell #5," said Lovecraft. "What happened there? That kid said he got pushed out of an empty cell."

Patrick and Stu looked at each other meaningfully.

"We need to tell them," urged Patrick.

Slowly, Stu nodded. "Right, we were hoping this wouldn't be an issue, which is why we didn't mention it earlier in the infirmary. And to be fair, we probably would've been safe there. But here..." Stu screwed up his face in thought. "You have to understand that there have been several riots here."

"The last one closed the jail, didn't it?" asked Hurston.

"It did," confirmed Patrick.

"But, the one we need to talk about happened over forty years ago," said Stu. "Guards were taken captive and everything."

"What does that have to do with now?" asked Hurston, but Tibbons just shushed him.

"The riot was broken, and the guards were freed," said Stu. "But, there was no therapy for the guards, because...well, these were big, tough guys, so they can handle it, right? So, they were sent right back to work the next day. Now, Randall Hodds lived in Cell #5, and he was one of the prisoners who had taken several guards captive, including Jim Barrett."

"Why do I know that name?" asked Hurston absently.

"Barrett had suffered pretty badly as Hodds' captive, and Hodds liked to tease him about it from his cell," said Stu with a sad, solemn voice. "Well, one day, I guess Hodds went too far...or something else possessed Barrett."

"Wait!" said Hurston in surprise. "You're talking about *that* guard!"

Stu continued his story, ignoring the Reporter. "Barrett

walked away and brought back a can of kerosene while Hodds was still locked in his cell for the night. I don't know where he got the kerosene from, but...the other guards found Barrett standing outside Cell #5 watching it burn."

"What happened to the guard?" asked Tibbons.

Stu sighed. "Well, he finally got the help he needed. Spent the rest of his life in the funny farm. But Cell #5 was cleaned out and put back to use. Since then, a lot of strange stuff has happened in that cage. Prisoners stuck in there have gone insane, or killed themselves or both."

"What're we talking about?" asked Hurston.

"Unfortunately, we're talking about the paranormal," sighed Lovecraft, and then he gave a shiver. "Which totally freaks me out."

"That's why we need to study it," said Patrick adamantly.

"What?" asked Max.

"If we can quantify these weird happenings, then we can understand them," explained Patrick, but everyone just looked quizzically at him.

"I think you need to add more," said Stu kindly.

"Really?" asked Patrick, and he looked from Stu to the rest. Patrick wracked his brain as he tried to think of a better explanation.

"Break it down into bite-sized bits," consoled Stu kindly.

"Okay," shrugged Patrick. "What we don't know often scares us. But if we can explain why people see ghosts—or think they see ghosts—that would calm a lot of nerves. We're not scared by thunder and lightning because we understand what it is. Or eclipses."

"Good solid psychology," nodded Tibbons.

"Going into spooky places, though? Crazy, I say," muttered Lovecraft as he folded in on himself. "If you hear creepy noises from an unlit basement, don't go down there!"

"Or, bring two flashlights," countered Max, who was taking comfort in this. Not in a mean way, but it was nice to see that even Mr. Lovecraft was scared of something.

"Or! Just *don't* go down into the spooky basement!" argued Lovecraft forcefully.

"You aren't having a serious conversation about ghosts, are you?" asked Tibbons, as if he had not heard right. He glared at the Substitute. "You dragged me over here for this?"

"I'm not sure I can disprove them?" said Hurston, and the Councilman looked at the Reporter in surprise.

"You're kidding?" asked Tibbons.

"I did a story about a haunted house a few years ago with Patricia," said Hurston, and he motioned to his camerawoman, Icewater. "It was a Halloween fluff piece. Filler in case there was no big news. So, I interviewed some fellow..."

"Oh! I saw that," said Patrick excitedly. "It was Bak Zagans from 'Ghost Escapades.'"

"Sure," said Hurston, who was not really interested in remembering who it was. "Anyhow, as we were reviewing the audio of the interview...there was another voice."

"Distortion?" asked Tibbons. "Or, some inference."

"Nope," assured Icewater.

"We checked," said Hurston.

"Four times," added the Camerawoman adamantly.

"What did the voice say?" asked Patrick, who was leaning forward, completely enthralled.

"It actually answered some of the questions before this Bak fellow did," said Hurston.

"Intelligent responses?" gasped Patrick. "So, it was a spirit."

"What other type could there be?" asked Tibbons.

"Well, there are intelligent ghosts that can interact with their world," said Patrick. "But there are also residual hauntings too. Those are the noises, sounds, or words from something terrible that had happened in the past. But those don't interact. They just...make sounds."

Eyes wide, Lovecraft and Max, looked at one another.

"Like hearing someone fall?" asked Max in a hollow voice.

"You heard that too?" asked Stu with a sympathetic voice. "Scared the crap out of me when I first heard it."

"You're so lucky! I'd love to catch that on tape," said Patrick.

"I could go the rest of my life without hearing that again," moaned Lovecraft, and he wiped the sweat from his brow.

"So, what happened to Craig?" asked Max. "Was that something doing it purposely, or just a memory?"

"I think someone did not want him in that cell," said Patrick carefully.

"Why doesn't everyone stay out of the cells, especially #5, for the moment," said Lovecraft. "In fact, we should let Brick and Smithie out for the time being."

"Good thought," nodded Tibbons. "And really, those cells are probably not very clean." The Councilman looked over at Stu. "No offense."

"It's okay," shrugged Stu. "The ladies just did the infirmary. I don't think anyone bothered to clean this place after the last riot."

"So, let's reinforce the rule that people are not to wander off for their safety on multiple counts," said Lovecraft.

"Even if some of them are questionable," muttered Tibbons.

Lovecraft wisely overlooked that last comment and turned to the paramedic.

"How are the patients doing?" asked Lovecraft of Boyle.

"They're stable for the moment, but...we don't have a surgical kit," reported Boyle with a severe tone. "The bandages are going to hold for now, but eventually, we'll run out."

"How long can your patients last?" asked Lovecraft.

"Some could last a day or so before the blood loss becomes too severe, but most...," said Boyle, and she left it there.

"Including me," said Tibbons softly. Lovecraft looked up at the ceiling, deep in thought.

"Is it safe to open the front door again?" asked Hurston into the silence.

"That is the question," muttered Lovecraft unhappily, and then he looked down at everyone. The Substitute was about to speak when Stu cut in.

"What if we didn't have to?" asked the caretaker.

# 27

Lovecraft said with a manic laugh. "What did I say? Just five minutes ago, about NOT going into the spooky basement?"

And even the Substitute heard the nervousness in his voice.

To cover it, he squatted down and knocked on the old metal hatch on the floor of the laundry room. It looked like a small submarine hatch, complete with a wheel in the middle.

"At least no one knocked back," suggested Max gently, and he saw Lovecraft go very still.

Stu spoke thoughtfully. "Unlike the hatch in the pantry —which has wheels above and below—this one only has it on top, but not underneath."

"So, you could only go down," said Patrick in

puzzlement.

"Maybe they didn't want anyone coming up through this hatch," suggested Max.

Not wanting to contemplate that thought any further, the Substitute grabbed the hatch wheel. He tried to open it, but the wheel would not give.

Lovecraft looked up at the rest.

"A little help?" he asked. Icewater put down her camera, and she and Stu also took a part of the wheel.

With a strain, they pulled on it. Suddenly, the wheel shifted, making Lovecraft fall on his side. He gave a little laugh as he picked himself up.

"Good teamwork!" said the Substitute. "Now, let's look down there. Stu, could you lift it up?"

The hatch must have been a traditionalist because it made appropriate squeaking noises as Stu lifted it up. Icewater picked up her camera once again, and Max noticed that Lovecraft had loosened the gun in its holster. But nothing jumped out.

After a moment, Lovecraft took out one of his super glowsticks. Tory—from Downstairs at the office— had tweaked it so that when Lovecraft dropped glowstick down, it easily illuminated the tunnel below.

"How far do these tunnels lead?" asked Hurston.

"All over," said Stu. "At least that's what I heard. They've been sealed since I got here."

"So there was an escape tunnel in the laundry room?" asked Hurston.

"It was apparently chained up-- back in the day-- but even if a prisoner went down there," said Stu, and his voice trailed off. "There's really only two ways out, and well, no one ever came out the other side."

"What does that mean?" asked Lovecraft.

"They just sorta disappeared," said Stu. "So, word spread, but apparently, every decade or so, someone had to try it."

"Is that the only way underneath?" asked Lovecraft.

"There's also a door on the outside of this building which leads to the boiler and stuff," supplied Patrick.

Stu looked at Patrick with suspicion.

"I never let you see the blueprints," said the caretaker.

A little embarrassed, Patrick explained. "I found them at the library."

Since Stu was getting visibly riled, the Substitute cut in.

"So, what's down there?" asked Lovecraft.

Stu looked at him. "Oh. Maybe just some dusty corridors. But there were...well, I don't know what happened. No one talked about it, but I think at least one person died. They only said that it's restricted and muttered something about methane leaks."

"Which could just be methane leaks," said Lovecraft seriously. "That would be bad too. We're going to want to move in a loose group. That way, if something does happen, the rest can step back while I go after the fallen person. I can hold my breath for a while."

"*If* it's methane," said Stu in a worried tone.

"If it's methane," admitted Lovecraft, and then he turned to Icewater. "Can we borrow your camera?"

Soon, Icewater knelt by the hatch and lowered her camera down into the tunnel. She turned the camera to look down the hall. Lovecraft leaned over to watch the camera's little viewscreen as Icewater moved the camera back and forth.

"Looks clear," reported Icewater. "Dusty, but clear."

Lovecraft stood back while Icewater pulled her camera back up.

He did not look happy about the news.

"Guess we go down then," he said softly. "Close it."

"What?" asked Stu, who was still holding the hatch open.

"Close it!" snapped Lovecraft, and everyone looked at him in surprise. He stopped and squeezed his eyes shut. "I'm sorry. Stu, could you please close the hatch until we are ready to go?"

"S...sure," said Stu. The hatch dropped too quickly, and Stu winced as it clanged shut. He looked a little abashed. "Sorry."

"It's okay," said Lovecraft, kindly. But he did grab the wheel and wrenched it shut. It was already getting easier to turn. Leaning back up, his shooting hand was shaking, so he gripped the edge of his coat. "Let's go back. We need to talk to the rest."

# 28

I make no promises," said Lovecraft to the assembled refugees. "You heard the plan. But, if we don't go, people *are* going to die."

"But, if we go," countered Turk. "We could die."

"Maybe," said Lovecraft. "That's why we're taking a small group. Besides, we need food if we have to stay here longer than a few days."

That caused a general uproar.

Missy cried out. "Why? What've you heard?"

"Nothing you haven't heard," insisted Lovecraft. "I'm hoping they'll be here tomorrow. But, the soldiers moving toward us might meet more opposition with these new revenants."

"And...," said Rayton thoughtfully. "Since we are...*well*, relatively safe. We might not be on the top of their list to save."

"Unfortunately true," agreed Lovecraft. "We have sanitation and clean water, so that is great—Really it is!— We could be a lot worse off, but we need food, and more importantly, medical supplies. So, I'm looking for volunteers."

Missy elbowed Craig to volunteer.

"Go on," she urged.

But his eyes widened in panic.

"The High School students are not invited," interjected Lovecraft.

Some of the students—especially Craig—looked relieved at the news, but a few, like Patrick, were disappointed.

"My one chance to see the tunnels," grumbled Patrick.

"You were never going," insisted Stu with a paternal tone that brooked no argument.

The rest of the adults were thoughtful, and then Rayton stepped forward.

"I ran track," said Rayton.

"And coach it," added his student, Lydia, dutifully.

"And coach it, so I'd be an asset to the team if you need someone to move fast," said Rayton.

"That's good," said Lovecraft.

Brick called out. "I'd like to go!"

Lovecraft had let him and Smithie out before his big announcement. The two men were now standing uncertainly by their old cells. Lovecraft looked at Brick thoughtfully when Boyle spoke up.

"Are you kidding me?" asked the paramedic with disdain.

"Hey, anything to keep me outta that cell...," started Brick, but then he paused thoughtfully.

It did not look like something he did often, thought Lovecraft. However, he chided himself for being so uncharitable.

Brick looked up at him nervously. "Umm, can I talk to you...you know, man to man?"

Nodding, Lovecraft walked over to Brick. But, when he saw Hurston and Icewater following, he stopped.

"Can we have a minute?" asked Lovecraft politely.

"This is important to the story," huffed Hurston.

"You have more than enough story," said the Substitute firmly. "Back off. Please!"

Reluctantly, Hurston and Icewater backed away.

Lovecraft was sure that they would try to film from afar. But, at least the camera would not be jammed in his face.

While Lovecraft had been pushing Hurston away, Smithie had rounded on Brick.

"Are you nuts?" hissed Smithie. "Didja see that big thing out there?"

"And the serpenty one," added Lovecraft. "That thing that stuck its head in here; there are more of those out there."

"Well, yeah," replied Brick, but he looked at the Substitute with haunted eyes in his almost flat face. "Thanks for listening to me, especially after...well, we didn't mean for anything to happen to Tic. He's...um, well, he was a good guy."

"But carelessness gets people killed," said Lovecraft.

"I know, I know," replied Brick miserably. "And I'm really sorry. If I go with you, maybe...maybe it'll start making up for earlier. We were just having too much fun, an' it got out of hand."

Lovecraft looked at Brick, who stood with his big shoulders hunched. The Substitute then gave a quick nod, and Brick looked up in surprise.

"Come on," said Lovecraft. "We leave in ten minutes."

The Substitute walked back over to the group. "Okay, that's two. I'd like to have at least one more."

"I'm going," said Boyle.

"I'm sorry, no," said Lovecraft.

"What?" replied Boyle in surprise.

"You're our only medical person, and I remember what that surgical kit looks like," said Lovecraft.

"He's right," said Tibbons from the wall. "We can't afford to have you not come back."

Boyle looked at Lovecraft in frustration.

"You can be upset with me," replied Lovecraft quickly. "But we need you to stitch up all the wounds when we get back."

"I'll go," said Florence as she stepped forward. She nervously adjusted her horn-rim glasses. "I want to make sure we have something edible."

"Excellent," replied Lovecraft.

"You're not going," snapped Maddie quickly. Maddie turned her wheelchair to glare at Florence.

"Grandma, we need food," said Florence. "*You* need food."

"We can make do," said Maddie, but the heat was falling from her voice to betray a nervous spasm.

"They need help, and I don't want to eat old mattress," said Florence sternly. "I'll be right back."

Maddie finally sighed. "Okay, but...please be careful."

In the end, another refugee, Randy, offered to go as well.

That set, Lovecraft went over to Tibbons, noting that Max was still by his side.

"You sure about this?" asked the Councilman.

"Not sure what choice we got," shrugged Lovecraft. He turned to Max. "Can you help me move his bed a little? We want it right against the wall. Put his head by that exposed pipe there."

"Sure," said Max, and he grabbed the top of the mattress, adjusting it.

"The cavalry could come tomorrow," insisted Tibbons.

"Maybe," said Lovecraft. "But, I don't think so. We're in for a wait, and I need to make sure everyone makes it."

Lovecraft moved in a fluid motion over Tibbons.

Before Max realized it, a pair of handcuffs secured his hand to a pipe. The kid looked at it in surprise, and then anger flooded his face.

"What the hell do you think you're doing?" demanded Max as Lovecraft moved away. The Substitute knelt by Tibbons' hand.

"Here's the key," said Lovecraft to Tibbons. "Just in case."

"You can't do this!" shouted Max, and people started to look over. He became embarrassed and continued in a harsh whisper. "Why?"

202

"I'm not taking one of my students down there," said Lovecraft. "I can't justify it to myself now; I certainly won't be able to justify it to my boss later."

"Don't I have any say in this?" asked Max.

"You're not even 18 yet," said Lovecraft.

Tibbons just watched the two as they argued above him.

"You need me down there," said Max.

"There's probably nothing," said Lovecraft.

"But you don't believe that!" insisted Max, and he did not mention that Lovecraft's gun hand was shaking.

"Your gun hand is shaking," said Tibbons.

"What?" asked Lovecraft as he looked down. He saw it shaking and grabbed the edge of his coat to stop it.

"I'm not scared of ghosts," said Max.

"Right. What about your dream, Dickcheese with the noose around his neck," countered Lovecraft.

"Dickcheese?" asked Tibbons in confusion.

But Max replied to the Substitute.

"He's just a bully," said the kid. "And you have to stand up to bullies."

"Still...," said Lovecraft.

Max continued. "Everyone else going down there would not believe it—even if we told them the truth—until it was too late."

"The kid has a point," said Tibbons. "Hell, even I don't believe it, but you do." Tibbons handed Max the key to the handcuffs. "Go quickly and bring back some food. I'm

203

hungry."

Max undid the handcuffs and handed them with the key to Lovecraft. The Substitute hesitated for a moment.

"If there are any problems," said Lovecraft to Max seriously. "I need you to run back here and seal the entrance."

"Okay," replied Max honestly. "Deal."

# 29

I don't wanna go down there," whined Turk as Lovecraft walked him to the hatch.

Turk shuffled along like a condemned man.

"For the last time, you don't have to go down there," said Lovecraft. He just managed to keep the irritation out of his voice. Instead, he worked to bolster the man up. "I just need a big, hulking guy who can drop something heavy onto the hatch."

"Why?" asked Turk as he furrowed his brow. "Aren't you coming back through here?"

"That's the plan," said Lovecraft to reassure him. "But, plans have a way of unraveling. And I don't want any revenants coming up through this hole and biting us on the ass. Or anything else coming through, for that matter?"

"Anything else?" asked Turk uncertainly as they walked into the laundry room.

"If it isn't us," continued Lovecraft. "Close the hatch and lock it. If necessary, drop something heavy on it."

"I can do that," said Turk, who missed that Lovecraft had scooted around the question.

"Appreciate it," said Lovecraft, and he slapped Turk on the shoulder. "With you here and Stu operating the front door, we should be good."

They walked up to the hatch on the floor. Brick was picking through a junk pile in the corner of the laundry room.

"You good over there?" asked Lovecraft of him.

Brick straightened up and hefted a two-foot length of pipe.

"Just in case," he grinned, and he walked over to the hole. Lovecraft nodded, and then he looked at Max, Florence, Rayton, Randy, and Brick.

"We're going to go down and head West towards the kitchen," said Lovecraft. "There's a hatch there, which is located just off the main kitchen. In a pantry, to be exact, according to Stu."

"Do we know what's there?" asked Rayton.

"No," replied Lovecraft. "That's why we kept this group small, so we can move quickly and change plans, if necessary."

"And our goals?" asked Florence.

"Simple. Food and medical supplies, but most of all, stay alive," said Lovecraft.

"I like that plan," nodded Max.

"I like to keep my plans simple," said Lovecraft, and he looked at Turk. "Okay, open the hatch."

The big man, Turk, easily turned the wheel himself and pulled it open. Lovecraft's glowstick still illuminated the ladder below.

Brick stepped forward.

"I'll go first," he said helpfully.

Lovecraft just gave a tiny nod as the man carefully climbed down the ladder while holding onto his length of pipe. He reached the bottom and looked around.

"Empty," reported Brick.

Rayton, Florence, and Randy went down next.

Then Max looked up at Lovecraft, who was peering at the hole.

Out of Turk's hearing, Max whispered. "Mr. Lovecraft." But there was no response. The kid raised his voice to a harsh whisper. "MR. Lovecraft!"

Lovecraft blinked and looked at him.

"Follow me, and I will keep you in one piece," said Max seriously.

"Oh! Okay," said Lovecraft. He nodded quickly and took some deep breaths, which calmed him down.

Max went down the ladder, and Lovecraft followed. The tunnel was minimally lit with bare light bulbs. And those bulbs were sparse—and randomly—set apart. Everyone, but Max, jumped when the hatch closed above them.

"We go West, right," said Max with authority.

"Ye...yeah," replied Lovecraft with a minor stutter. "After this turn."

"Okay then," said Max as he stepped forward, and everyone followed. Their footsteps sounded loud on the dusty cement floor.

They walked down the brick corridor and away from the ladder until they reached a sharp left. Shortly, the corridor took a sharp right. Rayton, for his part, ran his fingers over the walls as they walked.

"These walls seem older than anything else I've seen," muttered Rayton. "These bricks are easily over a hundred years old. Maybe even older than that."

"Is that important?" asked Florence nervously.

"I don't know," said Rayton thoughtfully.

"Because you're creeping me out talking like that," said Florence, but without much malice.

"Sorry," said Rayton abashed. "It's the curse of a curious mind."

"This isn't good," said Max from the front, and they glanced at the passage ahead.

"I thought I saw a depression in the ground when I was looking around the jail grounds yesterday afternoon," said Rayton.

The depression in the ground had been part of a tunnel caving in. The way forward was blocked by brick and dirt.

"Shit," spat Florence.

Max walked forward and looked at the cave-in.

"Careful," said Rayton automatically to the kid. The

science teacher slid to the front of the group. Inspecting the blockage, they could see that there was no safe way through.

"There's a way around," said Lovecraft in a small voice, and Max looked back at the Substitute. Lovecraft pulled out his phone and opened the map app.

"You have it on your phone?" asked Max in surprise.

"It downloaded just a little while ago," said Lovecraft.

"And someone just happened to have a map of this place for you?" asked Rayton suspiciously.

"When I called in," explained Lovecraft. "I was talking to my people."

"Homeland Security sent it to you?" asked Brick suspiciously.

"Hey. I'm not going to complain," said Max as he moved over to the Substitute. "Where are we on this map?"

Lovecraft pointed to a red dot. "That's us, and that's where we need to go."

The Substitute poked a blue dot at their destination, but the route went straight through the cave-in. Creating a line across the path—where the cave-in was—the app automatically created a secondary course that went down some stairs.

"We've got to go back and down," explained Lovecraft.

"How far do we need to backtrack?" asked Max.

"Not far," he replied.

"I wish we could see what was down there," mused Max. But then he noticed a thoughtful look on Lovecraft's face. "What?"

"Okay," said Lovecraft as he made a decision. He grabbed the map with his fingers and pulled it up.

The edges of the phone case glowed blue. A wire grid of the map suddenly appeared above the face of the phone. Expanding his fingers, the map grew larger, beyond the width of the phone.

"Where'd you get that phone again?" whispered Rayton breathlessly, who was suffering from a severe case of tech envy.

As much as Lovecraft wanted to give Grant—from Downstairs at the office—the recognition he absolutely deserved, the Substitute lied, as per protocol.

"Got it with my digital plan," he shrugged off-handedly. "We go back to this door and down a flight. It should be a quick walk over to these stairs and up to the pantry."

"Sounds like a plan," said Max. "Let's move out."

The kid started to walk towards the door going down. Everyone looked at Lovecraft, but he just followed the kid. Reluctantly, they all followed him to the old metal door, which they had just passed. Then it was down some stairs until they wound around to the next floor. The air here was stale and musty.

Florence pulled her powder blue cardigan a little closer. "Why is it so cold?"

"We are underground," suggested Rayton.

"I'm starting to miss my cell," said Brick with a nervous smile. His brow furrowed, and then he gave out a tiny cry, which made Lovecraft jump a little. "That's what it is?"

"What?" asked the Substitute, a little sharply.

"The air," explained Brick without explaining.

"What about it?" asked Max patiently.

"It reminds me of my crazy grandfather's house," shuddered Brick. "I had to visit him every summer. Gah!"

"We need to get through here quickly," said Lovecraft, with a shiver that had nothing to do with the cold.

Max moved into another corridor. Everything looked even older here, and the lights were even more sparsely set. The corridor turned sharply to the South. Cautiously moving along, the corridor ended in a T junction, which rounded slightly away from them on either side.

"What's that?" hissed Florence, and everyone froze.

"What?" whispered Max.

"I...I thought I heard something," said Florence softly. "Like, something moving."

"I don't...," began Max.

Suddenly, he heard it too and stilled. Something was coming from the West, moving slowly. He hopped across the corridor and put his back to the West wall. He motioned for everyone else to do the same and be quiet.

Lovecraft pressed his back against the wall as they heard a leathery sound getting closer. The light flickered above, and then it blinked out. Everyone—but Max—jumped while uttering little noises, and the leathery sound stopped.

"Shhh," whispered Max, and he prayed fervently. The creature moved again, and now it was almost upon them.

Something reached around the corner by Max and

210

touched out tentatively. The kid leaned back as long fingers quested for a moment but then withdrew.

The creature moved forward into the dark corridor, but they could only see a bare silhouetted that confused them. Was it man-shaped, or no? they wondered. Long, spidery fingers ended on powerful arms. Then it moved again and kept going. After a moment, the light flickered back on.

When it was out of earshot, Rayton opened his mouth to speak, but Max shushed him.

"Not until we're out," whispered Max quickly. "Let's go."

"What if there are more of them?" hissed Florence.

"Then we run like hell," hissed Lovecraft

Pushing away from the wall, he strode confidently up to the intersection. Lovecraft drew his gun, Rikke, which Jaime from Downstairs had modified. Then, he looked at Max with a confident smile. That was a monster. Monsters were something that Lovecraft could deal with.

"Come on," said Max, and he went around the corner, moving quickly. Like a guard dog, Lovecraft followed the kid. After a moment, the rest followed—if a trifle reluctantly—down the curved corridor. It led to another corridor going West, and after checking it out, Max led the group that way.

They found the metal stairs going up. Everyone relaxed a little more, and Florence felt the knot of tension in her chest loosen up. While the corridor went on farther, they found a ladder that had been bolted from floor to ceiling. It led up to a metal hatch with a wheel in the center.

Lovecraft holstered his gun and quickly shot up the ladder. Leaning back, with one hand on the ladder, he pulled on the wheel. It stuck, but he gave it a harder tug.

"Need help?" asked Brick from below.

"Maybe you can loosen it," said Lovecraft. Since the ladder was free-standing, Lovecraft swung around to hang onto the other side. Brick went up the ladder and pulled at the wheel. It did not give.

That cheered Lovecraft a little. "Well, I feel better that I couldn't get it right away."

"I'll open it," replied Brick, who now saw this hatch as a personal challenge. Gritting his teeth, the man pulled on the wheel. With a pained groan, the wheel finally gave. Smiling, Brick started spinning the wheel to open the hatch.

"Wait!" said Lovecraft quickly, and Brick paused. The big man looked at him questioningly. The Substitute continued. "We don't know what's up there. Let me go first."

After a moment, Brick shrugged and moved back down the ladder.

Lovecraft swung back around beneath the hatch. He hooked one arm in a rung and moved the wheel just enough to undo the lock. It made a soft noise. Drawing his gun again, Lovecraft used his upper back to push up the hatch.

The hatch lifted into a dark room, and only a little light came from underneath the door. Taking out his Klarus flashlight, Lovecraft flicked it on. He found that he was in a small pantry with bulk canned goods.

"Nice," whispered Lovecraft with a smile. "We found supper."

"Yah!" cheered Florence, quietly from below.

Lovecraft carefully lifted up the hatch, and he set it gently against a wall. Stepping up into the room, he moved to the door feeling the tension in his neck lessen. It felt so damn good to get out of those tunnels. He heard the rest coming up behind him, and he shined the light at the floor while they came up.

"I'm turning off the light for the moment," whispered Lovecraft when they were all up. He flicked it off and opened the door just a crack as the light peered in.

Outside, he saw a revenant facing away. The creature was pawing at the giant walk-in freezer. Lovecraft turned back to them and handed the flashlight to Florence. "I'm going out to take care of that poor soul and anyone else. Wait here until I give the all-clear."

Lovecraft said that last part directly to Max, who was staring out mutely at the revenant. The Substitute nudged the kid's shoulder, who looked up in surprise.

"Wait here," ordered Lovecraft softly but firmly.

"Sure," whispered Max quickly. The kid did not want to go anywhere near that thing.

Lovecraft nodded at last when he was sure that the kid would listen. He holstered his gun. Slipping through the door, Lovecraft closed it carefully behind him. Thankfully, there was no one else in the room.

The kitchen was a mess with food and pots scattered about. The cooks had been preparing breakfast when they were hit. In one corner, a gnawed body slumped against a wall. Their head had been almost severed. Stepping around the metal island in the middle of the room, he grabbed a long thin knife that lay next to a head of lettuce.

Swiftly, Lovecraft shot forward. The revenant turned, and Father Jennings looked at him with dead, white eyes. Frozen, Lovecraft stopped for too long. The revenant Jennings jumped at him, snapping at his throat.

Lovecraft shook himself, and his training kicked in. He shoved his forearm, which was covered by his tear-proof coat, into the revenant's mouth, and it bit down hard. The fabric held, but it hurt like heck. Grunting, Lovecraft plunged the cook's knife through the revenant's eye and pierced the brain.

Slowly, the revenant's jaws went slack. Lovecraft took the back of the priest's head and laid him gently on the floor.

"I'm so, so sorry," whispered Lovecraft.

Straightening up, Lovecraft stared numbly ahead at the little window in the freezer door.

A face slammed against the inside w.

"Gah!" cried Lovecraft as he jumped back. Then he saw that it was one of the cooks in the window. A live cook, no less. He pulled open the door, and a slender woman leaped out and bear-hugged him.

"Oh, Thank God!" cried Marta softly. "I thought our soufflé was going to fall for sure."

"No problem," said Lovecraft, and he tactfully pulled out of the ferocious hug. For a moment, he had to

214

concentrate on getting air back into his lungs. Marta might not be big, but she was strong. He looked at Marta and the rest of the cooks. "You all okay?"

"Yeah," said Marta, but then she glanced over at the gnawed fellow laying on the floor. "Chet gave us enough time. Fought those serpent things. Poor guy." She looked over at Jennings, and her face grew red with anger. "You stabbed the priest in the eye?"

"Unless you wanted me to start shooting," said Lovecraft. "The knife under the chin thing doesn't really work."

"I just...," started Marta.

"I know—believe me!—I'm not looking forward to my next confession," said Lovecraft miserably. "But, he was already gone."

Marta shook her head. "Okay. So, was he the last of them?"

"Actually no, so we need to keep our voices down," said Lovecraft, lowering his voice. "We're back in the jail, in general population. You can come with us."

"Better than the freezer," hissed Marta fervently. "At least we could turn down the temperature, so we didn't freeze, but that food's going to get ripe soon. Yuck."

"Okay, then over this way," said Lovecraft, and he noticed that the pantry door was already open. Max had his head out.

"Hurry," hissed the kid.

Marta shooed her staff towards the pantry.

Inside, Florence was already giving orders.

"Everyone take at least one can of food," ordered Florence softly, who was already cradling a big can of Lima beans in the crook of her arm.

"Don't forget the baked beans," suggested Lovecraft.

"That could be dangerous," chuckled Brick.

"Maybe we could fight the revenants off with that!" added Rayton with mirth. "Biological warfare!"

"That's enough of that," said Florence archly.

"I just thought that you could eat them heated or cold," said Lovecraft defensively.

Florence fixed Lovecraft with a business-like look.

"I'll take care of things here," ordered Florence. "Go get whatever else you need."

"And don't forget, there's a lot of cereal in that medical room!" said Marta.

"That's right," replied Lovecraft.

"We could use that," said Florence.

"I'm not sure how much I can get as well as the medical supplies," said Lovecraft.

"We'll help get the cereal," offered Rayton.

Lovecraft did not argue as Rayton, Randy, and Brick followed him. They moved quickly out of the kitchen and towards the examination rooms. Before Max realized it, they were already gone, and he was stuck.

"But...," started Max as he saw them spirit away.

"Here," said Florence as she put a great big tin in his

hands. Max looked down at the big can of lima beans. He looked up at Florence in horror.

"But...," he started.

"No buts," she replied quickly. "They're a good source of protein, and that will help people feel full for longer after eating them."

# 30

Sliding into the examination rooms, Rayton whispered. "Why do I feel safer out here?"

The medical supplies were right where Lovecraft had left them with Boyle.

"Me too," admitted Randy.

"Odd that," agreed Lovecraft. "Do you guys want to grab as much cereal as you can carry while I get the surgical kit?"

"Sure thing," said Rayton.

"Then quickly and quietly," said Lovecraft.

Rayton led Randy and Brick to the left into the cereal room, while Lovecraft went for the medical supplies and dug around.

A moment after they passed out of sight, there was movement in the corridor. Three runners zipped past towards the kitchen, serpentine tails trailing behind them.

Lovecraft only had to dig around for a minute to find the

surgical kit. It was the size of a medium purse. He opened it up and found that it still had the sterile pre-wrapped syringes and local anesthetics.

Rayton, Randy, and Brick came out of the cereal room with a large net bag over Randy's shoulder.

"Brick scrounged a bag," explained Randy.

"Like a magician," smiled Rayton.

"I found it earlier in the laundry room. Thought it might help," shrugged Brick, a little bashfully.

"Great work," grinned Lovecraft. "Now, let's head back."

Moving out into the examination room, Lovecraft handed Rayton the surgical kit.

"If it all goes wrong, you run like hell to the front gate and get this to Boyle," said Lovecraft.

Rayton nodded solemnly. "Okay."

Following Lovecraft's lead, they moved quickly back towards the kitchen.

The Substitute suddenly screeched to a halt, and the guys nearly plowed into him.

Standing spread out in the kitchen were the three revenant runners.

The serpent-like creatures were growling at Max, who stood defiantly in the doorway of the pantry waving the tin of Lima beans menacingly. Past Max, Lovecraft saw the last person drop through the hatch. The closest runner bunched up its hind legs, ready to pounce at the kid.

But Lovecraft's gun cleared its holster and fired. The

218

shot went down underneath a stove. The three runners whipped their heads around towards Lovecraft.

Max jumped back. He dropped down the ladder slamming the hatch behind him. A moment later, it locked with a metallic clang.

The runner closest to the panty turned to look for Max and then screamed in frustration to see him gone.

"Run. Run," hissed Lovecraft.

"What?" asked Randy, but Rayton tugged on Randy's arm.

"Why'd his bullet miss," moaned Brick as he, Randy, and Rayton ran off.

"I'm not sure he did miss," said Rayton. "Run faster."

The first runner turned towards Lovecraft, who was backing away from the door. With his free hand, he pulled a road flare from his satchel. He struck it against the wall lighting it.

As the runner crouched to leap at him, Lovecraft threw the flare at the stainless steel oven. The air beneath the stove was already distorted by gas fumes, fumes from the pipe that he had just been ruptured with his bullet.

Turning, Lovecraft sprinted away as the kitchen suddenly became a fireball. A shock wave rolled out of the kitchen.

The Substitute was knocked to the ground. He lost his grip on his gun, Rikke, which skittered across the floor. He tried to move, but his body would not respond. He felt heat near his boots.

219

Two pairs of hands, Rayton and Randy, pulled Lovecraft up and away from the fire. There a metallic thunk as Brick's pipe brained a revenant. After a moment, Lovecraft's legs started to cooperate. He wobbled for a moment on his feet as Rayton observed him.

"I'm okay," said Lovecraft. "Shock wave just rang my bell a little."

Lovecraft shook his head, and the fog in his brain lifted. He saw Rikke on the ground, ran over to her, and scooped up the gun.

Straightening, the Substitute found himself face to face with a revenant.

"Rayton," said Lovecraft softly, absolutely still.

"Yeah?" replied Rayton.

"You still got that surgical kit?" asked Lovecraft.

"Got it," assured Rayton.

The revenant bared its teeth. Lovecraft jumped forward and punched the creature with a solid left hook. As it staggered back, he fired a double-tap into its head.

"Then RUN!" howled Lovecraft as he sprinted through the infirmary. Both sections were now teeming with revenants. He fired at several revenants without slowing down, but only to clear a path for them.

Kicking open the infirmary door, Lovecraft went out into the bailey and jumped onto the hood of a car. Revenants were shuffling between the vehicles.

"Get to the jail!" ordered Lovecraft.

"What about you?" asked Rayton as he hesitated.

"I'm going to buy some time!" replied Lovecraft, and he shot a revenant in their path.

Rayton nodded. He did not like it, but he nodded. As Lovecraft ran on top of the cars, the Science Teacher went around the parked vehicles' perimeter.

The revenants appeared to be more interested in Lovecraft due to the noise he was making. But Randy was wandering too close to the cars.

"We should cut across," said Randy as he shifted the bag of cereal on his shoulder.

"What?" asked Rayton in surprise. "No, we shouldn't. Don't go near the cars."

"That's an old myth," laughed Randy, and he hopped in between the cars. He took a diagonal path towards the entrance to the jail. Brick twitched as if to follow.

"He's going to get himself killed," growled Brick while Randy dodged through the cars.

"Maybe," said the Science Teacher, and the next words tasted as if he had just thrown up. "We can't save him. Come on!"

Rayton put on speed and ran around the outside of the cars. Brick followed, but he was not as fast; too many walks to the fridge and not enough around the block.

Brick looked for Randy, but he was nowhere in sight. Suddenly, there was a rending scream from somewhere between the vehicles.

"Randy!" cried, Brick. He rounded the parked cars' edge and was heading towards the jail entrance when the screaming stopped. He and Rayton slowed. "Randy?"

A figure with a bloody leg burst out from between the cars. It screamed wildly. Brick jumped away as Randy fell and let go of his bag of cereal. Randy reached out and grabbed Brick.

"It came out from underneath the car!" blubbered Randy.

"He's bit!" cried the Science Teacher. "Grab the bag!"

But Brick tried to get an arm under Randy and pick up the cereal bag simultaneously. Several revenants stepped from between the cars. They stood in Brick's path to the jail.

The Science Teacher shook with frustration because he did not have a weapon.

Brick, for his part, threw the bag of cereal over the revenant's heads. It crashed in front of Rayton, distracting the creatures. While the revenants were watching the bag, Brick hit the nearest one in the back of the head with his pipe. However, while it crumpled, more revenants moved between Brick and Rayton.

Brick put down Randy, who had become dead weight, and started swinging. The Science Teacher grabbed the cereal bag and backed—reluctantly—towards the door when a figure jumped down beside him.

The teacher let out a cry, but then he saw it was Lovecraft.

"What are you...," started Lovecraft, but then he saw Brick fighting. The smile melted off his face. "Oh."

"Randy's in there too," said Rayton.

Lovecraft lifted his gun and fired at the revenants, but more and more of them were arriving. Brick backed up towards the infirmary.

"Get out of here!" screamed the big man.

"No!" shouted Rayton. "See if you can run around."

"There's too many," replied Brick. "Go on!"

"But...," started Rayton. Lovecraft tugged on his arm. The revenants nearby were beginning to look at him and Rayton hungrily.

"We gotta go," said Lovecraft because he was eyeing the runners who were ducking and dodging to get behind Brick.

"Fuck," cried Rayton as Lovecraft lead him into the jail. Tears of anger and sadness formed in Rayton's eyes. "Fuck!"

As they went through the door to the jail offices, Lovecraft heard a short, sharp cry from Brick, who collapsed as he bled out. Safe inside, Rayton shook with rage.

"That asshole Randy tried to run between the cars," explained Rayton.

Lovecraft shook his head. "Thanks for not joining in that idiot maneuver."

"Brick was just trying to help him," growled Rayton, grinding his teeth.

"I'm sorry," said Lovecraft. "But we've got to go."

"I know," said Rayton, and he followed Lovecraft through the pile of bodies outside the gate.

"There you are!" cried Stu, who pressed a grin to the metal gates. "Hurry!"

Tiptoeing around the bodies, Lovecraft slowed as he looked carefully at the bruiser's profile. The bone plates did indeed separately cover the face, neck, and chest. He noted that the bone plate on the face hung down in front of the neck. So, unseen from the front, there was a gap at the top of the throat between the face and the neck.

A plea from Stu pulled the Substitute from his study.

"Hurry!" said the Caretakeragain.

Lovecraft and Rayton went safely into general population.

As Stu slammed the metal gate shut, Rayton dropped the cereal bag in front of the caretaker. Then he and Lovecraft collapsed onto the ground.

"I didn't think we'd make it," said Rayton in a hollow voice.

"Too close for comfort," agreed Lovecraft. He did not even mind when Hurston ran up with the camerawoman, Icewater.

"What's going through your head right now?" asked Hurston in his deep baritone.

"I'm going to Disneyland," grinned Lovecraft, and Hurston looked like he was about to explode. He turned to Icewater and made a slicing motion across his throat.

"Kill it," huffed Hurston. "If he's not going to take this seriously."

"You asked," said Lovecraft smugly, and he saw Icewater's mouth twitch with a fleeting smile.

After Icewater and Hurston wandered away, Boyle came

up. Rayton held up the surgical kit almost reverently.

"May your hand always be steady," said Rayton solemnly. Boyle stopped for a moment, and then she took the surgical kit carefully.

"Thank you," said Boyle. "Thank you both."

"I'm just looking forward to some dinner," said Lovecraft as he hauled himself up. "Is the rest of the grub here yet?"

Everyone looked oddly at him.

"What rest? You mean, besides this?" asked Stu carefully as he held up the bag of cereal.

"We were just bringing the cereal when we got cut off from the rest," explained Lovecraft. "They should be coming back with the canned food."

Rayton glanced at Lovecraft.

"You need help?" asked the Science Teacher, who was still sitting on the floor.

"Can you help Stu cover the front?" asked Lovecraft.

"Absolutely," replied Rayton, and he relaxed a little. He had had enough excitement for one day.

Lovecraft took off at a steady gait towards the laundry room with his hands in his pants pockets. His stomach grumbled in protest.

"Shhh," he told his stomach. "Almost dinner time."

The past general population, he walked a little quicker through the next set of cells, Death Row. They seemed ominous, even in the daylight. But he slowed in front of the execution room.

"Dickcheese," he muttered and then moved on.

Stepping into the laundry room, he saw Turk scramble up from where he sat near the hatch.

"What're you doing there?" asked Turk in confusion.

"I took another route," explained Lovecraft. "Is anyone back yet?"

"Not yet," said Turk, quickly and urgently. The big man radiated nervousness. "And I haven't moved from this spot."

"It's okay," said Lovecraft soothingly. He did not want to make it seem like he was blaming the man. But he also felt a sharp stab of anxiety. He realized that the kid was still down there. "I was hoping that they'd be back by now."

Someone—hopefully a person, thought Lovecraft desperately—banged on the bottom of the hatch. Turk nearly jumped a foot. There was a muffled cry from underneath. Lovecraft ran over as Turk grabbed the wheel.

"It's them," said Lovecraft. Even though he could not say the words, he could faintly tell that it was the cook's voice. Distantly, he searched his mind, and then he remembered that her name was Marta. He called out to her, and the pounding stopped as the wheel turned.

Turk pulled back the hatch, and several cooks scrambled out of the hole. They looked panicked and scared. Marta was the last one through, and she turned to Turk.

"Close it!" snapped Marta. "Close it now!"

Turk looked at Lovecraft, but the Substitute was looking for Max and Florence.

"Where are they?" asked Lovecraft of Marta, but the cook ran over and tried to grab the hatch.

Turk held it open. Finally, Lovecraft nodded, and Turk let it go. The cook pushed the hatch down—which closed with a clang— and then she laid on top of it.

"No one goes back down there," ordered Marta.

"What happened?" asked Lovecraft, and his voice had grown so dark and cold that it cut through Marta's fear. She froze and then glanced up tentatively.

"I...I don't know," she replied honestly.

Lovecraft caught himself about to snap. He took a moment and made himself examine the situation as he had been trained to do. Here was a person who was—probably rightly so—scared out of her wits. He had to put aside his fear for the kid.

In a softer, calmer voice, he started speaking again.

"Please tell me what you saw," he said.

Lovecraft crouched down beside Marta so that she did not have to look up awkwardly at him. She was breathing heavily for a moment.

"We were almost back when the lights went out behind us," said Marta in a calm voice. "It grabbed for Max and got his coat. It had such long fingers." Lovecraft's heart froze. "But Max squirmed out of his coat." And his heart started beating again. "That lady who came with you..."

"Florence, I believe," said Lovecraft.

"Yeah," said Marta as she looked down. "She told us to run. So, we did. We just ran and left!"

227

Marta's voice hitched at the end. Lovecraft could see the pain and embarrassment on her face.

"Do you have a gun?" asked the Substitute.

"What?" asked Marta in surprise.

"Did you have a gun down there?" continued Lovecraft seriously.

"N...no," said Marta uncertainly.

"Then your best option was to get back here and tell me," said Lovecraft, and he could immediately see some of the tension leave her face. "Because I have a big ol' hand cannon, and I've dealt with things like that. So, I'm going to go back down there and get them."

"But, they might...," started Marta uncertainly, and her words trailed off.

"True," admitted Lovecraft. "They might. But regardless, I gotta go down. I need to know. Can you please move off the hatch?"

Marta saw the steely look in Lovecraft's eyes. Quickly, she rolled off the hatch as Lovecraft looked back at Turk.

"We're going to open the hatch," said Lovecraft. "If I'm not back within an hour, I need you to drop something heavy on this hatch and don't open it. Ever. Do you understand?"

"I...okay," stuttered Turk.

"I can't hear 'okay,'" insisted Lovecraft, gently but firmly. "I need you to tell me that you will cover this hole if we do not come back."

"I will," said Turk with a reliable voice.

Lovecraft smiled gently. "Don't worry. It'll take more than a blocked exit to stop me. Now, let's open this bitch." He stopped and looked sideways at Marta with a shy smile. "Pardon my French."

The cook just shrugged, unconcerned.

Turk hauled up the hatch, and Lovecraft dropped through without even touching the ladder. He hit the ground in a crouch and waited a moment. But, nothing attacked him. Large tins of food lay on the ground, forgotten in their haste. But he did not have time to deal with that.

Moving fast around the corridor, Lovecraft drew his gun. Quickly, he reached the door going down. Stepping down the stairwell, he came out onto the next floor. It was dreadfully quiet. There was not even the sound of the machines that ran the jail. Too far from everything.

Lovecraft controlled his breathing as he went down the corridor. He focused on finding the kid and Florence. He did not let himself think of what he would find when he did. He could not think about that now.

As he came close to the rounded corridor, he saw the scuffle on the dusty floor. He snapped on his flashlight. Lovecraft could not recognize the third set of footprints and deduced it must have been one of the creatures that they saw earlier. The impressions looked vaguely humanoid. But only vaguely.

Quickly, Lovecraft got a sense of the swift battle that had taken place. Max had gotten loose from the creature by slipping out of his coat. Lovecraft picked up the kid's discarded Tigers jacket and hung it on his satchel. Florence had tugged the kid away. But something had picked both of them off their feet. Then, it was just the footsteps of the creature, which disappeared at the rounded corridor.

And something had walked that rounded corridor so much that the dust had not collected on the floor. Lovecraft moved left, where the creature had gone earlier. Following the curvature of the wall, he found another open door.

Through that door was a set of stairs leading down, but the room was so dark, he could not get an idea of its size. He turned off his flashlight.

Cracking a super glow stick, Lovecraft tossed it to the bottom of the stairs. It lit up only a small portion of what felt like a large chamber. At the edge of the light, possibly in the middle of the chamber, the glow stick reflected off a pond of dark water. Leaning forward, Lovecraft saw that the steps were at least stable. He would not have to worry about anything grabbing him from beneath the stairs.

Starting to walk down, Lovecraft suddenly stilled. Whispers rolled by him, and a cold sweat broke out on his back. He was plummeting towards gibbering fear when his thumb brushed Max's nylon coat.

Lovecraft looked down to see it hanging on his satchel, and his fear quickly blazed into fierce resolve. Max was one of his students, and he was not going to leave the kid down here.

Baring his teeth, Lovecraft stalked down to the rocky ground, sprinkled with gritty sand. He glared at the darkness, and he could feel that the chamber was huge.

"You come here looking for a fight?" asked a voice from the dark. The voice was like ancient vellum: smooth, dry, and very, very, very old.

Lovecraft froze, and his eyes darted around.

The voice bounced from all over, so the Substitute could not tell where it had come from.

"A kid and a woman were taken," said Lovecraft in careful tones. "They are my responsibility. I'm here to bring them back. But, if I can do this peacefully, that'd be great."

Water splashed.

Something was moving, which caused ripples at the edge of the shallow pond. After a moment, a figure moved into the green light. It was an ancient man in a large antique black suit. He stepped out of the ankle-deep water. Shackled to his left ankle was a rusty metal cuff that had a big chain fastened to it. The chain, which went off into the darkness, jangled as he stopped near Lovecraft.

"Who are you?" asked the old man with the voice.

"I am called Lovecraft," said Substitute.

"But, that's not your real name," replied the old man.

"No." And that was all Lovecraft said.

The older man smiled as if Lovecraft had passed a test. "Names have power."

"And what should I call you?" asked Lovecraft.

"Mr. Abyssian," said the old man, and he paused for a moment. "Yes. That will suffice. But, I have seen all that you have brought here."

"Me?" asked Lovecraft in surprise. "I did not bring this. We were told to come here. We were supposed to be at City

Hall."

"But you trespassed down below," said the voice in the dark.

"We did not know that we were trespassing," said Lovecraft. "We desperately needed food and medical supplies. If I had known, I would have asked."

Mr. Abyssian squinted at Lovecraft with eyes clouded by glaucoma. The older man leaned forward and suddenly sniffed the air. Out of the corner of his eye, Lovecraft saw something big, moving just past the light. It took all his restraint not to draw a weapon. He had a feeling that that would be a foolish move right now.

"Your words smell untainted by lies," said Mr. Abyssian at last.

"My Mom was very big on 'not lying,'" said Lovecraft, a little wistfully. His eyes grew distant for a moment as he remembered her. "Lies always get people into deeper trouble."

"Then, why are you here?" asked Mr. Abyssian.

"To save as many people as possible," said Lovecraft.

"Including the two who trespassed," asked Mr. Abyssian.

"They mean no harm to you or yours," said Lovecraft.

"And if I don't let them go?" asked Mr. Abyssian.

Lovecraft just gave a small shrug. "I will tear this place down upon your ears."

Mr. Abyssian suddenly gave a dry chuckle. "You would, wouldn't you?"

As if the darkness had disgorged them, Max and Florence suddenly appeared at the edge of the light. They stumbled haphazardly. Lovecraft managed to catch Florence as Max fell. She was shivering from a deep cold. Her lips were almost blue.

"What...what...," she murmured.

"No time," whispered Lovecraft. "Can you walk?"

"Yeah," said Florence straightening up. Once he was sure that she would not fall over, he let her go and hauled Max.

"Wha...what took you so long?" grinned Max through his shivers.

"Shut up, kid," said Lovecraft gently, and he wrapped the kid's jacket around his thin shoulders. Max immediately pulled it tight. "We gotta go. Up the stairs, you two."

Florence and Max began to go up the stairs. Lovecraft turned to follow, but he stopped. He picked up the super glowstick and turned to Mr. Abyssian.

Lovecraft almost said 'Thank you' but then stopped himself. Some old things would take 'Thank you' as a sign that you owed them a debt, which would never be paid off.

"I will leave you to your peace," said Lovecraft.

"Do not come back down here," warned Mr. Abyssian.

"I can do that," agreed Lovecraft, who was only too happy to comply.

Swiftly, Lovecraft shooed Max and Florence up the stairs. He whispered to them as they left the dark chamber.

"We've got to walk quickly but not run."

"Hard to move," mumbled Florence.

Max just had his head down, trying to put one foot in front of the other.

"I know, but we gotta go," whispered Lovecraft urgently. "This is just a temporary truce."

Lovecraft helped them until they reached the ladder that led up to the jail.

"Turk!" shouted Lovecraft up. "We need help!"

After a brief scrabbling up above, the wheel started moving. Turk pulled open the hatch.

"You're alive?" exclaimed Turk in surprise.

"So far," said Lovecraft. "And, they need a hand."

"I'll help," said Marta, and she knelt next to the hatch.

Lovecraft lifted Max first, and Turk and Marta hauled the kid up the rest of the way. Farther away, he heard whispers growing. Maneuvering Florence, he helped her up, but he looked aside as her poodle skirt billowed. As Turk got her up, Lovecraft hesitated.

"Come on!" said Turk urgently, but Lovecraft looked back at the big cans of food. The whispers were getting louder, but the food was so close.

"One more moment," he said to the air as he ran to grab a can of food. He did not even look at what it was. Running back to the hatch, he looked up.

"Coming up," shouted Lovecraft.

"Whoa," said Turk, and he jumped out of sight. The

234

Substitute heaved the first can up and through the hole.

Without even bothering to think of where it landed, he ran back to grab another large can whose lid was as wide as his outspread fingers. He picked it up but noticed that the whispers were closing in on him. He could almost make out the words. And something told him that if he made out what the whispers were saying, then he'd be dead meat.

Lovecraft threw the second can up through the hatch and then jumped up to grab the ladder. He looked up just as something ethereal and screaming shot towards the ladder.

The Substitute dove aside as a chill wind passed. Whatever it was, it was swooping around for a second shot. Lovecraft scrambled up the ladder. He hauled himself up and over the edge of the hatch, just as something tugged at his boot. But it lost its grip, and he collapsed to the ground.

Turk slammed down the hatch and pulled the wheel tight. Grabbing a large washing machine—which he had dragged close—Turk tipped it on top of the hatch. Only then did Turk take a breath of relief.

Something about that breath gave Lovecraft the man-giggles, and he could not stop laughing for a minute.

Turning on his side, Lovecraft looked at the kid who was still huddled in his Tigers jacket. But Max was slowly warming up.

"You gonna survive?" asked Lovecraft of the kid.

"No," grumbled Max.

"Well, that's good," said Lovecraft with a gentle smile. He looked up at the cooks, who all were still there. "Can

235

we get something to wrap these two up in?"

"How did they get so cold?" asked Turk with concern.

But Marta did not want to know the answer. "There're some old linens over there. That should help."

Under Marta's orders, the cooks got the linens and piled them around Florence and Max, whose lips were returning to a standard shade.

One of the cook's picked up a can, which was now dented from its impromptu space shot.

"Baked beans," said one of the cooks, Zoe, dismally. "Why couldn't you have saved the tin of hot dogs?"

"I couldn't save everyone," said Lovecraft. "Those hot dogs gave their lives so that we could get away." He snapped off a crisp salute. "God bless you, Hot Dogs! God bless you."

"I was just saying," responded Zoe testily.

"I know. Sorry. We'll do the best with what we have," said Lovecraft, a little more seriously.

# 31

Max pulled off the last layer of linens as his temperature returned to normal. That made Lovecraft feel better as they sat next to Tibbons, who was freshly stitched up but still laying on his mattress.

Hurston and Icewater were getting people ready to do a

series of interviews by the first floor cells. That reminded Lovecraft, and he pulled out the tin of cream to apply more to his face.

"Is that a good idea?" asked Tibbons, and Lovecraft looked at him questioningly.

"It's just skin cream," replied Substitute.

"No, I mean the interviews," growled Tibbons. Across the way, Maddie was primping herself for an interview. Tammi and Missy walked up to her.

"I have a little makeup?" offered Tammi. "Do you want to share?"

"Thank you!" said Maddie gratefully.

"I wish my top wasn't such a mess," said Missy sadly. Someone's blood had gotten splashed on it. Nearby, Craig peeled off his letter jacket and took off his shirt. He replaced the coat and handed his shirt to Missy.

"Here," said Craig. "For the interview. It was fresh out of the dryer this morning. Honest."

"As long as it doesn't have any blood on it," said Missy happily.

"In here," said Maddie, and she nodded to Cell #3. As Missy went in, Maddie stood up out of her wheelchair. Looking away, she held onto the bars as she and Tammi guarded the door. Missy grabbed the bottom of her shirt and stopped. Maddie noticed the pause out of the corner of her eye.

"What?" asked Maddie.

"What if something's...you know, watching?" asked

237

Missy, though the jail cell appeared empty.

"No one's going to see you in here," said Tammi. "We've got the door blocked."

"Not them out there," said Missy. "I mean—you know —IN here."

Maddie snorted. "There's no such thing as ghosts."

"I know that," said Missy quickly. "But, do they know that?"

"Just change quickly," suggested Tammi.

Missy turned to the blocked door and quickly whipped off her shirt, and put on Craig's.

But she had not needed to worry. The moment she stepped in, the ghost in cell #3 had recognized that Missy was one of the high schoolers and had averted his eyes.

Back across general population, Lovecraft thought of Tibbons' question regarding letting people be interviewed. After a moment, he shrugged.

"Everyone loves to be interviewed," said Lovecraft. "And it'll take their mind off our predicament."

# 32

Boyle walked up to Lovecraft—who was lightly dozing —while the interviews were finishing up nearby. Probably only he could spot the worry in her manners because otherwise, she looked calm and professional. Lovecraft looked up with an open, curious expression.

"Can I speak with you for a moment?" asked Boyle.

"Sure."

"I mean...alone," said Boyle, and she nodded to an empty area in the general population.

"Okay, sure," said Lovecraft, and he stood up.

When Max started to stand, Boyle just gave him a curious look, but then she shrugged. The kid took that as acceptance and followed along.

Boyle strode towards an empty area of concrete. Lovecraft strolled alongside her with his hands in his pockets.

"That bad is it?" asked Lovecraft when they were out of earshot. Boyle stopped by a wall, and then she leaned against it. She had a lithe frame, and for a moment, she let Lovecraft see the exhaustion behind her eyes. But then her professional face returned.

"It's about Councilman Tibbons," said Boyle.

Lovecraft sighed. "I was afraid of that."

"I followed protocol with anyone bitten—or even just scratched—by the revenants and poured pure Hydrogen Peroxide in their wounds," explained Boyle.

"Did the CDC ever prove that that helped?"

Boyle shrugged. "They haven't gotten definitive proof that it's stopping it, but it might slow down the spread of the R-Virus."

"R-Virus?" asked Max, and then his face lit up. "Oh yeah, revenant virus. Sorry. Nevermind."

239

"And since animals can't get infected...," started Boyle, but she left that thought out there.

"Animal tests are kind of out of the question then," finished Lovecraft. "I wonder if the Hydrogen Peroxide is killing a lot of the virus, or any?"

"For some, it seems to kill the virus completely...of course, that's IF they were infected in the first place," said Boyle.

"So Councilman Tibbons?" asked the Substitute.

Boyle just nodded.

Shit thought Lovecraft.

"Shit," said Max.

Lovecraft almost commented on the swear but instead asked the paramedic. "Okay, how long?"

"Not long," said Boyle. "And I don't want to panic anyone..." Again, she let that thought hang out there.

"But this needs to be taken care of," finished Lovecraft. "We could move him." The Substitute nodded towards the cells.

"Too dangerous," said Boyle with a shake of her head. "He might turn en route. And I don't want to truss him up like an animal, off to slaughter..."

"True," agreed Lovecraft wholeheartedly. "So, how're we going to get the privacy?"

They all looked around thoughtfully, and Max's eyes wandered up. Suddenly, the kid whipped around to look at Lovecraft and Boyle.

"Mattresses!" he yelled out.

"What?" asked Boyle.

"From the beginning of that thought?" asked Lovecraft gently.

"We take everyone upstairs to hunt for mattresses to sleep on," said Max.

"And, you have to stay in large groups for safety," added Lovecraft with a nod. He looked at Boyle. "How long do you need before we do this?"

"I have everything. We need to do this as soon as we can," said Boyle sadly. "He does not have long."

"Yeah, poor guy," said Lovecraft sadly, and he turned to the kid. "Okay, you're up!"

"Wha...what do you mean?" asked Max in surprise.

"It's your idea," said Lovecraft. "Go and wrangle everyone yourself."

"But...by myself?" asked Max nervously.

"Sure. You can do it," nodded Lovecraft with a smile, and that made Max stand a little taller.

The kid made a confident, chuffing noise and strode off towards the refugees.

"Excuse me!" Everyone!" shouted Max. And to the kid's surprise, most everyone turned to him. "Since we're going to be here a little longer, Councilman Tibbons thought we should have more mattresses to rest on. He asked me to lead everyone upstairs to collect as many as we can."

"Is this because you're afraid to go alone?" sneered Craig.

Max shot back. "Aren't you?" And some people chuckled at that. The kid turned and started towards the stairs. "Follow me, and we will all be safe *IF* we all stay together. If you need to break off to collect a mattress, bring a friend!" He paused to look back with a severe expression. "Make that two friends. No one wanders on their own!"

"Do we all need to go?" asked Rayton.

"I figure one mattress per person," said Max. "If you want a bed tonight, come on."

For a long moment, no one moved to follow. Lovecraft struggled inwardly because he wanted to step forward and help. But then Tammi, Stu, and Patrick went to pursue, and more went with them.

Max directed people up the left-hand stairs. Maddie rolled her wheelchair over to the stairs and stood up. Florence reached out to help the older woman.

"I can get your mattress," suggested Florence.

"I'm not so sick that I can't get my own mattress," snapped Maddie. She held onto the rail and moved slowly up the stairs. But Florence hovered close behind.

"Stay together," reminded Max as they moved.

Leading everyone to the next floor, Max did not see Craig snag Missy's hand. And Lovecraft and Boyle had their heads bowed in quiet conversation, so the bully was able to lead her into Death Row.

"Is this a good idea?" asked Missy as Craig led her towards an empty cell.

"It's one of my best," admitted Craig modestly.

"But, is this dangerous?" asked Missy, and she stopped at the threshold of a cell. As he walked into the cell, she pulled her hand out of Craig's. He turned around, first in surprise but then with a flash of anger. She continued, though. "Max said..."

Craig interrupted her. "Max said to stay together, and we're certainly staying together. *And* it's been too long."

Stepping up to her, Craig reached out and caressed her hip. She gasped softly as he nuzzled her neck.

"Way too long," she agreed in a husky voice. She let herself be steered into the cell. They collapsed onto the bed pulling at each other's clothes. Soon he slid into her, pressing against her body.

Engrossed in each other, they did not see it.

A shadowy figure appeared near the ceiling, outside the room. It was formed of smoky darkness, which looked vaguely humanoid. The shadow creeper reached the top of the door and climbed over the lip. It scuttled across the ceiling on all fours and stopped over them. Slowly, its head twisted 180 degrees to look down upon them.

Missy looked up and saw the horrible grin on its smoky face, and she let out a shriek. But the walls seemed to eat up the sound.

"I love it when you scream," crowed Craig.

Missy bucked against the Bully, and he let out a whoop. Her nails dug into his back.

"Careful there!" he said, and his face strained with pleasure. "Don't worry! Almost finished!"

The shadow creeper dropped from the ceiling.

243

# 33

As everyone appeared to go up the stairs, Boyle spoke quietly and urgently to Lovecraft.

"We don't want to make a mess of it, but all I have are local anesthetics," she said.

"It's okay," replied Lovecraft. "I...I have a painkiller."

"What is it?"

"It's something I'm field testing," said Lovecraft. "Kinda like an Epi-pen, but for pain. If I'm hurt really badly, Dr. Landers said that one of these cocktails would stop the pain. It's supposed to work long enough so that I can finish the job. But, he warned that if I take two at once..."

Lovecraft stopped speaking, and they stood there in an uneasy silence.

"I'm not a doctor, but I have to know if this will do more damage than good," insisted Boyle.

"I don't know," admitted Lovecraft. "And that's the truth. But Dr. Landers said that two of the pens would...well, put me to sleep forever."

"What if the Councilman still comes back?" asked Boyle.

"Then I have a knife," he said simply.

"Okay," she said.

As soon as they saw that everyone had reached the second floor of cells, Boyle and Lovecraft moved quickly over to Tibbons.

"I didn't think you'd ever stop dithering!" snapped the Councilman as they drew near.

Both stopped in surprise.

"What?" asked Boyle.

"Come on!" said Tibbons. His voice softened as he waved them over.

Lovecraft and Boyle knelt on either side of Tibbons. His face had gone gray. "I mean, you didn't think that I couldn't figure it out? That I'm dying from a zombie bite? I thought I was going to croak before you all quit dicking around."

But Lovecraft looked Tibbons square in the eye and spoke in a gentle rebuke.

"Hey! Lay off her. Most people aren't exactly comfortable with euthanasia, especially when they have to take a direct part of it. People have enough trouble with Fido."

Tibbons started to speak, but then he gave a little nod. "You're right." The Councilman turned to the paramedic. "Sorry, Boyle, it's been a long day."

"For all of us," reminded Lovecraft pointedly.

"Right," agreed Tibbons sheepishly, and his face turned thoughtful. "A bullet's going to scare people...and I do not like the idea personally."

"We already thought of that," said Boyle.

"You did?" exclaimed Tibbons. "Great job. What's our solution?"

Lovecraft took out two large pens from his satchel. The pens were covered in so much medical terminology that they—at first blush—looked like hieroglyphics.

"You're going to take a nap," said Lovecraft.

Tibbons chuckled darkly. "Like an old dog being sent to the farm."

"Like a member of the family who deserves to go out peacefully," corrected Lovecraft.

"Don't get sappy on me," grumbled Tibbons. "Now, let's get a move on; I haven't got all day."

Lovecraft took the first pen and removed the cap to reveal a small needle. He turned it towards Tibbons, who flinched. Lovecraft looked up questioningly.

"What?" he asked.

"Sorry," said Tibbons. "I just...hate needles."

"I'll make it quick," assured Lovecraft.

"Councilman Tibbons?" asked Boyle, and he turned to look at her. She gave his nose a big kiss. While he was distracted, Lovecraft injected the first pen into Tibbons' arm. The Councilman stiffened in surprise and then turned to glare at Lovecraft.

"Hey! That wasn't fai...," started Tibbons when he stopped. A slow, lazy smile spread across his lips. "Wow, that is some good stuff."

"May the road rise to meet you, and may you be in Heaven a half hour before the devil knows you're dead," said Lovecraft.

Tibbons smiled lazily. "I always liked that old Irish

saying. You kids take care of yourselves."

Lovecraft injected the second pen into Tibbons' arm, and this time the older man did not even flinch.

The Councilman slowly closed his eyes.

Shifting, Lovecraft moved to kneel by Tibbons' head. Boyle looked at him questioningly, but Lovecraft just took out his folding knife, and then he turned Tibbon's head to expose the base of the spine.

"If he opens his eyes, shout!" said Lovecraft softly.

But they waited, and nothing happened. Cautiously, Boyle checked his vitals while Lovecraft held the Councilman's head firmly in place.

"He's gone," whispered Boyle. "I think we're safe."

"Let me carry him into Cell #6 and lock him in there, just in case," suggested Lovecraft.

# 34

Out of the corner of his eye, Max looked at Lovecraft, Boyle, and Tibbons. But nothing seemed to be happening there.

Max turned to the next cell and stumbled to a halt. Next to a cell door, Max Chow saw a piece of paper that read: Chow, Cole.

"Something wrong?" asked Rayton helpfully.

Max pushed his feelings down and turned to give the

teacher an easy smile.

"It's all good," lied Max convincingly.

# 35

Patrick was the first to start crying when Lovecraft told everyone the news about the Councilman. Others soon joined in. Boyle and Lovecraft had waited until everyone had gotten back with their mattresses.

"Councilman Tibbons passed away," explained Boyle. "But, he went peacefully."

"We should all be so lucky," said Max sadly.

Lovecraft stepped forward. "I think we should make good use of the mattresses and get some rest. The Councilman would want...did want us to take care of ourselves."

# 36

The moment Max put his head on his balled-up Tigers jacket, the kid was out like a light. Lovecraft was happy that the kid was getting some rest because they deserved it after working so hard.

However, Lovecraft was too tired to sleep. And his mind

was whirring at a breakneck speed.

Tibbons' eyes were slowly closing.

And the white eyes of Reverend Jennings, who he had thrown against a car.

Brick falling amongst the zoms.

The Substitute almost jumped when Icewater appeared before him.

The Camerawoman crouched in front of him. She did not have her ever-present camera with her. He must have looked surprised because she gave a rare grin. She held out her hands to show that they were empty.

"I come in peace," she said softly so as not to wake anyone. She had on well-worn blue jeans that looked like they were distressed from real life rather than from a manufacturer. Underneath her Scottevest, she wore a lime green top.

"Do you, do you need some help?" asked Lovecraft quickly. He was worried that something else had gone wrong. He started to get up, but she put out a hand to gently stop him.

"Nothing bad. I promise you," said Icewater quickly to reassure him. "I needed to talk to you quietly for a moment."

"Okay," said Lovecraft wearily.

"By the way, my name is Patricia Carroll," said the Camerawoman. "Icewater's just a nickname I got in Iraq, and it kinda followed me."

"People thought you had ice water for blood?"

"I don't get rattled easily. So yeah, it's something silly like that," said Icewater, but then she gave a happy little shrug. "Could've been worse."

"I think it's cool. Closest I ever got to a nickname was 'kid,'" smiled Lovecraft genuinely, and they shook hands.

Icewater continued. "And, it's not your fault."

"What?"

"What happened here," said Icewater. "Why we had to hide here in the jail."

"Why do you think I'm worried about that?" asked Lovecraft.

"An old boyfriend was a major in the Army. He'd get that same look when he reviewed past actions and wishing the outcomes were different. Coulda, woulda, shoulda."

"He never dropped the ball like this."

"You did the best you could with what you had. You saved a lot of people."

Lovecraft just sighed.

"In time," said Icewater. "You'll see that you saved so many. Now what I'm wondering is why I can't see your face?"

"What," replied Lovecraft in confusion.

"I was reviewing the footage from today," said Icewater.

"Oh," was all that Lovecraft would say.

"And I have great footage. Clear as a bell," said Icewater. "Except for you. When my camera looks at you, there's this big fuzzy blur where your face is. Almost as if something

250

was messing with my camera."

Lovecraft did not add anything. He just sat quietly and wondered where this conversation was going. He resisted the urge to grab his tin of face cream.

"It's probably just a glitch in the camera," shrugged Icewater nonchalantly. "By the way, what is that face moisturizer that you use?"

"Smooth Criminal," replied Lovecraft quickly and immediately chided himself. But that was the first thing that popped in his head.

"I'll have to check it out," smiled Icewater. She stood up and twisted her back sideways to pop a few vertebrates. But then she looked straight at him. "Now, you get some rest. You've earned it."

"Yes, ma'am," smiled Lovecraft, and he relaxed. Icewater walked back to her camera with a smile. The Substitute glanced over to Max, but the kid was still sleeping.

# 37

A cell door slammed shut.

Max sat upon his ancient mattress. But, everyone was gone.

Slowly, Max stood. The jail looked almost new. Fresh paint covered the walls.

In front of the first floor cells, Max saw two inmates talking casually. However, they did not seem to notice the kid as he cautiously walked by. His eyes darted up to where he had last seen his father's cell.

Max took off running.

Pounding up the steps, the kid dodged around inmates, who had a slightly faded look. He suddenly skidded to a halt before his father's cell. His heart thundered. Taking a deep breath, he looked around the corner. His father, Cole Chow, was sitting on the edge of his bed but jumped up when he saw the kid.

"Max!" cried Cole happily. He leaped out of his cell and hugged his son warmly. "And look at you! You look like me when I was your age, though I hope better behaved."

"Dad?" asked Max tentatively.

"We don't have much time," said Cole quickly. "Something's coming. It's too dangerous."

"We saw the man with the noose...," started Max.

Cole interrupted. "Oh, Him? That's just my old partner. We didn't part on good terms. But no, it's...there are other things here that...well, it's not safe to say more, but you have to get..."

"The guy in the basement?" asked Max.

"Shhhh, don't even whisper about him," hissed Cole fearfully. "I can't believe you went down there once."

"We had too," insisted Max.

Something crashed above on the topmost row of cells, and Cole looked up in horror.

"Go!" he cried to his son. "Get back down to your friends and warn them! Now!"

"But...," started Max.

The lights on the floor above went out, and they heard wild, panicked screams.

On the right-hand side, liquid darkness flowed down the stairs like a wave. It extinguished light as it crept along. Finally, the smokey darkness settled into the form of a shadow creeper.

The creature crept forward, and wherever it passed, the walls turned old and frail.

"Go! Go! Go!" cried Cole desperately. "And for God's sake, don't go back down into that basement again!"

Max sprinted towards the left-hand staircase, which was still lit.

An inmate-- standing by his cell-- suddenly screeched in terror as the shadow creeper grabbed him. The prisoner aged instantly from a young man to dried old bones, which clattered upon the cement. With an enthusiastic hop, the shadow creeper resumed its pursuit of Max.

Cole tried to stand in its path, but the creature just shoved the father back into his cell.

As Max ran, he felt the creeper right behind him. It snatched at him.

Reaching the left-hand staircase, Max grabbed the metal rail and used that to make a hard turn. He jumped out over the stairs and sailed downward.

Up above, the Shadow Creeper was unable to stop in

time. It ran into the wall and splashed into it. Momentarily, it lost its smoky cohesion.

The kid hit the ground hard and stumbled. Recovering quickly, Max turned to leap down the next flight of stairs.

But, the kid saw something waiting on the floor below.

"Boo," grinned the man with the noose, Dustin.

Max scrambled back up the stairs. The shadow creeper —still pulling itself back together—tried futility to grab at him.

Looking for safe harbor, Max saw that there were no shadow creepers near the right-hand staircase now. Panting with exertion, he ran that way. Behind him, Dustin followed languidly with a rotten grin on his face.

Bolting past the cells, Max saw several shadow creepers on the landing below. The kid turned and ran up the stairs. With an almost-human cry of glee, the creatures below joined in the chase.

Reaching the third floor, the kid ran to the first couple of cells, trying to think of a place to hide. Nothing, but in desperation, he looked into the fourth one.

The man with the noose leaped out of that cell and cut off the kid's escape.

Stumbling back, Max looked behind. The shadow creepers that had been following him were now patiently waiting on the landing.

"Max?" cried a voice from the right staircase. "Max!"

The kid's heart leaped as he saw his father, Cole, fighting to get up the stairs to him. A third shadow creeper jumped

Cole from behind. It started to drag his father back down the stairs.

But Cole tugged on the railing of the staircase even as the smoky darkness was reducing him down to old bones. Losing his grip on the railing, Cole was pulled back, but the bones still fought the shadow creeper.

"He's my son, Goddammit!" growled the skeletal Cole, but he slid down the stairs and out of sight.

A quick glance over the balcony rail showed that the wire mesh was not there. It would be a long plunge to the concrete below.

Two more shadow creepers were crouched by the left-hand staircase, ready to spring. Max figured he might be able to dodge one, but who knew how many more were hiding behind them.

The man with the noose, Dustin, grinned. "Little, little boy, time for your dirt nap."

"Thank you for the offer Dickcheese, but I'm not sleepy," said Max, and he saw Dustin's face grow red with anger. A stupid plan snuck into Max's head, and he tried-- desperately-- to think of a better one.

The man with the noose growled. "I'm going to tear you apart!"

"The hell you will," screamed someone behind Dustin. The man with the noose whipped around just as Max's skeletal father punched him in the jaw.

Dustin stumbled back towards Max.

The kid shot forward. Max grabbed the noose around Dustin's neck. The kid leaped over the edge of the balcony.

There was no wire mesh to slow him.

Above, the shadow creepers let out a screech of surprise.

Using the noose like a rope, Max swung out and then down to the floor below. The rope jerked as Dustin slammed into the rail above. As the man with the noose began to tip over the rail, Max reached the next level, and he leaped to the lower balcony safely.

There was a scream of rage as Dustin fell past.

Darting back to look over the side, he saw the man with the noose pinwheeling towards the concrete below. Distantly, the kid noticed two people walking towards the gate out of the general population, but his focus was on the man who had tried to kill him.

"Dickcheese!" crowed Max triumphantly as Dustin hit bottom with a sickening crunch.

Relieved, Max turned towards the stairs when a shadow creeper grabbed him and bore him to the ground.

# 38

A hand shook the kid awake.

Wildly, Max looked around. Lovecraft, who was leaning against the wall nearby, pulled his hand back.

"Bad dream?" asked Lovecraft sympathetically.

Max blinked the crust from his eyes. He suddenly jumped up, scanning general population.

It was still night. People slept all around him. It seemed peaceful.

"Something's coming," whispered Max, and he tried to keep his voice calm.

Lovecraft regarded the kid for a moment but then stood up. He winced. His ankle—which that darn runner had chewed on—had grown stiff and sore.

"Why do you say that?" asked Lovecraft carefully as he moved his wounded ankle to get it limber again.

Max hesitated for a moment before speaking. It felt stupid. "My Dad warned me."

"This would be the father that is...," started Lovecraft, but he let his voice trail off.

"Ah...yeah," replied Max, a little sheepishly, and the Substitute pondered this for a second.

Lovecraft nodded. "Okay, I'm willing to go on a little faith here."

The Substitute crouched near Boyle and touched her shoulder gently. She jumped.

"What?" asked Boyle sleepily.

"I think we're in trouble," whispered Lovecraft.

"What is it?" asked Boyle in a low voice.

"I'm not sure...yet," admitted Lovecraft. "But..."

There was a massive crash at the main gate.

The noise rebounded through general population waking up Hurston.

"They're back!" squealed the Reporter in terror.

257

"Damn," said Lovecraft. He turned and ran down the general population. He hopped over several occupied mattresses along the way. "Excuse me! Pardon me!"

Lovecraft pulled out his gun, Rikke, and loaded a red-tipped bullet into the chamber. Skidding to a halt by the gate, he fired one round through the bruiser's head. The dead behemoth fell back. Behind Lovecraft, there was a great cheer.

But then another mass of revenants walked around the corner with a second bruiser.

"Aw crap," swore Lovecraft, and he loaded another red-tipped bullet. When the second bruiser got close, Lovecraft shot it dead. The people behind him gave a ragged cheer this time, but Lovecraft said nothing. Then he heard the heavy footfalls, like the heartbeat of an ancient and terrible god.

Around the corner came a third bruiser.

"Oh, not fair," moaned Lovecraft as he backed up.

Once this bruiser found the gate, it swung at it hard. But the gate did not move, for now.

"Shoot it already," screamed Hurston in a near panic.

Lovecraft turned back to general population. He was happy that everyone who had been hurt was now ambulatory. He honed in on Max.

"Grab everyone," ordered Lovecraft. "Get them to the laundry room."

The gate started to buckle.

"Okay, everyone!" called out Max. "Move this way.

We're going to the laundry room!"

Max backed towards Death Row, waving people in his direction. Lovecraft almost chuckled because the kid looked like a tour guide.

"Come on," continued Max. "Walk this way!"

"But...?" started Hurston. The bruiser hit the gate so hard that dust came down from the ceiling high above.

Lovecraft glared at the Reporter.

"Move!" he barked.

Tammi hopped off her mattress. She was going to run for it, but she stopped and helped up Lydia from bus #9.

"Again?" moaned Lydia.

"I know," agreed Tammi sympathetically. "What the hell, right?"

Just inside Death Row, Max stopped outside a cell to direct people to keep moving.

"Just this way," instructed Max. He gestured towards the hallway past the morgue. "It's going to be alright. Go around that bend, and you'll see the laundry room."

Turk stopped in front of Max.

"I'm going to find something heavy to put in front of the door when we close it," said Turk.

"Great idea," said Max.

Turk grinned and walked on past the morgue. He, too, urged people around the corner to the laundry room. Max shooed the last people past, and he turned to see Hurston and Icewater lagging behind. The camerawoman, Icewater,

259

was still filming. The kid opened his mouth to yell at them when someone grabbed him.

Max was yanked off his feet and pulled back into the cell.

# 39

The bruiser hit the metal by the front gate, and the top right bent down a little. A runner leaped up onto the bruiser's shoulder.

It squeezed through the opening like a snake and sprang for the wire above. Clinging upside-down to the wire mesh, it hung between the first and second floor.

Immediately, it scrambled deeper into general population.

Calmly, Lovecraft aimed at it, but his gun clicked empty.

"Last clip," he called out reflexively as the creature drew close.

Slipping in a clip of regular bullets, Lovecraft lifted his weapon, but the runner's muscular tail swiped at him. The creature's tail gave his head a love tap, which made him stumble. Lovecraft shook the cobwebs from his noggin as the creature escaped.

Twisting around, the Substitute tried to shoot at it, but his shot only grazed its flank. And that only made the damn thing scuttle faster.

Lovecraft suddenly realized that Hurston and Icewater were still back there as well.

"What're you two still doing there?" shouted Lovecraft in exasperation, but the bruiser started pounding on the gate again. Lovecraft turned back towards the door and tried to keep an eye behind him as well.

"It's coming towards us!" screeched Hurston

"The cells," said Icewater as she stepped smoothly to the side, without jiggling her camera. She kept filming as the bruiser beat on the door. "If we're out of its path..."

But Icewater did not see the look of disbelief that Hurston gave her. He turned and ran, and over the din, she did not hear him go.

Hurston did notice Max being dragged into the dark cell, but he was too scared to stop.

The runner moved quickly past Icewater, who was partway inside a cell. The Camerawoman kept the focus on the front gate, believing that Hurston was somewhere safe in a cell behind her.

Following Hurston, the runner kept going, enjoying the thrill of the chase. It let go of the wire mesh and twisted in mid-air. As soon as it hit the ground, it sped into Death Row.

With the runner hot on his tail, Hurston left Death Row and ducked into the first room past it.

Against one wall were rows of metal drawers. Grabbing one of the metal doors, he yanked it open and scrambled onto the large tray inside. Closing the door behind him, he heard the runner slam into the metal door a second later. It started to scrape its claws against the metal, but in its primitive stupidity, it did not pull on the door handles.

Hurston sucked in huge gulps of air, which tasted of ancient antiseptics. Recognizing that he was in absolute darkness, the Reporter reached for his cell phone, but then he realized that he had left it by his mattress. He fumbled through his pockets and found the compact video recorder that Icewater had given him earlier. She said it was 'in case of emergency' or to get additional footage. As if he, Reporter and anchor with the Number 1 station in the state, would take B roll shots.

It took him two tries to get the small video recorder on. Hurston fumbled through the settings with no built-in light until he managed to switch it to night vision.

That was when he noticed the dead man.

Yelping, the Reporter reared back until he realized it was only Tic, that idiot who had gotten himself killed earlier. Tic was wrapped up in plastic now, patiently waiting for a coroner.

"Stop that!" snapped Hurston at the corpse.

Once he got his breathing under control, the Reporter looked around the metal compartment with the night vision. Inside, there were no walls to separate the rows of seven-foot metal trays. It appeared empty, but he soon felt a deep chill.

Regardless, Hurston felt innovative and proud of himself. Smugly, he turned the camera towards himself.

"This is Rick Hurston for Channel 2 News reporting from Fallen Oaks jail. I have been forced—Forced!—to find refuge from the revenant plague sweeping our town. I am hidden in a set of metal containers, but—Thank The Lord— I am safe."

"No, you're not," said a voice in the darkness.

Hurston blinked. He turned the camera to look around. His view slid quickly past Tic's still corpse. But, there was no one else visible.

"Is...is anyone there?" asked Hurston tentatively.

There was a tearing sound, and Hurston let out a little screech. He moved the camera around to make another sweep. He froze when he saw a bundle of shredded plastic, plastic which had encased Tic.

Swinging the camera, he saw something above him.

Tic— now a shadow creeper—dropped down upon him with a grin.

# 40

The metal door shook as Hurston shrieked inside.

Outside, the runner sniffed at the door when it suddenly popped open. The runner scampered back a foot.

Out of the door fell a compact video camera. The runner sniffed it carefully and then the inside of the morgue drawers. But, it found that the container only had some shredded plastic in it. Otherwise, it was empty.

Disappointed, it headed out of the morgue and turned

towards the laundry room as it followed the huge scent trail. The runner turned the corner and saw Boyle guarding the doorway with a length of pipe.

For a moment, neither took a breath.

# 41

Dragged into a Death Row cell, Max was thrown back.

He fell between a musty bed and a desk. A shadow creeper hopped on top of him, holding the kid to the floor.

"Your fault!" hissed the shadow creeper. "All your fault!"

And that was when Max's jaw dropped.

"Craig?" asked Max.

"You did this," snarled Craig, the shadow creeper. "Not my fault."

The bully's hands found Max's throat and started to squeeze. The kid tried to punch Craig's sides, but it was like hitting a wall. Then the kid stilled, and he tried another tack.

Max slammed his knee into Craig's wontons, and the bully doubled over.

"Sucks being solid," spat Max with a vicious grin. He pushed Craig off of him and into the desk.

Scrambling to the door, the kid almost made it. But Craig threw himself forward and grabbed Max's leg. The kid fell forward but managed to get ahold of the doorframe. Craig tried desperately to drag the kid back inside.

"This is all your fault," growled Craig, and the kid finally understood what the bully was saying.

"MY fault!" cried Max, and he twisted to look back at the shadow creeper. "You dumb son of a bitch! You left the main group, didn't you!"

"No," lied Craig reflexively.

"Yes," whispered a woman's voice from the darkness, but Max was too focused on Craig.

"You idiot! We were trying to keep you safe, and you get yourself...," started Max, but he could not find the words. "Whatever the hell you are! Damn it." Realization clicked in. "Wait! Where's Missy? I haven't seen her."

Craig tried to pull himself up Max's leg, but the kid kicked the shadow creeper in the face with each word.

"What!" Kick. "Have!" Kick. "You!" Kick. "Done!"

"Not my fault!" whined Craig shakily.

"I was trying to save all of you," growled Max. "Even your sorry butt!"

Craig's hands loosened, and it was just long enough for Max to scramble back, away.

The bully tried to shake off the kicks as he grinned horribly. "Now, you'll join us!"

A voice screamed from the back of the room. "You asshole!"

Max saw another shadow creeper spring off the bed onto Craig's back.

"Did you get me killed?" demanded the new shadow creeper, and Max immediately recognized Missy's voice. Her fingers sprang claws, and she started to attack Craig. Strips of him were flayed off as he howled.

"Not my fault!" cried Craig as he tried to throw her off, but she wrapped her legs tightly around his middle. Her fingers became a blur on his upper half.

Max almost—almost!—felt bad for Craig, but he kept the hell away from that fight.

The kid leaped out into the corridor, only to be grabbed immediately.

# 42

After the first runner had escaped, Lovecraft saw another crawling through. Firing quickly, he killed it. It dropped to hang halfway through the gate and temporarily plugged that hole. The other runners behind it quickly backed from the entrance and disappeared. He turned to look for the other one, but it had already run off.

"Dammit," he spat.

The bruiser hit the gate again, and the dead runner wobbled in the hole.

Lovecraft took several steps back.

The next punch knocked the gate off its hinges. It toppled slowly into the room, falling partly on top of the dead runner.

The bruiser and the revenants looked from the fallen gate to the Substitute.

"Well?" growled Lovecraft. "I ain't got all day. Who's first?"

The revenants shambled forward on unsteady legs while the bruiser brought up the center. Taking a skip backward, Lovecraft started to pick off the Revenants on either side with his gun, but his focus was on the bruiser.

"Well, time for plan...wait, is it B, or are we on plan C," wondered Lovecraft aloud as he holstered his gun. The bruiser was closing in on him. "Doesn't matter. Plan S for 'Stupid' is more like it. Well, let's see if this works."

Lovecraft shot forward, running directly towards the bruiser, which lumbered blindly forward. As he closed on the creature, the Substitute sprang up and just managed to grab the wire mesh between the floors. He swung his legs over the bruiser's head. The beast began to pass under him. Lovecraft let go of the wire, and he twisted like a cat in mid-air.

Taking off his satchel, he looped the strap over the bruiser's head. He slid it between the armor plates on its face and neck. The strap cinched around its throat. Lovecraft pulled back on the strap like a garotte, and the creature seized up as its oxygen was suddenly cut off.

The bruiser tried to reach up to claw at its throat, but the bony plates made it impossible to get a hold of the strap. More Revenants tried to grab at Lovecraft, but he kicked them away.

Slowly, the creature dropped to its knees. Lovecraft rode it down until it fell forward dead. A hand grabbed his shoulder, and Lovecraft ducked away from it. He drew his Gurkha knife and took off the outstretched hand of a Revenant.

With a smooth motion, Lovecraft cut the strap of his satchel and scrambled away from the mass of Revenants. One of them lunged and bit Lovecraft's arm, but it could not break through his coat.

Whacking it in the face with the hilt of his Gurkha knife, it let go of Lovecraft. He was scrambling free of the creatures when he spied Icewater standing near Death Row.

"Run, dammit! Run!" cried Lovecraft. Icewater looked up from her camera and turned to look behind her.

"Come on…," she began, but the Camerawoman did a double-take when she realized that Hurston was not there. "Where…?"

"No time!" said Lovecraft, as he ran up to her, urging her on.

Icewater glanced forward and saw the horde of revenants staggering behind the Substitute.

"Probably best," she said.

The Camerawoman spun around. But she twisted her camera onto her shoulder so that it shot backward. Icewater took off towards the laundry room, and Lovecraft had her take the lead so that no one was left behind.

The Camerawoman passed a cell, and a moment later, Max jumped out.

Lovecraft ran up to the kid and grabbed his shoulder.

Max cried out in surprise.

"What the hell are you still doing here, kid?" demanded Lovecraft.

Max opened his mouth to answer, but then he saw the Revenants behind, and his blood froze.

The Substitute cut in. "Never mind. Chit chat later. Here. Hurry and hold this!"

Lovecraft pushed his broken satchel into the kid's arms and propelled the kid along. They ran towards the bend, which led to the laundry room. Lovecraft drew his sidearm. He fired back on the oncoming Revenants as the three turned the corner.

"Holy crap!" swore Max as they all skidded to a stop.

Icewater turned her camera around to film.

Lovecraft suddenly remembered the other runner. With growing horror, the Substitute turned to look and braced himself for the sight of mangled bodies.

The runner had made it to the laundry room door all right.

But standing above its carcass was Boyle holding a length of bloody pipe. She looked surprised, delighted, and nauseous all at once.

When Max, Icewater, and Lovecraft drew close, Boyle raised the pipe with a wild look.

"Whoa!" said Lovecraft with an amused look. "It's just us, Slugger."

"It...it attacked us," explained Boyle with a distant voice.

"And you made it sorry for that," said Lovecraft gently.

"I...I've never killed anyone before," moaned Boyle.

269

"First the Councilman...and now this..."

Icewater's eyes widened for a moment at the mention of Tibbons, but she kept her peace.

"I know," said Lovecraft softly. "But, once someone is infected, there's no coming back. Not for Tibbons. Nor for that creature. You did what you had to do. Thank you."

"They're closing in on us!" cried Max, who had glanced back around the corner.

"Come on!" cried Turk from inside the laundry room. He and Rayton were levering an industrial laundry machine closer to the door.

"Let's go inside," said Lovecraft, and Boyle nodded. She turned, and they went through the door just as the Revenants came around the bend. Icewater filmed the paramedic as she went past.

Turk slammed the door as soon as they were all inside.

Lovecraft spun around and grabbed the laundry machine with Rayton on the other end. They pushed the industrial appliance awkwardly into place. Once it was set in front of the door, Lovecraft leaned gratefully against the machine.

The Revenants slammed into the door outside, but the heavy laundry machine barely vibrated with the impact. Lovecraft's heart was pounding, and he suddenly gave a little yelp of joy.

People looked at him in surprise, and some of those looks turned into stern glares.

"Sorry," said Lovecraft, abashed.

Boyle turned back at him, but her face was that of a professional again.

"What about those big things?" asked Boyle.

"That last one is dead, and I didn't see any more outside," said Lovecraft, and then he looked up to Heaven. "Please, God, don't let there be any more."

While he was looking up at the skylights in the tall ceiling, the Substitute saw that the glass and bars were still over the windows. No one was going to sneak up on them.

"And we're missing people?" said Simp anxiously. "Where's Craig and Missy?"

"They're gone," said Max with a solemn voice.

Lovecraft looked over at the kid, but Max was looking sadly at the floor. The Substitute did not say anything, but he did put a comforting hand on Max's shoulder for a moment.

"We did the best that we could do," said the Substitute softly. And Lovecraft said it for both of them.

Squaring his thin shoulders, Max looked up at the Substitute and put on a brave smile.

Icewater looked up from her camera. "Oh no! Rick isn't here either?"

"Who?" asked Lovecraft.

"Rick Hurston, the reporter," elaborated Icewater.

"Oh...damn," said Lovecraft honestly. He was trying to think of something nice to say, but his brain was getting tired.

"He was not a great reporter," said Icewater softly so

that only Lovecraft and Max heard. "Or, even-- really-- a good reporter. But, he could be a great person."

The Substitute touched his chest where, beneath all the layers, his cross hung.

"Amen," said Lovecraft.

Pushing off with his shoulder blades, the Substitute walked over to one of the sinks and turned on the water. As cool water pooled in his cupped hand, he took a drink.

Straightening, he turned back to rest. "Not exactly Perrier, but at least we have that."

Lovecraft took his satchel from Max and fished out a roll of duct tape. He started to construct a makeshift shoulder strap for his satchel out of tape. Soon, he had reattached the Mythtesters-Esque strap and slung it across his chest.

Boyle came over and spoke softly.

"When do you think they'll be here to rescue us?" she asked.

"I...I don't know," admitted Lovecraft. "But, for now, I recommend that we rest."

# 43

Lovecraft and Max sat against a wall. The Substitute was in quiet contemplation of a steak, medium-well.

"I need to give more money to feed people," whispered Lovecraft. "Hunger should only ever be a choice, such as

when you're trying to lose weight. It should never be forced on anyone."

Max was making a sympathetic noise when a pane of glass dropped down in front of them. The kid and Lovecraft just looked at each other and then up. A runner knocked out the glass. Lovecraft grabbed Max, and they dove out of the way of the falling glass.

Safe, the Substitute turned and drew his gun. The runner was pulling at the bars when Lovecraft put a bullet through its brain. It slumped down.

There was a surge of noise as people began to look around frantically.

"What was that?" demanded Boyle as she stood up. Everyone's eyes went up to see the runner, laying bonelessly over the barred window.

"Can they even get through those bars?" asked Florence with concern.

"I don't know," replied Lovecraft.

The runner was suddenly jerked out of sight, and most people relaxed, but Lovecraft stayed on his toes. A moment later, another runner appeared and grabbed at the bars. It began to pull at them.

"Well, fire at it," demanded Maddie from her wheelchair, but Lovecraft just waited. He pulled the clip from his gun, looked inside, and then slid it back into place. More runners appeared and started to smash through the glass on the other three windows.

As the glass fell like a waterfall before Lovecraft, he watched the things. The others, including Max, scrambled back in a panic.

Grabbing at the bars, the runners pulled at them with surprisingly strong jaws. In the first window, one end of a bar broke free. The bar made a low metallic groan throughout the laundry room as the runner began to pull it out of its way.

"Why aren't you shooting!" accused Maddie.

"Not enough bullets," said Lovecraft.

"What?" asked Boyle.

"I only got two bullets left," said Lovecraft. "I have to make every bullet count."

"Save a few for us then," said Stu dismally.

"Hell no," replied Lovecraft fiercely. "I'm going to use the last two bullets to ventilate those bastards. Then I'm going to use this gun as a hammer and cave their brains in."

Lovecraft looked around quickly, trying to formulate a plan that did not include the words 'Last Stand'. Reluctantly, his gaze settled onto the hatch in the floor. The laundry machine was still on top of it.

Max's gaze followed curiously, but then his eyes widened.

"Oh no," said the kid in horror.

"What?" asked Maddie. She squinted at the metal hatch. "What's wrong?"

"I'm open to a better plan," said Lovecraft to Max, without any heat in his voice.

Above, the runners began to peel back more bars. The Substitute holstered his gun and went over to the hatch. He put his shoulder into the laundry machine and pushed it off with a deep grunt.

Turk spoke up as the laundry machine crashed to the ground.

"Is that safe?" he asked.

"No," said Boyle as she walked forward. "But, it's safer than up here."

"I don't want to go back down there," said Florence in a small voice, and Max nodded quickly in agreement.

"Neither do I. Ever, ever again," said Lovecraft patiently. He bent down and tried the hatch. It gave more freely this time, and he opened it up. "Now, I need people to climb down in a calm and orderly fashion."

"What's down there?" asked Maddie suspiciously.

But before Lovecraft could answer, they heard another bar come loose. The runner was almost through the first window.

"We don't have time," said Lovecraft. "Everyone down!"

Boyle sped forward and went down the ladder first. That broke the spell, and more people went. Lovecraft eyed the runners above. They would have enough room to squeeze through in minutes if that.

"Hurry," urged the Substitute.

Seeing Maddie and Florence struggling with her wheelchair, Smithie—to Lovecraft's surprise—stepped forward.

"Here, let me help you," said Smithie, and he easily

picked up Maddie.

"Thank you," said Florence sincerely.

And Smithie kind of shrugged, but he would not look at Maddie.

"You kinda remind me of my grandma," was all he said. And he helped her down the ladder.

Near Stu, Patrick sighed.

"I'm getting to go down in the tunnels; why am I not happy?" moaned Patrick softly.

"Because you're a smart young man," said Stu gently.

As people waited to go down, Turk's chest constricted. He moved like a condemned man towards Lovecraft when Rayton ran up.

The Science Teacher asked Lovecraft. "Does that hatch only close from the top?"

"Yes," answered Turk with grim resolve. "One of us has to stay up here."

"Oh," smiled Rayton, and he stretched his shoulders. "I figured as much."

Perturbed, Turk did not know why Rayton was so happy. Turk had already realized that he needed to stay up here. He wondered if he could find a length of pipe as Boyle had. His eyes cast around for a weapon.

"I'll close the hatch behind you," said Rayton, and Lovecraft and Turk looked up at him in surprise.

"What?" asked Turk. "I...I can stay up here. I'm the one who's been manning the hatch."

"But, I can take it from here," said Rayton smoothly.

"But, I can't let you do that," insisted Turk. A small part of him wanted to jump down into that hole, but he could not let Rayton take his place and die. "I mean, if it's my job, I can't let you stay up here and get eaten."

"What?" asked Rayton in surprise as he did a quick jog in place. "I'm not hanging around."

"Come again," asked Lovecraft curiously.

"Lydia knows I don't like to brag, so she was downplaying it when she said I was just the track and field coach," explained Rayton. "I almost qualified for the Olympics, twice."

"No shit," replied Lovecraft.

"And when I close that hatch," said Rayton. "I'm going to move that laundry machine away from the door and run like hell!"

"There will be a lot of them," said Lovecraft.

"I'll let a few in here to loosen them up," said Rayton. "But, once I'm through the door, it's a short sprint to the front gate, and then I'll settle into a comfortable jog. Besides, I don't want to go back down that hole again."

Lovecraft nodded. "Okay, you get closing duties." He looked at Turk. "You good?"

"Better plan than I had," shrugged Turk.

"Okay," said Lovecraft to Turk. "So, you're below."

As Turk went down, Lovecraft crowded Florence and Max towards the hole.

"We need to go, now!" said Lovecraft, softly but

277

urgently.

"Aw man," moaned Max, but he went down the hole. Florence hesitated for a moment, but then she reluctantly followed.

"This is a terrible plan," she grumbled.

"Agreed," said Lovecraft, and he took out his Snapphone. He sent a quick text that read: 'Gone South. Laundry Room. Down the hatch.' He added a heart emoji, and then he hit send. Lovecraft looked up at Rayton, who nodded.

Whipping around, Lovecraft darted over to the laundry room door. With a big push at its top, he toppled the laundry machine. The door broke under the press of bodies. Revenants spilled into the room. Lovecraft ran back to the hole.

"Godspeed," he saluted, and then he jumped down into the hole.

The teacher locked the hatch, cutting off all the sunlight.

Below, Lovecraft hit the ground in a crouch and waited there for a moment, breathing deeply. After the sunlight, the tunnel seemed impossibly dark. Resisting the urge to tense up, he straightened as his eyes got acclimated.

"What now?" asked Boyle softly.

"We wait," said Lovecraft.

"What if...," started Florence. And she looked meaningfully towards the bend in the corridor, which led deeper into the basement.

"We're okay," said Lovecraft firmly. "I sent a message to

278

my people, so they know where we are. So, we wait."

"O...okay," said Florence, but she did not seem convinced.

"Remember what Reverend Jennings said," piped up Tammi. "That if we have faith, we'll make it."

"Yeah, but where is Reverend Jennings?" asked Florence uncertainly.

And Lovecraft's chest clenched at the thought of the reverend, but he spoke calmly.

"This too shall pass," he said with steel in his voice. "The reverend was right. We just need faith."

"Remember when the reverend talked about Noah having to sit around for forty days with a bunch of animals, who probably all smelled bad because they had gotten wet?" asked Tammi. "At least we won't be down here that long."

That produced a small chuckle from several people.

"And we're not surrounded by wet animals," added Maddie. She reached out and took her granddaughter's hand. The older woman gave it a reassuring squeeze.

Florence's smile was stronger this time. She nodded. "Okay."

"Though I'd say this was more like Daniel and the Lions," said Maddie.

"What about Jonah and the Whale?" suggested Stu as he weighed in.

And that turned into a discussion over which Biblical parable best described how screwed they were.

Unobtrusively, Lovecraft stepped back. He did note, though, that the super glowstick that he had dropped earlier was almost out. Taking out his last glowstick, he cracked it. Lifting it up, the glowstick gave him at least a little more light than the bare bulbs.

Back past the ladder, the tunnel ended in a wall, so that end was secure. But then Lovecraft remembered the pissed-off spirit from earlier, which had dove at him through the ladder. Well, more or less secure, he conceded to himself.

Moving away from the ladder, there was the 'L' corner. Lovecraft looked around the corner and found that it was clear. Farther along, he could see that it turned again. He dropped the glowstick halfway down the corridor. He remembered that there had been more food tins, which he had had to leave behind, but most seemed to be gone now.

But then he spied a couple on the ground and grinned.

Picking them up, Lovecraft turned right into Max.

"Hey, watch it," complained the kid as he took a few steps back.

"You shouldn't sneak up on people," said Lovecraft with reproach. But then he smiled. "Look what I found."

"Oh no," said Max quickly as he took one of the large cans. "We should save this one for later, just in case, okay? Please!"

"Hide it where we can find it," smiled Lovecraft indulgently.

Max went back to the "L" corner to squirrel away the giant can of lima beans for now. Hopefully forever.

Trucking back, Lovecraft presented the other large can to

Florence.

"See, we're not completely lost," he grinned.

Florence looked down in surprise.

"Oh no, the hot dogs made it!" she chuckled. "Where did you find this?"

"It had rolled against a wall and was trying to hide from us," said Lovecraft as he took out his Swiss Army knife.

"What's that can?" asked the cook, Marta, and she looked over Florence's shoulder. "Is that a tin of hot dogs?"

"Yep," said Lovecraft. "Cut in half; it should be almost enough for everyone."

"And at least some water," said Marta with reservation.

"But hot dog flavored water?" moaned Florence.

"At least it's clean," shrugged Lovecraft.

After opening the tin, he handed it to Florence and stepped back. Walking around the corner, he leaned his shoulder against the wall and faced the far corridor. But, the Substitute listened contentedly to the happy noises behind him.

All was quiet for 5 minutes.

In the far corridor, a light winked out.

Lovecraft could not tell if there was anything there in the darkness. Flexing his fingers nervously, the Substitute waited, but nothing happened.

After a moment, the light came back on, and that glow gave him hope.

A short while later, Max, Boyle, and Turk came to stand

by him.

"Everyone's settled," reported Boyle.

Lovecraft turned so that he could still see down the far corridor. Then, at the same time, look at Boyle out of the corner of his eye. It was an awkward position. But, he did not want to turn his back to the far corridor.

"Good to hear," he responded.

"What's the plan?" asked Turk.

"Plan?" asked Lovecraft in confusion. "What do you mean?"

"We can't just stay here," said Turk slowly, as if he were speaking to an idiot.

"Yes," replied Lovecraft. "We can. And we will."

Turk waved his hand down the hall. "But, there might be another way out through there."

"It's not safe to walk around here," said Lovecraft.

"That's for sure," added Max urgently.

"Why not?" asked Turk.

Lovecraft hesitated for a moment, wondering how much to tell Turk, and more importantly, how much he would believe. "It's an old building and falling apart. I don't want people wandering around."

"I'll be careful," said Turk.

The big man started to step past Lovecraft, but the Substitute turned to face him.

"No," said Lovecraft firmly.

"Turk," warned Boyle. "I think we should listen to him.

He's been down here before."

"And I really did not want to come back down again," said Max truthfully. "Really, really did not..."

"I'm not scared," huffed Turk.

"I am," said Lovecraft.

Turk paused, and his brow furrowed like crumpled paper. Slowly, it sunk in what the Substitute was saying.

Lovecraft leaned forward to continue. "I am scared of what is down here."

"Me too," added Max.

"Well, why did we come down here—okay, I know why we came down here—but, if it's that bad...," started Turk, and then his voice trailed off.

"If I had had any other choice...," started Lovecraft.

"You'd have done what?"

Lovecraft managed not to jump.

The dry, weighty voice had come from right behind him. He was proud of himself for turning around slowly. More precisely, that he did not scream out like a little kid.

Yay me, he thought.

Mr. Abyssian was now standing in front of him, just a few paces away. He was still in that old, dark suit, which seemed two sizes too big for him. The suit was neat, except where the iron chain was locked around his left ankle. There the chain had left rust stains on the pant leg. The chain itself coiled back down the hall and into the now darkened corridor with its big links.

283

When he was reasonably sure that his voice would not squeak, Lovecraft said. "Hello."

"You're here," commented Mr. Abyssian.

"Yes," said Lovecraft carefully. He felt like a kid caught with his hand in the cookie jar. "But, not by our choice."

"I'm pretty sure I told you not to come back down here," said Mr. Abyssian in a calm tone. "But sometimes I mumble, having been alone for so long."

"You did not mumble," said Lovecraft. "I..."

However, Abyssian cut him off. "And you agreed."

"I did. And now we're only here— quietly— staying in this corridor until we are rescued. Which I hope is really, really soon."

The older man tilted his head in thought. He spoke thoughtfully. "You have kept everyone here."

"And I hoped we could just stay out of your way," said Lovecraft. "Very quietly. Like church mice."

Boyle picked up on Lovecraft's concern.

"Think of us as refugees," added Boyle. "Who will be gone as soon as possible."

"I...could see that," agreed Mr. Abyssian.

Puzzled, Turk looked between the ancient man and Lovecraft, and the big man was unsure of what was going on.

"Wait? Who the hell is this guy?" demanded Turk petulantly.

Lovecraft flinched. He began to look at Turk in shock.

Mr. Abyssian started to quake with rage. The chain at his ankle jangled. Looking back, Lovecraft began to sputter.

"Sorry, he doesn't understan..."

But Mr. Abyssian cut him off with a roar, which shook the walls.

"WHO AM I?"

Mr. Abyssian reached for his face. His hand, with its skinny, alabaster fingers, covered his face and dug in just outside the eyes. With a pull, the face started to separate from the rest of his head.

But Lovecraft had stopped watching. He spun around.

"What the...," started Turk in confusion.

"Don't look!" cried Lovecraft. He did not know why, but his gut was telling him to 'Not Look.' He grabbed Max's head with his left hand.

"Wha...," started the kid.

Lovecraft pulled Max's face to his chest. The kid struggled, but Lovecraft held him fast. At the very least, maybe his body would act as a shield so that the kid could survive.

Boyle, seeing the look of terror in Lovecraft's eyes, turned and covered her eyes.

Only Turk watched as the face fully detached, and he saw what lay beyond in that gaping maw of darkness. There was a violent thrum—like locusts—somewhere deep inside.

"They asked me that at Roanoke too!" snarled the face in Mr. Abyssian's hand.

And Turk began to shriek wildly.

The big man fell back. He bounced off a wall and began to tumble to the floor.

Time seemed to slow down for Lovecraft. It did that. Sometimes an event was a blur, like when the Runners first attacked in the Infirmary, and sometimes it was like this.

Turk's hair had gone as white as snow between hitting the wall and collapsing on to the floor.

Distantly, the Substitute knew that hair was not supposed to do that, normally.

Collapsing to the ground, Turk just lay there twitching.

From the ladder, the Substitute heard people running forward.

"Stay back!" cried Lovecraft urgently. "Don't come any closer!"

Most of the noise stopped at that, but Icewater still ran around the corner. Or at least tried to. Boyle sprang out and knocked the Camerawoman back. The paramedic pushed her out of sight of Mr. Abyssian's maw.

"What're you....?" complained Icewater.

"Please don't! It's too dangerous!" pleaded Boyle. She was happy to see that Patrick was staying back with Stu. Admittedly, the caretaker held the kid's arm firmly, just in case.

Lovecraft looked down and back. He saw Mr. Abyssian's legs just a few feet away. Pulling his gun, he fired two shots, one into each shin. The bullets knocked Mr. Abyssian's legs out from under him, and he fell forward.

As the older man hit the ground, the face of Mr. Abyssian bounced out of his hand. It clattered to a stop — farther down the corridor — with a sound like porcelain.

Letting go of Max, Lovecraft whipped around. He saw that the maw was momentarily facing the ground.

The Substitute slammed his big boot on the back of Mr. Abyssian's head, pushing the maw into the dirt and sand on the floor. Mr. Abyssian's feeble hands scrabbled at Lovecraft's leg.

Beyond the man on the ground, the lights dimmed further down the corridor. Only the glow stick lit the passageway.

Lovecraft saw one of the creatures streak out of the darkness. He drew his Gurkha knife and ducked under the monster's claws. They slashed right at the space where his favorite eyeballs had just been.

Lashing out, Lovecraft sliced open the creature's side with his massive blade. He heard noises farther back in the dark. The rest of the creatures would be here momentarily.

"Everyone back," called out Lovecraft, as time seemed to return to normal once again.

"We need to run!" cried Maddie.

"Nowhere left," said Lovecraft, and he flipped the empty gun around to use it as a hammer.

Out of the corner of his eye, the Substitute saw Max appear at his side. The kid held up the only weapon available to him. Anyone who came near was going to get walloped with a tin of lima beans.

A moment later, Boyle was at his other side. Her pipe

was ready.

Baring his teeth at the creatures in the dark, he howled. "So we stand. We stand and fight! But first, I'm going to break this guy's neck with my boot."

Lovecraft started to bare down on Mr. Abyssian's neck, which made brittle noises.

"Wait!" cried the face of Mr. Abyssian.

The Substitute stopped bearing down but did not release any pressure either.

"One...good...reason?" asked Lovecraft through clenched teeth.

"Maybe I was hasty," said Mr. Abyssian quickly. "A chipped shin is one thing, but I'd rather not go through the next millennia holding up my head. My existence is humiliating enough as is."

"We just want to wait out the storm," said Lovecraft. "As soon as we can, we will leave, but not a moment sooner."

As Mr. Abyssian thought, the creature that Lovecraft had slashed tried to stagger upright. Bright blue ochre trickled from the wound in its side.

Boyle tightened her grip on her pipe. The creature was giant. A quick estimation by Lovecraft figured that they could maybe take one, but not a horde of these things.

"Okay," said Mr. Abyssian.

"Okay?" asked Lovecraft, without taking off any pressure. But it was getting awkward to stand like that.

"Yes, yes," replied Mr. Abyssian testily. "If the boy would just retrieve my face, gently."

Max realized that the face was closest to him. He began to turn towards it. But he had his lima beans ready, just in case.

"You okay with getting that kid?" asked Lovecraft with concern.

The kid looked at the Substitute and nodded with more confidence than he felt. "I got it."

When the face didn't do anything more terrifying than just existing, Max put down the lima beans beside it.

Carefully, the kid picked up the face, and it gave him a pained smile. The kid almost started to lose it, but he managed not to drop Mr. Abyssian's face. Walking over, Max pushed the face into his hand.

Mr. Abyssian grasped his face, and, as Lovecraft let up a little pressure, the older man slid it over the maw. As the face snapped into place, the insect-like buzzing stopped.

Lovecraft moved back and away from the older man. Unconsciously though, he stopped between the chained man and the kid.

Surprisingly, the frail-looking man hopped right up, which made his chain jangle. But then, he got an odd look. Turning his head away from them, the Chained Man unsnapped his face. After quickly rubbing the edges, he snapped it back on.

"This cursed sand gets everywhere," he muttered with disgust.

Mr. Abyssian looked back at Lovecraft, who tensed. However, the older man turned and walked into the darkness without another word.

The creature that Lovecraft had cut twisted menacingly towards him. It had no eyes, but the Substitute could tell that it was seeing him just fine.

"Dennis," warned Mr. Abyssian from the dark.

Reluctantly, the creature turned and limped back into the dark. Shortly thereafter, the lights came back on.

"The fuck," breathed Boyle in relief, and Max gave a little, maniacal laugh.

"Okay," said Lovecraft. "Everyone stay back. Let's not push our luck any further."

# 44

Turk made little noises.

His head lay in Boyle's lap, and she gently stroked his hair to comfort him. But his eyes haunted Lovecraft. Eyes that said that the big man would never be right again.

Turning to look back at the hallway, Lovecraft saw that the glow stick was starting to dim. The lightbulbs were all still on, but once that glow stick went out, there would be no more light if Mr. Abyssian and his pets returned.

Sighing softly, Lovecraft tried not to worry about all that. He looked over. Max's head was bowed in sleep. The kid snored gently. To his surprise, a smile came across the Substitute's face.

In the far corridor, the light went out.

Lovecraft was watching the darkness when someone shouted near the ladder.

"Noises!" cried out Florence by the ladder. The shout woke Max up. Lovecraft clamored up, but he was not feeling as spry as he had forty-eight hours ago. His tired eyes hurt, and his ankle was sore.

The Substitute looked down the corridor at the darkness, but it did not move.

Boyle saw his look.

"What's wr....?" she asked softly, but Florence interrupted.

It was only by sheer force that Florence managed to keep her voice from trembling.

"Um, Mr. Lovecraft? I think something's trying to open the hatch," she said.

Lovecraft turned towards the ladder and moved through the nervous crowd as the refugees began to rise. Max was now up and following closely in Lovecraft's wake. Hastily, the kid wiped his face in case of drool.

Checking his phone, Lovecraft saw that he still did not have any signal. The hatch above unlocked.

"Everyone back, but Do Not Run!" called out Lovecraft. "I can't help you if you run."

The hatch peeled back, and Lovecraft drew his Gurkha knife ready for anything.

A young corporal from the National Guard looked down.

"Y'all okay, sir?" asked the corporal in a soft Southern

drawl.

Lovecraft grinned. "I am now."

The corporal leaned up and spoke into his walkie-talkie.

"We found them! Alive!" said the corporal. "I repeat, Alive."

# 45

Once Max was up, it was only Lovecraft left in the tunnel. But the Substitute hesitated. He moved back to the intersection. Sheer habit almost made him say 'thank you,' but he stopped himself.

Stopping, he looked down the corridor to where there was no light.

"We are leaving," said Lovecraft. "I'll see if I can't get people out of this jail as quickly as possible. But...well, I'll do my best."

Unsure what else to say, the Substitute finished quickly. "I will leave you to your peace."

Turning, Lovecraft went to the ladder and up it.

Back in the shadows, a dark figure stood there, backed by his beasts.

"You know Dennis," said Mr. Abyssian. "That was the most fun we've had in ages."

"Huh. Better that they're gone" grumbled Dennis, whose side was still smarting.

The dark figure turned, and the shadows immediately lifted.

There was no sign of them.

# 46

Soldiers with Z-sticks had created a ragged path through the jail. Agent Kate Swift navigated carefully through and into general population. It was not like her gray suit was still perfect. There were already spots of mud and blood. But her Mother's continuous lectures about keeping her clothes neat had become ingrained in her.

All the survivors, save one, had been brought to a hastily erected tent outside the jail.

One living person had still not left the penitentiary.

Even though the jail made her shiver, Swift had gone in. A part of her was happy that she had not been here. But, she was more than a little worried about the person who had been.

Swift started down the row of cells until she found an open one. Inside lay the body of Councilman Tibbons on an old, musty mattress. Beside the body sat Lovecraft on the floor. He looked up and saw her. That brought a little smile to his face.

"Thought I'd find you in here," said Swift, and Lovecraft just slowly nodded. She walked into the cell and looked down at Tibbons. "Who was he?"

"Tibbons," said Lovecraft, and he thought furiously for a moment. "Councilman Tibbons. I...I don't know his first name. Shit. I can't believe I didn't even know that."

"If he was a Councilman, then it's Roger," said Swift. "We were wondering where he was when we found the rest of the city council."

"Well, the idiots at city hall really messed this one up," growled Lovecraft.

"For what it's worth," said Swift as she crouched down beside him. "You guys were the lucky ones."

That made Lovecraft blink in surprise. She put her hand on his knee.

"We were running late because the defenses at City Hall were falling quickly," said Swift.

"Wait?" asked Lovecraft in confusion. "Who was at city hall? I thought that was supposed to be the rally point, but then it wasn't."

"The city council was at city hall," said Swift. "And they were living in style there."

"A real party?"

"Champagne, big-screen plasma, and a ton of food."

"What happened?"

"When we got there, the sheriff had been thrown through—all the way through—the big plasma, and he was the lucky one. He went quick."

"So, that's where the 20 million went."

"If only they had put some cash into a studier door."

"From what I saw, it might not have mattered."

"True, I saw your big friends out there."

"They don't go down easy," nodded Lovecraft, and then he sighed. "We should call the Chief."

"I already called," replied Swift. "I saw a camerawoman out there. We need to intercept the film?"

"Actually not," said Lovecraft. "I used that tin of face cream that Adam from Downstairs came up with. The camerawoman even complained to me about it messing up her shot...well, sorta."

"You're kidding," grinned Swift, and her bright smile cheered him.

"I kinda felt a little bad," said Lovecraft. "But, this way, she gets to keep her footage. And she worked hard for it. So, is the military cataloging the site?"

"Yep, and we need to go," said Swift. She reached out and helped him stand up. He moved painfully, but then he paused and looked down at Tibbons.

"Sorry, sir," he said softly.

Swift gave him a moment but then led him out of the cell, which was now empty.

They headed out of general population. However, Lovecraft did pause long enough to leave the extra set of jail keys on Stu's desk, as promised.

Once outside, they quickly snuck away towards Swift's rental.

"Where to?" asked Lovecraft.

"Found a little hotel not too far from here. And it's right

next to a Ruth's Chris' Steak House," she replied.

"You're kidding," exclaimed Lovecraft joyfully, even though he was almost too exhausted to smile.

"A little drive," shrugged Swift.

"But worth it," sighed Lovecraft happily.

Swift smiled, and she put her arm in his. "So first, you'll shower as I order food. And if you're a good kid, I'll bounce up and down on you."

"Yes, Ma'am," said Lovecraft, but then his face grew thoughtful. "Do we have anyone else in the area?"

"Lamour is nearby," said Swift.

"I need to call in a favor once we're on the road," said Lovecraft, and then a smile came to his face. "Then, I gotta tell you about this kid I met."

"Who's this?" asked Swift.

"The biggest help I had was from this teenage kid named Max," laughed Lovecraft. "He was tough as nails."

"You're kidding."

"I wouldn't."

"And he has your real name?"

"Scout's honor."

"I've got to meet him now," said Swift.

"That...can be arranged."

# 47

Max hit the ground and yanked up the bottom of the triage tent. He slid under to escape the confines of makeshift examination rooms. The people inside were friendly, but he needed to find someone. He slid through the crowd of soldiers and survivors.

In one of the tents, he saw his fellow student, Tammi, being given a sandwich by one of FEMA's people.

The doctor, who had checked Max for bites, had told the kid they had followed the National Guard across the city.

Boyle was still running around. The paramedic handed a bottle of water to Lydia from Bus #9.

Turk was now curled up into a ball on a cot, staring blankly ahead. Boyle went over to him and picked up a wool blanket, which had fallen to the ground. She tucked it around the shivering man once again.

"Max?" called out a voice. The kid turned, and his jaw dropped.

"Mr. Rayton?" exclaimed Max.

The Science teacher trotted up, beaming.

"You made it," laughed Rayton in relief. "I was really worried about you."

"Me?" cried Max with a laugh. "You're the one who got left up there."

"It was a little dicey," admitted Rayton with a shrug. "But, once I got out of the jail, I just fell into a nice, comfortable run. I met up with the National Guard near city hall and told them where to go."

The rest of the survivors noticed Rayton and happily crowded around him.

Slipping out of the crowd, Max ducked past Icewater, who was filming the reunion.

Further along, Max spotted two guys in dark suits talking to a colonel.

"Colonel Whipple? We're from Homeland Security," said the taller of the two men, Alford, as he showed his ID. "We're here to assist."

"We appreciate any help," said Colonel Whipple sincerely. "We're going to need to go house by house to..."

Max ran up to them, speaking a little breathlessly to the Homeland Security agents.

"Are you with Agent Lovecraft?" asked the kid. "I'm trying to find him."

"Who?" asked Alford.

"Agent Lovecraft, with Homeland Security," said Max as his speech slowed down. He began to feel confused. "He was here with us."

"Lovecraft?" asked Alford in confusion.

"Some of the other survivors mentioned him," mused Colonel Whipple. "And we rode in with an Agent Swift from Homeland too."

"You did?" asked Alford. "As far as I know, we're the first Homeland agents on the scene."

Max blinked in confusion. "But...then...who was he?"

"A spook?" murmured Colonel Whipple thoughtfully.

"What?" asked one of the agents.

"In Vietnam, we called American agents that didn't use their real identity 'spooks,'" said Colonel Whipple. "You know, like a ghost."

# 48

That evening, a burly man in a gray suit walked into the high school gym, which had been converted into a temporary shelter. He approached a FEMA doctor.

"Hi, my name's Nathaniel Lamour, from Social Services," said the man in the gray suit with a Texan drawl. "Looking for a young man. Chinese-American. Name's Max Chow."

# 49

The Secretary of State watched the man at the front of the room. She saw that there was still fatigue in Lovecraft's eyes. But, she also noted that he did not seem as haunted as he had at the beginning. She wondered if reporting what had happened at Fallen Oaks had been cathartic for him in some way.

"So, the kid's okay?" asked the four-star general. He was trying to keep his tone agreeable, but the Secretary of State had to suppress her smile.

The big softie is worried about the kid, she thought with amusement.

"He's in good hands," assured Lovecraft.

"Good," nodded the general.

And Madame Secretary was happy as well to know— with certainty—that the young man would be cared for.

"As you're aware," continued Lovecraft. "Most of the town's structures survived. Whether the town will be...well, we don't know that yet. Around the hospital, the National Guard found cocoons that transformed people into runners and bruisers. As for those—and any new revenants—they've been taken to the CDC's dark science facility, Kipperling Falls. The initial reports are inconclusive. When they're finished, you'll all have those reports as well. When you have finished those reports, usual precautions are to be taken."

"What does that mean?" whispered the Madame Secretary's aide, Vicki.

"Burn it," hissed the Secretary of State. "Now shush."

"This is why I asked you to be here, Madame Secretary," said Lovecraft. "Sorry about the last notice."

The Secretary of State just waved off his apology, as it was not needed. "You need me to tell the other countries what I heard here today so that they can prepare."

"Yes, please," said Lovecraft.

"But, what are your thoughts on this matter?" asked Madame Secretary.

"We're recommending widening the vector of possible hot spots and a forensic auditing trail of monies going into any town in that vector...," started Lovecraft.

Madame Secretary spoke up when he took a breath. "Pardon me. I mean, what are your personal feelings about these incidents."

"Oh," said Lovecraft, almost in surprise. He thought for a moment. Finally, he looked at her thoughtfully. "This is all far, far from over."

# 50

The Secretary of State and Vicki walked down the hall, lost in thought. A new marine was leading them out but at a respectful distance.

"I just realized," murmured Vicki. "That that guy never gave his name."

"We'll talk later," replied Madame Secretary.

"But, who was he?" asked Vicki.

"Best not to ask too many questions," urged Madame Secretary. "Just listen to his intelligence."

"It would be funny if he were one of those Gaslight guys," smiled Vicki.

Madame Secretary grabbed Vicki's arm and pushed her

against a wall.

"Where'd you hear that name?" asked Madame Secretary with clenched teeth. The marine looked around to see what was wrong, but then he saw the look on the Secretary of State's face. Moving farther down the corridor, the marine waited a reasonable distance away.

Vicki was shocked. "Wha...what?"

"Where did you hear that name?" repeated the Secretary of State.

"I...I don't know," sputtered Vicki. "Around. People talk about them."

"Well, don't," said Madame Secretary. "People who talk about them disappear."

"You're kidding," said Vicki, and then she looked down at the Secretary of State gripping her arm. "Um, you're hurting my arm."

"Good," said Madame Secretary, but she did let go of the arm. "Maybe it'll help you to remember this talk because this is not a game."

"But....," said Vicki.

"You're a bright person, and I like you," said Madame Secretary. "Do the smart thing."

Vicki's chin wobbled. "I'm sorry."

"It's okay," said the Secretary of State more softly. "My apologies. My husband and I knew someone who got too close. Bill tried to warn him not to poke too hard, but they...they got too intrigued. Obsessed even."

"What happened?" asked Vicki in almost a whisper.

"He disappeared," sighed Madam Secretary. "And I don't want you to disappear." She gave a small smile. "Come on; there's still time for lunch. My treat."

"How...how can you eat after that meeting?" asked Vicki. "I mean, those people."

"It was horrible. No question that those people suffered," said Madam Secretary. "But, starving ourselves won't help them. The first rule of politics, eat when you have the chance. You don't know when your next meal will come. And after that meeting..." She sighed again. "...I need some pancake therapy."

# 51

Max wandered past the sign that said 'Welcome Parents to Exeter School.' He pulled at his school tie and headed around the side of the main building. Behind, kids were running to see their parents. He had been invited to lunch with his roommate's family, but he did not feel like it.

Finding a bench, Max leaned back and closed his eyes. He thought back to Fallen Oaks and then further back to Toledo. They seemed so far away. And yet, they were still less dangerous than Mr. Sanders' math exams.

After a while, he heard footsteps coming towards him. Maybe if he ignored them, they would go away.

"Sorry we're late, kid," said Lovecraft.

The kid's eyes snapped open.

303

Lovecraft and Swift were really standing there. They were even dressed like ordinary parents, in boring fall clothes.

Max grinned. "What took you so long?"

## About the Author

## Walter G. Esselman

*Apparently, I'm supposed to write this bio to humanize me.*

*It is bold of them to assume that I am a carbon-based lifeform from Earth, but regardless...*

I grew up in Michigan, practically on the campus of MSU. Not that I follow sports, humorously enough. I've been writing forever but never really sent anything out. So, I pushed myself to get short stories out there and became a regular contributor at World of Myth and Dark Dossier. I recently started turning my eye towards novels, which is the first step in that process.

My wife Amy and I still live in Michigan because it's the most beautiful state. Not that I like to go outdoors, humorously enough. I mean, seriously, there are bears out there, Sharks! I even saw a Bearshark once. A chilling sight.

After tooling around the Commonwealth with Cait for many years in Fallout 4, I'm back in the land of Skyrim once again.

*Khajit will shoot arrows if you have the coin. Or, it's a dungeon with a lot of loot.*

I hope you have a wonderful day!

## Author's Notes

You made it!

Thank you for reading me!

I appreciate it, even if it wasn't your favorite.

This story was inspired by an episode of Ghost Adventures, Moundsville Penitentiary. Before their Lockdown, Zak Bagans goes across the street from the old gothic jail. And there are these really lovely homes, all in a row, across from this spooky jail.

And I thought, what if there was some event that forced those poor people to take refuge in a haunted jail. Immediately I thought of zombies because what more do you want between you and a horde of zombies but a big thick wall. If not, two walls.

I believe by that point I already had written a screenplay with him ". So, I put him in.

I didn't know if this would ever see the light of even an overcast day.

I did have the barebones of the story, but mostly I just started writing it. I thought that the kids from the classroom might play a more prominent role, but what came out of the writing was the formation of this Father/Son bond between Lovecraft and Max. So, I followed that thread, which was the brightest and most enjoyable. Lovecraft opening up to tell the kid about his traumatic event when he was the same age. And I liked Max's attitude of "I'm scared, so I'm going to do what I can about it."

# Discussion Guide

1. Was the Setting of the book unique?  How did it impact the story?  Did it evoke any sort of feeling?

2. Was there enough depth to the characters to make the book palatable?

3. What was the plot?  *The plot of a story is what drives the action.  Called by Hitchcock a 'Macguffin,' or by Spiderman a 'goober.'  Han Solo and Luke Skywalker have to save Princess Leia.*

4. What was the story?  *The actual core of the story itself.  In "Star Wars" and "Into the Spiderverse," it is a young man finding his own way.*

5. How well did the plot and story mesh?

6. Was the book grounded in reality or very fanciful?

7. What was the evolution of Lovecraft and Max's relationship?

8. Did Lovecraft's actions make a difference?

9. Are the female characters well-drawn, or merely props?

10. Do any past the Suri test?  *That they have a goal independent of the man, or men, at the center.*

11. Or, the Bechdel Test?  *That two women have a conversation that is not about the man, or men, at the center.*

12. Were minorities represented?  *But, I might have been so*

*low-key that I'm not sure that people might have realized that Councilman Tibbons and Icewater were African American. Still, an important question to have.*

13. Was the reporter, Rick Hurston, a bad guy?

14. How was the character of Reverend Jennings handled? Was Lovecraft right to treat him the way he did? Did the Reverend make a difference?

15. What was underneath the jail?

16. Best real weapon to use against a zombie? Best fictional weapon?

17. Where is the best place to go during a zombie outbreak to stay safe? Have you located a place close by that you could go to?

18. What does an ideal location need to have to be the best spot?

www.ingramcontent.com/pod-product-compliance
Lightning Source LLC
Chambersburg PA
CBHW070547260626
47161CB00002B/529